INTANGIBLE

INTANGIBLE

INHUMAN PROTECTORS
Book One

A. Samson

Intangible
Paperback Edition

Love N. Books Press
An Imprint of Wolfpack Publishing
1707 E. Diana Street
Tampa, FL 33610

www.lovenbookspress.com

Edited by My Brother's Editor

Paperback ISBN 978-1-969876-32-5
Ebook ISBN 978-1-969876-31-8
LCCN 2026937879

INTANGIBLE
(IN'TANJəB(ə)L)

Adjective:
Unable to be touched or grasped.
Not having physical presence.

INTANGIBLE

PROLOGUE

Thayer woke with a gasp to an almost stifling smell. Through the fog in her head, she knew she was no longer in her bed nestled among the flannel sheets infused with lavender fabric softener she had just put on in preparation for the chilly fall nights.

No, this was definitely not her bedroom. Wherever she was smelled of spoiled food, motor oil, wet dogs, and male sweat. With a moan, she tried to sit up. It was no use, between whatever held her hands secured firmly behind her back and the nausea, she had to admit defeat after a few minutes.

Settling back on her side, she took slow, steady breaths to keep the nausea at bay. There was a piece of cloth shoved in her mouth that she couldn't push out with her tongue, no matter how hard she tried. It was obviously held in place with something, and the last thing she wanted to do was to be drowned in her own vomit.

She fought to tamp down the growing panic racing

through her. How had she wound up here? Even more importantly, where was here?

When the nausea had settled, she slowly took an assessment of what she knew. The last thing she remembered was falling asleep in her empty dorm room. Her roommate had left for the weekend, allowing for some much-needed privacy. Vaguely, she remembered something waking her before she quickly fell back asleep.

No, she hadn't fallen asleep. Something had knocked her out. The same thing that now had her head pounding in pain.

Trying one more time to push the foul-tasting cloth out of her mouth, she admitted defeat when it didn't budge. Trying to open her eyes, she realized that not only was her mouth gagged, but she was also blindfolded.

She felt a small glimmer of hope. Hadn't she read somewhere that if they didn't want you to see them, you had a better chance of being let go? Or was that just some Hollywood hype to sell tickets to the latest blockbuster? No, she would choose to hold on to even the smallest hint of hope.

Thayer lay still, listening to the noises around her for a few minutes. There were no voices that she could hear, nor was there anything that sounded like people shifting around. If there were, surely, they would have noticed she was awake by now.

She did hear the sound of tires on a highway slipping away underneath her. Whatever she was lying on did not do much to deaden the vibrations traveling through her body either. It was also hard enough that her shoulder ached from lying on her side. She could confidently rule out an upholstered seat of any kind.

Rolling onto her stomach, she tested the binds that held her hands securely at her back. If she could just wiggle out of them, maybe she could escape or at least try to wave down a passing motorist.

Tugging as hard as she could, she let out a small yelp when she felt the skin break at her wrist. Even with what had to be her blood making them slick, she couldn't fight out of her restraints. Upon further examination with the tips of her fingers, she decided her hands must be held together with cable ties. That meant, if she could just find something sharp, she could cut through them.

Stretching her legs out, she began to feel around, searching for anything that could help her. Slowly working herself around in a circle, she used her feet to scope out her surroundings.

It was exhausting to push her body around, and her head still felt like it was splitting in half from whatever they had given her.

Finally, her right foot hit something that made a rattling sound like metal inside metal. With a prayer it was a tool chest, she began squirming over until her back lay against the object.

Feeling with her bound hands as best as she could, she felt her heart almost give out when she found a lock. Wrapping her fingers around it, she rattled it, praying it would be unlocked. It was no use. The lock was firmly closed.

Thayer thought for a second of curling up and crying. Could you die of crying with your eyes covered? She doubted it, but it wouldn't do her any good anyway.

Maybe the corners of the chest were sharp enough to use like a reverse saw.

Using her toes, she shoved herself forward until she found the edge. It wasn't sharp, but it was worth a try. The only other items she had found would be of no use at all. Unless she could figure out how to use the remaining special sauce from what felt like a Big Mac container.

She pushed herself into a modified sitting position, banging her head on the roof of whatever she was in. Closing her eyes, she remained still, hoping she wouldn't vomit from the pain in her head. The chocolate popcorn she had eaten while watching a movie in her room earlier threatened to reappear several times before she managed to convince her stomach it needed to remain where it was.

Reasonably recovered, she began the tedious task of rubbing her wrist up and down against the chest. It was an exhausting system of working the ties against the edge until her muscles screamed, then taking a short break before giving herself a pep talk to keep going.

Her shoulders felt like they were on fire. Thayer shook her head, thinking at twenty, she was entirely too young to be this winded from simply moving her arms up and down. She should probably get to the gym more as soon as she returned to school. Since heading to college, working out every day hadn't been a top priority.

She felt like she had been working at it forever when she was suddenly thrown against the other side of her prison. Lying still, she decided she was no longer on a paved road.

With every bump, she bounced around the floor.

No matter how hard she tried, she couldn't quite get back into position to work on her restraints more.

About the time she had decided she couldn't take banging around inside her box anymore, they came to a stop.

Lying very still, she listened intently, wondering what happened next. It was hard to not let every horror from every mystery she had ever read circulate through her brain. Taking a couple deep breaths, she calmed her mind. She would need all of her wits to fight.

Hearing footsteps coming closer, she could just make out voices when there was a loud bang, and cold air bathed her body. At least she was still wearing her pajamas. Relief flooded her at the thought of the alternative.

Someone grabbed her ankles and pulled her to the opening. When they released them, she brought her knees to her chest, kicking out like she had been taught by her self-defense instructor. She heard a satisfying grunt when they connected to something solid.

Before she could strike out again, hands wrapped around her ankles, pulling her outside. She hit the ground with a jarring thud.

"Fucking bitch," a man growled out above her.

She was jerked off the ground by two strong hands digging into her biceps before she could kick out in the direction the voice came from.

Fighting as best as she could while still bound, she tried desperately to headbutt one of her captors. He grabbed her hair, jerking it tightly in his hands to keep her still. The pain that radiated through her scalp made her cry out.

"It's about time you got here. I don't like to be kept

waiting." The voice was from a different man than the one she had kicked.

Neither voice had sounded familiar, but this one sent shivers down her spine. How was it possible that a person could sound so sinister?

"Sorry, boss. It was harder to get her out than we thought. Took us a little longer than anticipated," the first man said.

That made at least three of them. She knew she needed to gather any information she could about the situation.

"She had better not have been damaged," the man in charge answered as if she were just some object.

Bile rose in the back of her throat again at the realization that perhaps that was all she was to him. Something that could be used and then tossed out like the trash.

"I need them to believe they'll get her back in one piece."

She must have let out a whimper because her head was pulled back with a jerk on her hair.

"A few bruises, but nothing serious. What do you want us to do now?"

"I have someone hired to watch her. They'll be by later. Your money is being transferred. I'll be in touch if I need you again." The man stepped over to her, and she was suddenly surrounded by the sickly smell of a sweet cologne. "Behave yourself, and you might just make it out of this alive," he said, growling into her ear.

She flinched back as the men laughed.

The nauseating smell of cologne disappeared as quickly as it arrived. Hearing a car door open, then the growl of the engine moving away, she guessed the man had left.

Someone cut the ties that bound her feet together and she was suddenly marched forward. She listened to a rusty groan before stumbling down a set of stairs, the only thing keeping her from falling was the hands holding on to her.

The floor under her feet was cold, and her body began to shake. No doubt it was trying to go into some form of shock from everything that had happened, but she refused to give in to it.

"I suggest you get comfortable, princess. You won't be going anywhere soon," one of the men said, his mouth next to her ear. He laughed when she tried to pull away from him.

Running his hand down her body, he cut the ties, holding her hands together. With a nasty shove, she found herself crashing against something before hitting what had to be a wall. Her fingers crept up to the trickle of blood oozing down from her forehead where she had fallen.

The man laughed harder as he left the room with his accomplices.

Hearing a door slam shut, she rolled onto her back, reaching for the blindfold. Pulling it from her head, she was dismayed to find only a faint light coming from a weak bulb somewhere outside the room. At least she wasn't in complete darkness.

Climbing onto a cot covered with a scratchy, dirty blanket, she began to work the gag from her mouth. She was now shaking so badly that she had to fight to get her fingers to work the tape off. Once she had wrestled it free, she spit out the disgusting cloth.

Wrapping the blanket around her, she sat on the cot, curling her feet under her, hoping to get some warmth back in them.

She was in a cage, like the ones from the old westerns she used to watch with her bodyguard when she was in middle school. Only this one looked like a newer version with a modern lock. There was enough room for the cot, a bucket, and not much else.

The cage sat inside some kind of cellar with cinderblock walls and a rough-hewn floor. There was a bare bulb hanging from the ceiling that was turned off, but nothing else as far as she could see. With a shiver, she wrapped the blanket tighter around herself.

Reaching out, she pushed on the door, finding it firmly locked. Tears began to form as she closed her eyes. Quickly, she took several deep breaths, pushing the tears away. She had been taught that crying would only cause her to dehydrate, and she didn't know when she would get any water.

Straightening her shoulders, she vowed to stay strong. If her father and her tutor turned bodyguard, turned surrogate older brother had taught her anything, they had taught her to survive. She reminded herself that, without a doubt, the second they learned she was missing, they would leave no stone unturned until they found her. She just needed to do whatever she had to survive until then.

There were three things that she needed to remember. First, she was stronger than she knew.

Second, she needed to keep herself as healthy as possible. That included getting as much rest as they would allow, drinking any water they brought, and eating what she was given for nourishment.

Third, her mind was her greatest weapon. She needed to analyze every move to find her best attack. It's why her father had insisted on her learning chess and reading *The Art of War*. Her opponent always had a weakness, and she just needed to find it.

She sank down onto the cot, feeling exhaustion slowly winning its fight against her. In just a few moments, she fell fast asleep.

She had no idea how long she'd slept when she heard the hinges of a door moan. Quickly sitting up, she pushed herself as far back from the door as possible. Two men came around the corner wearing balaclavas carrying a sack from McDonald's with them.

"Flash me your tits, and you can have it," one of the men said, waving the bag in front of him.

"Just give her the sack," the other man said, pushing two bottles of water inside the cage.

"I'm just having a little fun," the first man said, smashing the sack inside the cage.

They didn't sound like the voices from before. These two sounded much younger, like high school or college age.

"Are we supposed to stay to make sure she eats?"

"Nah. We just get paid to bring her food and empty her slop bucket every day. That's your job." He laughed, walking back toward the door as his partner started to whine.

"Why do I always get the shit jobs?"

"Because you're younger, pissant."

She listened to them sparring back and forth until the outer door slammed closed.

Picking up the bag and one of the waters, she sat back down, pulling a burger out. Sinking her teeth into the Quarter Pounder, she soon began to eat like she was starving. She hadn't had anything to eat since the day before, and her stomach had finally settled down.

Popping open the water bottle, she drank half of it before setting it aside. In case they didn't bring her more for a while, she would have to be careful with how much she drank.

She lay back down on the cot, staring up at the ceiling. She was reminded of the time she had agreed to give a speech in middle school after the teacher had witnessed her being kind to a new foreign student on the playground.

Thinking it was just her class she was speaking to, she had poured her soul into her paper about embracing diversity. When the time came to give the speech, she was horrified to find the entire school and administration sitting in the auditorium, waiting.

Frozen in fear, she had begged her teacher not to make her go out from behind the curtain. Her father had tried every way he could to be there, but he'd had an obligation he couldn't get out of.

The duty of representing her family was given to the man who had been hired to be her caretaker. When the crowd began to whisper, he had stood up in the back of the auditorium and walked to the back of the stage.

Finding her terrified, he asked the teacher to stall for a few minutes while they discussed the situation. Pulling her into one of the empty classrooms, he stood her on a chair before crossing his arms over his chest, so they were eye to eye.

He speared her with his most serious scowl before having her repeat an oath. It gave her the courage, for some reason, to give that speech and continue to push forward anytime she was scared.

She began the oath he had made her repeat so many times, repeating the new ending he had added.

"My name is Thayer Kent. I will fear no man because I am stronger than I know. I will fear no problem because I am smarter than my opponent. A Kent never shies away from adversity. A Kent will not go down without a fight. When other lesser men flee, I will walk into the storm. I now promise to uphold the duty that has been thrust upon me and teach these little shits what it means to be accepting of others."

When she had straightened her shoulders and nodded at him, he pulled her off the chair. Taking both of her shoulders in his large hands, he looked down at her with one more scowl.

"Good, now get out there and show those assholes you have bigger balls than all of them put together." A very audible gasp from her teacher sent her racing to the stage. He had also taught her all of her best curse words.

"I'll try," she whispered as her eyes closed. "I'll try to show them they can't break me." Curling up facing the wall, she felt herself drift back into a restless sleep.

CHAPTER ONE

"Mr. Brown, you really should consider my suggestion about finding a smaller bull," Memphis told the older gentleman through gritted teeth. "It would make calving for these first years easier."

It was cold, even though they were inside the old barn, it had to be pushing below freezing already. Memphis barely felt it, however, as he strained to help the young cow deliver her first calf. He had slipped off his coat and rolled up his sleeves as he kneeled in the straw on the barn floor.

"I'm real sorry to get you out this late, Doc. I found her struggling when I came out to check on her one last time before bed."

Ray Brown only had a handful of cows. He was too old to properly work the farm anymore, but he managed to make just enough to keep a roof over his and his wife's head. He knew the vet kneeling in the middle of the barn at midnight would accept nothing more than a hot meal or a pie for his services for now. There was no doubt that the Browns would pay him as they could.

Memphis had considered himself lucky when he had moved to town to take over the small veterinary practice after the old vet retired, cold barns and pie for payment aside.

"It's fine. They never decide to calve when it's convenient, do they?" Memphis's voice was strained as he braced against the cow trying to help pull the calf out.

With one final push from her, he managed to pull it free, sliding it onto his chest as he fell backward. Standing, he picked the calf up, swinging it to drain the fluid from its nasal passages. Miraculously, it was still alive. Leaving it for the mother to clean, Memphis walked out of the pen.

"Come up to the house to clean up. I'm sure there is already a fresh pie and some coffee waiting for you," Mr. Brown said, picking up their coats. Memphis smiled to himself. There was always pie waiting.

"You know I can't resist Mrs. Brown's pies. Let me just throw this shirt in my truck on the way by." Memphis stripped off his warm flannel shirt, leaving just his damp T-shirt underneath before rolling it in a ball to set on his floorboard.

Walking into the Brown's tiny kitchen, his nose took in the aroma of freshly baked cherry pie. "Mrs. Brown, you truly know the way to a man's heart," Memphis said, flashing her his best smile.

She blushed at him before cutting two pieces, setting the largest of them in front of him. She had made a fresh pot of coffee and set a steaming cup of it in front of Memphis, watching as he wrapped his hands around it to warm them up.

Memphis liked the Browns. They were like most of the people in this area of Minnesota, just trying to live a quiet life while providing for their family. It's exactly why he had moved to the area when he learned of the old veterinarian looking for someone to buy his practice.

Memphis had gone to vet school in Oklahoma as soon as he left the Army. He had used the ROTC program in college, coupled with a baseball scholarship, to help pay for his undergraduate degree, but knew he would have to spend several years on active duty before he could afford the cost of vet school.

He had calculated that he could spend three years on active duty before, if he was very careful, he would have enough money to earn his vet degree.

It hadn't worked out that way, though, once they learned about his unusual gift. Three years had quickly turned into six before he was allowed to leave. He tried to look at it in a positive light, though. He had enough when he got out to not only attend vet school but also buy this small practice along with the two-room cabin he now lived in.

Memphis's plan was to keep his head down, try to keep control of his gift and live his life in quiet peace.

"Well, I had better head home. I have a farm call first thing in the morning. Thanks for the pie," he said, rising to his feet from the small table in the kitchen. He had already discussed everything from the weather to cattle prices with the Browns. But morning for a rural veterinarian in this area came early, and he could use some sleep.

After being easily convinced to take a second piece of pie, he headed home to get some sleep before work. The pie was sitting on the seat next to him when he turned into the driveway leading to his cabin. It wasn't a large house, with only one bedroom, but it was his.

Stopping in front of the house, he studied it for a few minutes, certain he had left the porch light on. Maybe the bulb burned out while he was gone.

With a shrug, Memphis gathered up his pie and wet shirt before climbing out of the truck. He had made one more stop by the barn just to make sure the calf was being taken good care of. It was dry, curled up next to its mama, so he had said his goodbyes before heading home.

Opening the door of the cabin with one hand, he set the pie on a table by the door. He was still singing the last song he had heard on the only radio station he could get on the drive home. Memphis had only a brief second of realization that his dog hadn't met him at the door before he heard a deep voice.

"Taylor Swift? Really?" Suddenly, his body contracted as he slid into darkness.

The lights in his cabin were on when Memphis woke up. With a groan, he raised his head up, prying his eyes open. He had only a few seconds to look at the handful of men standing in his living room before his stomach cramped, emptying his piece of pie into a bucket a large man held.

"Where's my fucking dog?" Memphis growled when he finally stopped retching.

"Sleeping in the bedroom. We had to sedate him before he ate us." The big man stepped back, handing the bucket to another man.

He had to be well over six feet tall with a scowl that would have most men quaking in their boots.

Memphis closed his eyes, waiting for the next wave of nausea to pass over him. He knew his body didn't react the way others did, but damn, this felt worse than normal. Opening his eyes once he had managed to quell the bile in his throat, it struck him what had happened.

"Did you taser me? What was it set on, kill?" Memphis asked, trying to get his mind to focus on what was happening.

Yanking on his arms, he realized he had been tied to the chair from his bedroom. If they were here to rob him, they had gone to an extreme amount of trouble. Besides, there was nothing of value here. Everything worth stealing was at the vet clinic, locked up.

"Figured it would get your attention the quickest. I didn't realize it would hit you so hard, though. My bad," the big man snorted.

Was that supposed to be some sort of apology? Memphis wondered/

Looking around, Memphis ignored the large man dressed in black standing in front of him. He might be the one talking, but Memphis could tell the man in the business suit sitting calmly in one of the living room chairs was really in charge.

"What do you want?" he asked, pulling at the restraints holding his arms to the chair. If he could just get loose, he would beat the shit out of all of them. "There's probably thirty bucks in there," he said, nodding toward his wallet the man was studying. "Just take it and get out. I don't have anything else."

"We have a situation we need your assistance with,"

the big man answered, placing a large hand on Memphis's shoulder to hold him still.

With a sinking feeling, Memphis realized they weren't in a hurry to steal his television. No, he was almost certain that they had come for something else, and he was in serious trouble.

"I'll ask again, what do you want? Get your fucking hands off of me."

His eyes stayed glued on the man in the suit, but he was talking to the big man as he grabbed his hair to pull Memphis's head back. With a quick look at his eyes, the man turned his head loose again.

Memphis was already pissed that he had become so relaxed about his safety in this sleepy rural area that he had let his guard drop. Looking around, he realized the men had military-grade weapons trained on him. They'd have to kill him before he would go back to the Army. He didn't care what they wanted.

"You're going to help us find someone."

Memphis's eyes grew wide for a fraction of a second before he could regain control, but it was enough to confirm something. He was the man they were looking for. They had finally tracked down the one man in the world who could find a needle in a haystack.

"Fuck you," Memphis growled at them. "You don't come into my home, tase me, and drug my dog. If you think I'm going to help you do anything, you're out of luck."

His outburst was met with a punch to the stomach from the big man.

"You'll do what I tell you to do!" he snarled.

Memphis just gasped, praying he didn't throw up

again. He didn't care how badly they beat him. He wasn't going back with them.

"Again, fuck you," Memphis wheezed out when he had regained his breath, earning a backhand from the big man. Memphis spit blood from his now busted lip at him.

"Stop. Knox, untie him." The man in the suit stepped forward, laying his hand on the big man's sleeve. "We'll find another way."

"Sir, he can find her. His abilities at search and rescue go beyond anything I've ever heard about. I'll make him find her if I have to."

It sounded to Memphis like this Knox character was pleading with the man in the suit.

"I know, but this isn't right. I won't torture someone to find her. If Dr. Prescott won't help us, we'll just have to think of something else."

"Sir, we've run out of something else. He's our last hope."

Against his will, Memphis started to find his interest piqued. These two men obviously weren't professional kidnappers or torturers, thank God. It was also now unlikely they were some branch of the military trying to drag him back in. But he would reserve judgment until he was certain.

"Untie him," the man in charge said, motioning to the other men.

When the cable ties were cut off, Memphis tried to stand but fell back into the chair, finding his legs asleep from being tied too tight.

"Get the fuck out of my house," he snarled at them. "I don't care who you're hunting, I won't help you."

With another push, he managed to rise, walking awkwardly toward the bedroom where his dog was.

Passing Knox, he managed to land a solid punch to his stomach, making the man grunt slightly. The man was solid, Memphis thought, rubbing his wrist. He'd give him at least that much.

"It's my daughter," the man in the suit said quietly. "I apologize for how we handled this, but we're desperate at this point."

When Memphis turned to look at him, he shoved a picture in front of his face.

It was of a beautiful young woman with long blonde hair. Her light-blue eyes were full of mischief as she laughed at the camera. There were trees just turning in the fall air behind her, making the picture look like a postcard of some small New England town.

When he looked from the picture to the man in the suit, Memphis could see the pain in the man's eyes making Memphis falter.

"Guys, give us a few minutes," the big man they called Knox said, opening the door to the bedroom.

Pushing Memphis inside, he closed the door behind the three of them, leaving the other two men in the living room. Finding his dog sprawled on his dog bed, Memphis fell down next to him, checking his vitals. "It was just a light sedative," Knox added, rolling his eyes.

"He's a fucking border collie. The most Murphy would have done was herd you into the house."

The dog was out like a light, but his breathing was unobstructed, so Memphis felt a little better. He had been arranged comfortably on his dog bed, which was something at least.

"You named your dog Murphy?" Knox asked.

"He was already named when I got him. He was payment for the surgery that delivered him and his littermates. The family didn't have any money, so I got Murph in payment later. I don't know why I'm telling you any of this."

Memphis stroked a hand down the dog before standing. Facing the two men, he crossed his arms over his chest, waiting for an explanation. He didn't owe them anything, but he could at least listen to what they had to say.

"I'm James Kent," the suit told him.

So, this was Senator Kent from Connecticut.

"My daughter, Thayer, was abducted two weeks ago from her college dorm. The FBI has been unable to find any trace of her, even with the information we've been sent. Knox mentioned he might know someone who could help us. I'm afraid I used my pull on the SASC, Senate Armed Services Committee, to request your file, which was heavily redacted. There were no specifics on how you are able to find people like you can, but you have an extremely high success rate."

Senator Kent motioned for Knox to hand him a picture. In it, Memphis saw the same girl, only this time she looked filthy. Even though she looked scared in the picture, he could see the slight raise of her chin in defiance. She was sitting in a chair with her hands bound and a newspaper dated two days ago on her lap.

"How much are they asking for?" Memphis asked, looking at the senator.

"They don't want money. They want information about our military that I won't give them." He laid his hand imploringly on Memphis's forearm crossed over his chest. "I love her more than my own life. I would happily give mine to get her back. But I won't jeopardize our men overseas for it."

Memphis was shocked. He never thought he would meet a politician with morals. It was good to know they still existed, but he couldn't go through this again. He had seen too many dead bodies, watched too many more die in front of his eyes.

"I'm sorry, but I think you've been misinformed. I'm not your man," he said quietly, turning back to his dog.

"Do you want me to tase him again, sir?" Knox asked. "Please let me light this piece of shit up again."

"No, Knox. We'll be going. There has to be another way to find her."

"Sir, we've exhausted all of our resources. That's why we're here."

Memphis listened as they walked through his house toward the door, arguing.

He thought about the two pictures, the one of the pretty woman laughing at the camera and the one of the scared woman glaring at her captors. They would find another way. He's a senator, for crap's sake. He had access to the very best resources. But if he did have those resources, why hadn't they found her yet?

With one more look at his dog to make sure he was okay, Memphis sighed before walking into the living room.

Knox had just reached out to close the front door when Memphis spoke. "If I do this..." There was a pause before he continued. "If I do this, I'm not responsible for what I find."

Looking up, Knox caught Memphis's eyes staring into his. Knox and Senator Kent stepped back into the cabin.

"You'll help us?" the senator asked, a slight quiver in his voice.

Memphis realized he really was their last option. With another sigh, Memphis looked up at the ceiling before returning his gaze back to them. With a slight nod of his head, the men closed the door behind them.

"First, the fewer people here, the better for me," Memphis stated, motioning to the extra men Knox had hired to help.

Knox crossed to one of the men, speaking quietly to him before they left the cabin.

"I sent them back to the hotel to get the command center set up," Knox said once they had left the cabin.

"Second, if she is still alive," Memphis continued, "I can't bring her back. It's not like *Star Trek*. I can't just beam someone out."

Knox and the senator settled onto the small couch, listening.

"You have to be prepared that I might find her dead." Memphis stared at the senator until he nodded his head once.

"I can only give you information on what I find. I can't physically get that far away from her. I can't touch her, but I will do my best to talk to her. If I can see anything that will help identify where she is, I'll let you know when I come back."

"I understand. We're not expecting a miracle, but we have to try everything," the senator answered, nodding anxiously.

"Third," Memphis said, ignoring the senator's words. "I can pull myself out, but I can't see what's happening here. You can't leave me. If you need me to come back, you have to get my attention pretty hard.

Not with a taser!" he added, looking at a disappointed Knox.

"Whatever," Knox said, putting his hands up in a gesture of surrender.

"Finally, this stays between us. I'm serious. No one finds out what I do here. Otherwise, I'd have to disappear for good this time, and I've worked too damn hard making a life here."

Memphis waited until he had received promises from both men to keep his secret between the three of them. Pushing his lips together in a thin line, Memphis silently debated with himself over what he was about to do one more time before nodding with conviction.

"Do you have something personal that belongs to her?" When the senator pulled a pink stuffed bunny out of his bag, Memphis rolled his eyes. "I have to do this holding a stuffed animal?"

"She got it when she was a baby. She never slept without it. She even took it to college with her. Knox said to bring something special to her," the senator said.

Memphis glared at Knox, who was trying to stifle his shit-eating grin. It was starting to worry Memphis how much the other man seemed to know about him. He knew the military had buried his file deep to keep it away from any combatants that might want to kidnap him. If these men had the ability to dig up a burned file, why couldn't they find one missing woman?

"Just set it on the coffee table."

They all looked toward the bedroom when they heard whimpering.

"Do you remember what I said?"

When they nodded, Memphis turned toward Knox.

"You'd better take care of my fucking dog," he added before focusing on the bunny.

Most of the time, when Memphis was hunting for a missing soldier or insurgent, he had to focus hard on the item he was given. It could take quite a while for him to find them. However, occasionally he seemed to have a special connection to the person. When that happened, he would be transported instantly to them. It was rare, but it did happen.

With a deep breath, Memphis reached for the bunny, clutching it in his hands.

CHAPTER TWO

The first thing that hit Memphis was the smell. There was a strong profusion of urine, body odor, and mildew.

Taking a minute to look around the room from his dark corner, he stopped on the small body lying on a cot in the large metal cell. Watching her intently for a few minutes, he relaxed slightly when he realized she was still alive, just apparently asleep.

Further investigation of her would have to wait, though, until he could finish his recon of the room. Taking in every detail, he eased out of the dark corner until he could look out the doorway into a dirt tunnel.

The room was dug out of rock like a root cellar used to keep vegetables cool through the summer months. It had been fitted with a cage in one corner that looked like a glorified kennel measuring approximately six by eight feet.

A cord stretched across the ceiling where a low-watt bulb hung to provide the little bit of light the room had. There was an open doorway leading out of the room and from the way it looked, a tunnel ran into the darkness.

Memphis guessed there was a set of steps to a door leading outside at the end of the tunnel. Whether the door led out next to a house in the city or in the middle of nowhere, he had no idea.

"They left a while back. No one will be back until later to bring me something to eat."

Memphis jumped at the sound of the hoarse voice behind him.

Spinning around, he met two large blue eyes staring back at him. She had propped herself up on the cot, watching him warily.

"Where did you come from? The door hinges creak, so I know you didn't come from out there," she said, waving her hand weakly at the doorway.

Her cage contained nothing but a small cot, a blanket, and a bucket he assumed was her bathroom.

"Thayer Kent?" Memphis asked, sticking his head out of the room to look down the tunnel. When she didn't answer him, he took a step back into the dank room. "Are you Miss Kent, Senator Kent's daughter?" he asked again.

She nodded without taking her eyes off him.

"My name is Memphis Prescott, and I'm here to try to help you."

Thayer watched as he walked down the tunnel before returning after a few minutes. There was something odd about him, but she couldn't quite put her finger on what.

"How do I know you're here to help me? You could just be another one of them," she said. "If you're really here to help me, then let me out." Her eyes narrowed as she took him in. "Who sent you?"

Memphis studied her for a moment. She definitely wasn't some poor, helpless victim. Thayer was thin-looking and filthy, but her eyes betrayed her intelligence, and her chin jutted up in defiance. He liked this woman. She was a fighter. A lot of women would just curl up in a ball giving up, but not this one.

"Your father and some big guy named Knox sent me. They brought a stupid pink bunny to help me find you," he answered calmly, trying to give her something that only she would recognize.

Her eyes lit up for a second. "Mr. Wiggles?" she whispered, her eyes glimmering for a moment with unshed tears.

For some unexplained reason, Memphis had a sudden urge to pull her into his lap to hold her. He was furious that someone thought they could just snatch her away.

"Oh, for fuck's sake. I'm holding a pink rabbit named Mr. Wiggles?" He relaxed, seeing the corners of her mouth twitch before wariness clouded her face again.

"Why didn't they come? Where's the cavalry I know Dad will send?" Thayer asked him.

Memphis stalked toward her until she shrank back in apprehension. He stopped immediately, his eyebrows knitting in concern.

"Knox would never send just anyone after me."

"Thayer? I'm not going to hurt you. Knox sent me because I can do what he can't." Thayer's look of fear cut right through him. "Here, let me show you." Stepping forward, he ran his hand through the bars of her cage.

"I'm like a hologram. Try it," he said, slowly stepping the rest of the way through the cage.

Holding out a hand to her, he waited patiently while she gathered up her nerve. Reaching out, she slid her hand right through his.

"How?" was all Thayer could get out as she scrambled back onto the bed.

Watching her clutch the blanket to her made Memphis step back through the bars. He could see how truly terrified she was, even though she was putting on a good show. The last thing he wanted was to add to her fear.

"I have no idea. I was just born like this. I'm back in my cabin with your dad and Knox, but I can appear to you." When she just stared at him, he finally sighed, plowing ahead. "I need to get any information from you I can so we can use it to find where you are."

He watched as Thayer considered what he said for several beats before sitting on the edge of the bed. With a nod, she scrunched her eyebrows together in concentration, determined to do whatever she needed to get home again.

"Okay. What can I do to help?" she asked.

Memphis couldn't help but be impressed. He swore he could hear the steel coursing through her veins.

"Tell me everything you can remember. Every smell, sound, anything that could help." He leaned up against the cell, waiting for her to answer.

"How do you not fall back through? I thought you were a hologram."

"It's complicated. I can make inanimate objects either solid or not, but people and animals are always intangible for some reason. We can discuss it later, but for right now, let's focus on getting you out of here."

Thayer nodded her head, looking at him in confusion. "Right. How they kidnapped me is all still a blur. I'm sure they drugged me somehow. One minute I'm in my dorm, the next I wake up in the back of a vehicle.

"I think I'm in a cellar or something. It smells dank. I'm almost positive we drove down a dirt road to get here. The vehicle slowed down, and I was thrown around some. I also remember being brought down steps while I was still blindfolded."

Memphis nodded his head absently in thought. He knew she could be anywhere. Without an idea of how long she was in the vehicle or which direction they drove in, it would be almost impossible to find her. He was shaken from his thoughts a few minutes later by her quiet question.

"Can't you hike out to see where I am, then bring back reinforcements?"

Looking up, he reminded himself not to get attached. It just gave a victim false hope in their rescue. But something about her just called to him. It wasn't just her beauty that shone even through the grime she was being forced to live with. Her strength called to him. He knew without a doubt that, if given the opportunity, she would fight her way out.

"I can't get that far from you, or I'll just disappear back home. It's another one of the weird rules that governs my...condition. Keep going. What else did you notice?"

"I've seen at least four different men, but they wear ski masks, so I don't recognize their faces. The men who abducted me were older, but the ones who bring me food are young, like high school. It smelled like pine when we arrived, like in the mountains but not in New England. I don't know what else I can tell you."

For the first time, Memphis noticed that she was dressed in nothing but a pair of flannel pajama pants with a tank top. Her feet were bare.

"They abducted you in your sleep?" he asked.

"They got into my dorm room somehow. My roommate was gone for the weekend, so it was just me. I think they broke in really early in the morning. They put something over my face to knock me out. When I woke up, I was in a vehicle like a van or truck. Maybe a truck bed with a cap?"

He nodded his head absently, deep in thought. It was pretty brazen to abduct someone from a dorm where anyone could see you, no matter what time of the day. Did they know her roommate would be gone, or was it just luck? If the roommate had been there, were they prepared to kill her?

"Memphis?"

He was jolted out of his thoughts.

"I'm scared I'm running out of time. The man who hired the other men came back a couple days ago. He was mumbling something about upping the pressure," Thayer whispered as a tear escaped down her cheek. She swiped at it with a stubborn motion. "The other men I can handle pushing me around, but something about him terrifies me."

"What else can you tell me? Did you catch this

man's name or the names of the others? Did he mention anything about what he meant by upping the pressure?" he asked gruffly, hating how scared she was.

He didn't really mean to come across as angry, but he couldn't afford to become too attached to this woman. He had learned early that he couldn't risk becoming emotionally involved in what he did because sometimes he was too late to save them. It was important that he be able to go back to his life no matter how this ended.

He watched Thayer as she searched her brain for something to add. Finally, she met his eyes, shrugging her shoulders.

"I'm sorry," Thayer whispered as she swiped at another tear rolling down her cheek. "I never saw his face."

"No, don't be sorry." Memphis took a step toward her, impulsively crossing back through the bars before stopping. "You're doing great. I'll get this information back to Knox so he can start working through it."

He walked back to the dark corner. Sometimes it completely freaked people out if he just appeared or disappeared in front of them. He had learned it was best to do it unseen, if possible.

"Memphis?" Thayer called out in panic. Stepping back into the little bit of light allowed by the bare bulb from the tunnel, he waited for her to continue. "Will you come back? I..." Her voice faded away as she looked around the room, desperately trying to find a reason for him to return.

"I'll come back," he finally said quietly before stepping back into the shadows. Thayer didn't actually see him leave, but Memphis heard the sob that escaped her as he faded away. She could survive until he returned, he told himself.

Memphis came back into his body with a gasp, startling Knox awake. After flailing for a minute with wild eyes, Memphis finally settled back into his chair.

"Easy, buddy," Knox said, handing him a bottle of water. "Did you find her?"

Memphis threw the rabbit at the coffee table.

"What?" Knox asked, leaning toward him with concern on his face.

"Where is the senator?" Memphis asked.

"Out walking your fucking dog. What did you see?" Knox leaned forward with a scowl, as if ready to pound the information from Memphis. It was obvious now just how much Thayer meant to these two men.

"She's still alive."

"Thank God," Knox said, leaning back in his seat with a deep exhale.

"She's not good, though. She looks thinner than the picture, and she's still wearing her pajamas. She's being held underground in a cell inside a root cellar or something similar somewhere. She won't last in the cold for too much longer."

Memphis stood, walking over to a small desk in the corner near the kitchen. Sitting down, he began to sketch out a picture. Looking over his shoulder, Knox watched as he drew a diagram of the room Thayer was being held in.

"There is a tunnel of some kind, but I couldn't get far enough away to follow it. There are no windows, but there is electricity." Memphis went on to relay everything to Knox that Thayer had told him.

"Okay. Yeah, this is good," Knox said, running his

hand through his hair. "I'll relay this information to my guys. The FBI will also need to hear this."

"No!" Memphis says, spinning around to catch Knox's arm before he could dial his phone. "They can't know I helped you." Panic must have shown on Memphis's face, causing Knox to nod slowly at him.

"I'll keep you out of it," Knox said resolutely. "But just so you know, the agent I've been working with in the DC office seems like a stand-up guy. I won't say anything about you though."

When the senator opened the door, Murphy bolted drunkenly toward Memphis. While he pet his dog, he listened to Knox relay the information to the senator. True to his word, Knox informed the FBI without bringing attention to how they got their intel.

"Thank you," the senator said sincerely, shaking Memphis's hand. "We'll leave you alone now. Hopefully we can use this information to find her." He gathered up the pictures of Thayer, putting them back in his bag. When he picked up the bunny, Memphis found himself stopping him.

"Leave that here. I'll try to see what else I can find out. Maybe she'll remember something else."

"We'll be staying at the hotel in town tonight. Please let us know immediately if you get anything else."

Memphis nodded at the senator. Since there was only one hotel in town, Memphis knew he could find Knox if he had anything new.

After they cleared out of his cabin, he collapsed on the couch. He knew he had to formulate a better game plan tomorrow if he hoped to help find her. Sleep was going to be necessary, however, if he stood a chance of learning anything new. It always made him exhausted when he projected himself somewhere.

His last thought was of the woman in the picture asking him to return to her as his heavy eyelids slowly closed.

CHAPTER THREE

Memphis groaned as he rolled over the next morning, trying to see the clock. Somehow, he had managed to make his way into the bedroom before passing out in bed.

"Fuck, that can't be right." Finally, hunting down the glasses sitting on the nightstand, he slid them on, looking at the clock again. "Shit!"

Jumping out of bed, he grabbed his jeans off the floor, pulling them on. He had forgotten to set the alarm and was already very late to feed the animals at the clinic. Choosing the closest Henley from the closet, he jerked it over his head, careful not to break his glasses.

He couldn't remember taking his contacts out last night and said a quick prayer in the hope they would turn up shortly. With any luck, he took them out when he'd kicked his clothes off.

With a pair of socks in his hand, Memphis slid to an abrupt stop when he reached his living room. Sitting on the coffee table was the pink bunny.

"Shit!"

"You already said that," a deep voice rumbled from the kitchen, making Memphis jump. "Can I have another four-letter word for four hundred, Alex?"

Spinning around, Memphis found Knox standing in his kitchen with a cup of coffee in his hand.

"How the fuck do you keep getting in here?" Memphis asked, scowling.

"So that's a no on the expanded vocabulary? If you're not going to bother to lock your door, I assume that's an open invitation. Coffee?" Pulling a cup from the open shelf, he filled it before offering it to Memphis.

"I have to get to the clinic." Memphis sat down in his lounge chair, putting on his socks.

"I had the kid who works there feed everything. Told him you thought you had caught the flu." Knox sat down on the couch, crossing his leg over his knee. "I assume that's who I asked. He's listed as 'vet tech kid' in your phone."

"He didn't ask who you were?"

"He did. I had to choose between an old college buddy or former lover. I thought the latter had more flair," Knox said with a smirk.

"Asshole," Memphis growled, snatching up his phone. "How did you even get into my phone?" When Knox grinned, Memphis shook his head. "You know what, I don't even want to know."

Checking his texts, he found that his high school assistant, Jonathon, had indeed confirmed he would check on the handful of animals this morning and have the receptionist reschedule his farm visit when she got in. Knox had simply been jacking with him since he had texted Jonathon this morning, pretending to be Memphis. At least he didn't have to worry about it getting done. Jon was more mature than most of the thirty-year-olds he knew.

"There we go. We're up to three words now." Memphis flipped the big man off.

Obviously, his high school kid was more mature than Memphis was. Knox just laughed before nodding at the coffee table.

"You going back to check on our girl? I thought I should be here to watch your back if you did."

After a few minutes of glaring at an amused Knox, Memphis sighed. "Yeah, I promised her I would. I have to eat first though. Do you want some Cheerios?" he asked, crossing to the kitchen to fish the cereal out of the cabinet.

"Honey nut or regular?" Knox asked.

"Honey nut. I'm not two years old anymore." When Knox just stared at him, he finally rolled his eyes. "Fine, I have both."

With a grin, Knox said, "I'm good with either."

Pulling two bowls off the shelf, Memphis added the milk to their cereal. Handing Knox his bowl, they both sat in the living room, eating in silence.

"Does it take a lot of energy to do what you do?" Knox asked, finally breaking the silence.

When Memphis nodded, Knox stood, taking the bowls to the sink. He sat back down on the couch as Murphy trotted in from the bedroom. Hopping onto the couch, he curled up, resting his head on Knox's leg.

"Really?" Memphis asked, looking at the dog. "Do you not have any loyalty?" With a roll of his eyes directed at Knox, he sat down in one of the armchairs as he reached for the bunny. "Try not to let him eat your face while I'm gone."

This time, the first thing that hit Memphis was not the smell, but voices. From his dark corner, he could see Thayer slowly come into focus, flanked by two men in ski masks. She'd been pulled out of her cell for some reason.

Looking at the corner, she shook her head so lightly that Memphis would have missed it had he blinked. He stayed silent in the dark, waiting as the men taunted her.

"Damn, she stinks like shit!" a third man said, looking at her.

Memphis could see Thayer shaking slightly. She had to be terrified, but somehow, she was holding it together.

"Give me that," the man said again, grabbing a bucket of water out of the other man's hands.

Dumping the first bucket over her head, he reached out for a second one, laughing when Thayer flinched. Pouring the other bucket over her head, the man leered cruelly at her.

"Shit, look at those tits! When do we get a piece of that?" the man asked, reaching out and pinching one of Thayer's nipples that had grown hard in the cold air.

Memphis took a step out of the shadows toward them. He wasn't sure what to do. He couldn't throw anything at them. There was nothing in the room to use. Knocking them out with his fist was definitely out. He guessed he could try to fuck with their minds, but from what he saw, he wasn't sure there was much there to fuck with.

He stopped when Thayer's eyes cut up to his over their shoulders. With a slight raise of only one of her fingers at her side, she motioned for him to wait.

"As soon as he has what he wants, he said we could do whatever we want with her."

Memphis took a deep breath, focusing on what information he could gather from the men. He decided quickly that they were very young, as Thayer had said. They all had the same accent, similar to the one Knox had, only slightly different. It wasn't as lilting as his Tennessee one either.

"Come on, man. We've got practice in an hour." Throwing Thayer onto the floor of her cell, the men stalked out, laughing.

Memphis slid over to the door of the room, listening until he heard a heavy door close. Crossing quickly to Thayer, he walked through the bars. Thayer was shaking so violently, he was certain her body temperature was dangerously low.

"Get up, Thayer, you'll freeze." When she ignored him, staying curled up on the floor, he kneeled down, getting as close to her face without touching her as he could. "Thayer! Get up!"

With a startled gasp, she sat up, swinging at him.

"That's it, come on." He watched as a second swing sliced through his body, but she was scrambling to her feet. "Thayer, look at me." His voice came out gruffer than he wanted it to, but he had to get her attention. He could hear her teeth chattering hard enough to break.

"I-I'm so tired," she slurred, looking at him. A stream of cold mist circled out of her mouth as she exhaled. "It's s-so cold."

"Hold your arms up," Memphis barked out at her.

She did it without thinking as she watched Memphis study her waist. He took hold of the hem of her tank top, careful not to touch her body. Her clothes he could make solid to his touch, but her skin he couldn't.

In one quick movement, he pulled it over her head, letting it fall to the floor. Thayer quickly pulled her arms down in front of her bare chest.

"W-what are you doing?" she asked as he dropped back to his knees.

Gently taking her pants in both hands at her thighs, he started working them down, holding the material away from her skin.

"No!" She tried to pull away from him, but he had a tight hold on her pants. With one hand, Thayer tried to push him away, her hand passing into his shoulder. With a gasp, she jerked her hand back to her chest.

"Hold still. I'm trying to get the wet clothes off of you before you freeze to death. It's not easy."

Thayer snorted out a laugh. He worried that she was beginning to lose her grip on reality.

When Memphis had her pants around her ankles, she stepped out of them, holding on to the bars. He crossed to the cot, picking up the blanket on it.

"Get in."

She lay down on the cot, facing away from him. When the blanket landed on her, she spun to face him, tucking it around her as best she could. Her teeth were chattering, and she looked so sleepy, but she kept an eye on him anyway.

Memphis picked up her clothes, wringing the water out of them before hanging them on the bars to dry. Crossing through the bars, he sat down in the door of the tunnel, leaning so he could see both her and the entrance.

"Thank you," Thayer whispered as her eyes started to close.

Memphis watched her in confusion as her eyes slowly closed. He could not understand why she would thank him for standing by when she was assaulted, then forcibly removing her clothes. Nothing about what had just happened was okay.

They needed to figure out where she was quickly before whoever the mysterious leader of this brain trust realized he would never get what he wanted.

But weren't there better ways to get national secrets than kidnapping a senator's daughter even if he was on the SASC? It didn't make any sense. In the end, would he simply leave her to the assholes who were supposed to be taking care of her?

Memphis settled against the opening to the tunnel. He was at least skilled at watching over someone. He was sure Knox would be pissed by how long it was taking, but he would just have to wait. Memphis knew he couldn't leave her.

CHAPTER FOUR

"What the fuck took you so long?" Knox barked out when Memphis finally came back with a gasp.

He would feel bad about growling at him if he wasn't so worried about Thayer, the guy looked exhausted. Senator Kent had joined him, leaving the rest of the men back at the hotel. While Knox had paced, the senator had sat quietly with his eyes glued on Memphis's blank face.

"I think I might have an idea of the area where they're keeping her," Memphis said, trying to get up to walk to the kitchen. "I need something to eat."

With a strong arm, Knox pushed him back into the chair, leaning over until he was glaring menacingly close to Memphis's face.

"Answers first," Knox said.

"Get away from me," Memphis growled, shoving at Knox. It was the first time Knox could remember not being able to intimidate someone.

"Here," Knox growled back, handing him a bottle of water.

"Knox, get him something to eat," the senator said, placing a hand on Knox's forearm. When he snorted in disgust, standing back up, the senator continued. "Where do you think she is?"

"I think maybe she is in the Appalachian Mountains somewhere." Memphis took off his glasses, rubbing his eyes before continuing. "The guys holding her have accents similar to Knox but even more hillbilly."

"I don't sound like a hillbilly," Knox grumbled, tossing a bag of chips at Memphis. "That's what, over two hundred thousand square miles? Might as well just say she's east of the Mississippi River for all the good it does."

"If you'll stop acting like a douche and listen to me, I can narrow it down," Memphis said. "I think we can rule anything north of the Pennsylvania border out, and it doesn't sound like a Tennessee accent. More near the Smokies. Their accents don't roll like North Carolina. My guess is West Virginia or Kentucky. You're from Kentucky, right?"

"Yeah, so?" Knox answered warily.

"There you have it, asshole hillbillies. Must be from Kentucky."

"I will knock your head clean off next time," Knox growled.

He had grown up in the shadow of Fort Knox, Kentucky. You could disparage anything about him you wanted, except for the beautiful state of his birth.

"Wait, that's a long way from her school to transport her," the senator said, ignoring Knox. "Did you see who took her?"

"I saw the men paid to watch her, but they had ski masks on. Thayer said the men who transported her were a different group. She said they were more professional. The guys bringing her food seem to be strictly hired idiots. There's also another man who's pulling the strings, probably the one who contacted you."

Memphis stood, walking on shaky legs into the kitchen. Setting Murphy's bowl with kibble in it on the floor, he picked up an apple, biting into it.

"I think she's in a root cellar or some kind of bunker. West Virginia is actually my best educated guess based on their accents and what Thayer described of her impressions of the time she was outside."

They were all quiet for a few minutes, mulling over the new information. Finally, Knox broke the silence.

"I think we need to move our focus to that area, Senator. I also think you need to return home." When the senator shook his head, Knox quickly added, "You need to be there in case he tries to contact you again. We're going to head to the mountains to start our hunt. Pack your bag, you're going with me," he said, looking at Memphis.

Memphis glared at Knox. "I'm not going with you. I can help from here, and I have people who rely on me to tend to their animals."

"How I see it is you have two choices," Knox said, pulling his taser gun out of its holster. "The nice way or the silent way."

"Put it away, Knox. I know you want to find her as much as I do, but this isn't the way," the senator said. Turning to Memphis, he said, "If you can make the arrangements, I will gladly cover any expenses at the vet clinic. Thayer is all I have. Her mother passed away when she was a girl, so I raised her on my own with the help of Knox. Please help us bring her home."

Knox could see Memphis mentally wrestling with the decision before letting out a weary sigh.

"Let me make a phone call," Memphis said, putting his glasses back on.

"I'll also happily pay for someone to watch your dog."

"The dog comes with me. That's a deal breaker." Memphis stood resolutely, staring at the senator with his arms crossed until he nodded.

Knox had already guessed that Murphy served as a kind of therapy dog for Memphis based on the interaction he witnessed between them. If he had to guess, Murphy helped Memphis wake from nightmares that still plagued him.

The senator crossed to the door, pulling it open.

"Sir," Memphis said. When the senator turned to look at him, he added, "It's really important that you buy us as much time as you can, okay?" With a solemn nod, Senator Kent left.

When the door closed, Knox grabbed him, shoving him against the wall. "What did that mean? What are you not telling us?" he growled, holding Memphis with a strong arm across his throat.

"It means that if we don't find her soon, those guys will rape and kill her. I didn't think her father needed to hear that."

Knox physically jerked like he had been slapped before he turned Memphis loose.

"When I got there, they were throwing water on her

so she wouldn't smell as bad before fondling her. One said as soon as the man got what he wanted, they would be allowed to do whatever they wanted with her."

Knox's jaw clenched as his teeth ground together. Memphis was right, her time was running out.

After making arrangements for the retired vet to oversee the office for him, Memphis threw some clothes in a bag, rejoining Knox in the living room. The big man had gathered up Murphy's food, bowls, and leash, carrying them to the SUV. The senator had arranged for a chartered jet to take them anywhere they needed to go.

Memphis hated to fly, he had lived through one crash in Afghanistan and figured surviving another one wasn't good odds.

He followed the rest of the men on board, choosing a seat toward the back. Sensing his stress, Murphy curled up in the seat next to him, resting his head on his leg as Memphis absentmindedly petted him.

"Not a fan of flying, I take it," Knox said, sitting down across from him. He watched as Memphis's knuckles turned white as they sped down the runway. "I'm not a fan of small spaces. Commercial planes are not a problem, but these little suckers..."

Memphis finally turned to stare at him, his eyebrows knit in concentration.

"Hey Murph, how are you hanging in there?" Knox asked as he leaned over to scratch the dog's head.

Murphy answered with a quick thump of his tail on the seat.

"What do you get out of this?" Memphis asked the big man with narrowed eyes.

He had been trying to figure out the relationship between Knox and Thayer for a while. Were they lovers? It seemed like Knox was a little too invested in her for him just to be her bodyguard.

Knox sat back, looking at Memphis with a scowl. "You're obviously more than just a hired gun. How do you know the Kents?" They glared at each other in silence for a minute before Memphis continued. "You've put me through hell in the last twenty-four hours. You don't think I deserve to know what your motivation is? I can understand if this is just a job, but I don't think it is. Are you sleeping with her?"

"Christ no, and keep your voice down! Those guys *are* hired guns that don't need to get the wrong idea." Knox crossed his arms over his chest, glaring at Memphis. "Jesus, what is wrong with you? I'm old enough to be her father. She's only twenty, you dick."

"Then what? Does he have some sort of blackmail on you? Are you hoping to become her fuck daddy or what?"

Knox swung at Memphis, connecting with his jaw. Memphis was grateful they were seat-belted in, since there wasn't that much force behind the punch. His taunting had had the desired effect, though, confirming his suspicion there was more to this story.

"So, it is personal," Memphis stated with a smile, rubbing his chin. "You have five seconds to tell me what it is, or I'm not finding her just to have the next depraved fucker get his hands on her."

"I was her math tutor, then her bodyguard, now...

I'm her friend. Nothing more, understand me?" Knox growled, spearing Memphis with a glare.

The punch had gotten the attention of the other men, but they quickly went back to minding their own business.

"Thayer is brilliant when it comes to the liberal arts. Mathematics, though, not so much. I started tutoring her in middle school when I was still serving under her father in the Navy. She would come to his office after school to do her homework until he was done. I would watch her struggle with her math until I couldn't stand it anymore. When I got out, he helped me get a job teaching math at the private school Thayer attended. I've known the family for years now."

"The fuck you say." Memphis looked at him with even more concern on his face. "You think you can lead a search and rescue effort as a math teacher?" Leaning back, he snorted, looking out the window. "A fucking math teacher," he said in disgust.

"I was the officer in charge of the engineering department for a nuclear sub before that, you dickwad."

"How did you ever fit your fat ass in a sub?" Memphis could see Knox thinking about taking another shot at him, but before he could take a swing, he caught the smile on Memphis's face. He wasn't sure why, but something about the big man made Memphis believe in him.

"So, what's the plan when we get there, squid?" Knox flipped him off before laying out his ideas. Memphis found himself forgetting about the flight as he asked questions about the plan.

"I need to find a way to have them leave her cage open. If she can walk down the tunnel with me, I might be able to get outside to give you a better view of the landscape," he said.

"Anything would help. How good are you at identifying trees or plants? If you can get outside, that might help us narrow the area down," Knox added.

"I took plant science in school, so I'm okay. Not a botanist, but I can tell the difference between a live oak and an Aspen pine. If it's poisonous to animals, I'll know it."

"Such a fucking nerd," Knox snorted.

"Says the math teacher," Memphis answered.

By the time the plane landed in West Virginia, they thought they had a solid enough plan to move forward. Knox went over the plan with the leader of the hired team on their way to the hotel. Arrangements were made to have several drones brought in to help search the area.

After a heated argument, Memphis finally had to give in to the idea of bringing the FBI into the current situation. Reluctantly, he agreed with Knox's assessment that they needed their resources to find the captors, but he still refused to meet with them.

Memphis was positive if the FBI knew what he could do, they would be standing on his doorstep every time someone went missing. It wasn't that he was cold-hearted, but he had spent six long years doing just that for the military. It had not only taken a physical toll on him but a psychological one as well. Finding a fallen soldier had been heartbreaking, finding a murdered child would be his undoing.

It was dark when the two men finally settled into their room. They had picked up a couple of sandwiches from the local diner, slumping across from each other at the small table in the room.

"You're going to make him fat," Memphis growled at Knox, watching him slip the third bite of ham to Murphy. With a sigh, he stood, walking over to his pack. "I'm going to go over the plan with Thayer. You're going to stay here, right?"

"Yeah, Murph and I'll be here. Might catch up on some TV since you don't believe in it in that shack you call a cabin." Knox smirked at him.

"I can't get any service! Oh, fuck it." Memphis sat back, tugging the rabbit out of his pack. His eyes glazed over instantly.

The first thing that resonated with Memphis this time was how dark it was. He knew there was a bulb that hung down somewhere near Thayer's cage. The bulb from the tunnel that cast a pale light on her usually had been turned off at this time.

"Thayer?" he whispered into the darkness.

"I'm over here. They unscrewed the bulbs when they came back in. I guess they don't want anyone to see it in the dark outside. I don't really know."

Memphis breathed a sigh of relief hearing her voice.

"Keep talking so I can find my way over. I remember about where the bulb is, I just have to find it."

"Okay. What do I talk about?" she asked.

"Tell me about yourself."

"Okay. Well, you know my name, so I'll go from there. I'm a sophomore at Amherst majoring in literature. My favorite class is on American literature between the wars. You know, the 1920s and '30s. I'm not very good at math or science, which I'm sure Knox was only too happy to share.

"I grew up in New London, Connecticut, where my dad was in the Navy before going into business after my mother died. He commanded a submarine, but he wouldn't leave me behind when he deployed, so he took early retirement. We have a dog named Dude, because he's always surfing the counters in the kitchen."

Memphis snorted out a laugh. He would give anything to remain in the dark just listening to her talk, but he soon found the bulb.

"Here we go," he said, screwing the bulb back in. "How are you holding up?" he asked Thayer as she blinked against the sudden light.

Waiting for her response, he looked around the room. When he didn't see what he was searching for, he walked as far down the tunnel as he could hunting for something.

"Thayer? You okay?" he asked again, walking back into the room.

"I'm holding it together. What are you looking for?"

"I was looking for a switch. I think this is just an extension cord run from outside. It means that the electricity is brought here from somewhere else." He shrugged, turning back to her. "Everything helps."

She nodded her head in understanding.

"There's something I need you to do for me, but it's going to be dangerous."

"If it gets me out of here, I'll do it," she answered without hesitating.

Memphis stopped his exploration to stare at her in disbelief. Just when he thought he couldn't be any more impressed, she knocked his feet out from under him. He hadn't even explained what he needed, but here she was jumping in feet first.

Shaking his head when he noticed her looking back at him with one eyebrow raised in question, he continued.

"I need you to tear a piece of material off your clothes to stuff in the lock when they open it to bring your food. I need to look farther down the tunnel, but you have to go with me. Do you think you can do that? They can't see you do it."

Thayer sat still for a minute, thinking.

"They rarely open the cage, preferring to just shove the sack through," she answered. "But I can do it. I'll convince them to open the door. How big a piece do you think I'll need to use?"

They studied the lock together, making a plan.

Memphis knew it was risky, and she would have to be fast, but there didn't seem to be any other alternative. He had to get her out of this hole before things changed for the worse.

"I'll be back early in the morning to hide in the corner until they're gone. If you think it's not safe, don't do it. I'll just come up with another plan. Okay?"

She nodded her head once, showing him she understood. He turned to wander back to the corner when she cleared her throat.

"Memphis?"

"Yeah?" he said without turning around.

"Will you stay until I fall asleep? Please?" Hearing the fear in her voice, he walked back over to the tunnel, sliding to the floor.

"Of course. Lie down."

"Can I say something...about last time?"

"Shoot," he said, situating himself against the doorway again so he could watch her while keeping an eye on the tunnel.

"I'm sorry I panicked. You shouldn't have had to do what you did. I'm just glad you were here, so I didn't freeze to death. I have to admit, I'm a little embarrassed about turning into a basket case."

He smiled gently at her as she watched him with her wide blue eyes.

"There's nothing to be embarrassed about. It was quite a shock to your system, plus I'm sure me jerking your clothes off didn't help much either. I'm sorry about having to do that. I didn't see anything if that helps."

"How did you not see anything? You were on your knees pulling down my pants." She chuckled slightly when Memphis's face turned slightly pink.

He prayed it didn't do that back in the hotel room, or Knox would know something was up.

"I wasn't paying attention. I mean, if I was taking your clothes off, normally I wouldn't have jerked them off that fast." He grew redder when she cocked her head at him, knitting her eyebrows. "Well, yeah, I might jerk them off quickly if I was desperate to get to what was underneath, but then I would pay attention to what I was seeing. Umm, not that I couldn't tell you were stunning, but yeah, slower would be better." He clamped his mouth shut with wide eyes as Thayer tried to hide the smile that was threatening her face. "Fuck, I'm..." He stood, walking back into the dark corner before sliding down the wall. He was such a fucking idiot.

"Memphis? Are you still here?"

"Yeah, I'm still here."

"You didn't have glasses on the first time you appeared."

Thankful that she had changed the subject, he jumped to answer. "I lost my contacts somewhere in my cabin. Knox dragged me to the airport so fast I didn't have a chance to look for them."

"You mentioned a cabin before. Where is it?"

"Small town in Minnesota. I live there with my dog, Murphy. I'm the local veterinarian."

"No wife or girlfriend?"

"Nope, just me."

"That's good. I'd like to meet Murphy." Thayer's voice was starting to slur as she crept toward sleep. "I also like your glasses. They give you a Superman look when he's Clark Kent."

Memphis could feel the red spread back up his face. "So, in a nerd kind of way."

"No, I think in more of a sexy superhero kind of way."

Memphis couldn't stop the grin from spreading across his face. "Now you're just trying to tease me. Pretty sure there is nothing sexy about a country vet wearing a pair of glasses." He laughed, watching her eyes slowly close.

"Then you haven't looked in the mirror."

He felt his heart thump hard as he stared at the small body in the cell with a stupid grin on his face.

"You'll be here tomorrow? I can do this if you're here with me."

"I'll be here," he said quietly.

"I think you can go now. You looked tired. I need

you to get your rest so you can rescue me." Memphis stood up, crossing to the light.

Reaching toward it, he paused. "Good night, Thayer."

"Good night, Memphis."

He unscrewed the bulb, leaving it how he had found it.

"Memphis?"

"I'm still here."

"Maybe next time it will be you who gets wet. That way, I can rip the clothes off of you. I think I'd like that."

Memphis groaned aloud, adjusting his growing erection before disappearing.

CHAPTER FIVE

"You'd better not be having any fucking ideas about her. I'll cut your balls off and feed them to your dog. Thirty-three is too old for her."

Memphis heard the gravelly threat from Knox when he came back, but it took him a few minutes to understand why it was directed at him. Looking down, he adjusted his seat when he saw the lingering erection.

"It's nothing. I don't ever get close to my finds. They often wind up dead," Memphis said.

Knox growled at him again before handing him a bottle of water. "It'd better fucking be nothing."

Memphis rolled his eyes at him, pissing Knox off even more. The big man crossed his arms over his chest, the muscles of his forearms bulging as he scowled down at Memphis. Memphis knew, however, that he couldn't find her without him, so he waited until Knox visibly started to calm.

"I had water and snacks delivered while you were gone," Knox said after a few minutes.

Standing, Memphis walked to the counter with the mini fridge, digging out a stick of cheese.

"How do you know how old I am?" Memphis asked, turning to look at Knox.

"I saw your file. It had your birth date."

"No, it didn't. My file has the hell redacted out of it and is buried so deep at the Pentagon, no one should be able to find it. The government doesn't want one of our enemies to discover what I can do. Just think of what Russia or North Korea could do with me. So, answer my question. How did you know how old I am?"

"I called in a favor." Knox shrugged like the information was no big deal.

"That's a fucking big favor. What else do you know about me?"

"I know you and your mom were abandoned by your dad when you were around three. She died of cancer when you were seven. You bounced around foster homes until you won a full ride to the University of Tennessee to play baseball. Joining the ROTC program, you entered the Army for six years before attending vet school at Oklahoma State University."

Memphis's heart rate sped up as he listened to Knox.

"I know exactly what you did for the Army, and I know why they finally let you out."

Memphis sank to the floor, putting his head between his knees. Knox had enough information to destroy him. He could simply sell him to the highest bidder.

When Murphy ran over, crawling under his legs, whimpering, Knox fell silent.

"What do you plan to do with me after this is over?"

Memphis asked when he had his breathing back under control.

He had to push the dog away to keep him from bathing his face with his tongue. Stretching across his lap, Murphy waited for Memphis to start petting him as he stared at the floor.

"What the fuck are you talking about? I'm not doing anything with you. I'm taking you home where you can live out your days expressing anal glands and cutting off balls. Shit like that." Knox stood up, worriedly looking at Memphis.

He knew his face was deathly white, and he was pouring sweat. Memphis also knew the dog had just saved him from another full-blown panic attack.

"I would never make you do what you did in the Army. The only reason we came at all was because we were desperate."

Memphis nodded at Knox unconvincingly. Knox could never understand how much Memphis's gift cost him. He didn't understand what it meant to constantly live in fear of being discovered by someone wanting to hurt him.

Holding a hand out to Memphis, Knox pulled him off the floor.

"Let's head to bed," Knox said. "You take the bathroom first while I feed Murphy for you."

Memphis watched the dog happily follow Knox to his food bowl by the door before walking into the bathroom. Splashing his face with water, his thoughts turned to Thayer shivering in that cold, dark cell. He didn't think he could survive even one more death played out in front of him without losing his mind. They had to find her soon.

THE NEXT MORNING, both men were out of bed at five. After dressing, they walked in silence to the local diner for breakfast. Memphis did little more than rearrange the food on his plate. He still felt wrung out from last night.

"So, I think they bring her food before they all have to head to practice somewhere. I need to be in place around six thirty, I think." Memphis kept his eyes focused on his plate.

They had left Murphy in the room, so Knox wrapped up a couple pieces of bacon to take back to him.

"I should have just enough time to walk Murph before going back."

"Yeah, sounds good. You about done?" Knox asked.

They walked back to the room the way they had come, in silence. After walking the dog, Memphis settled into the chairs in the room.

"Okay. I'll be right here."

"Whatever," Memphis muttered, grabbing the bunny. He was going to be sick.

"Memphis? Is that you? What's wrong?" He could hear the rising panic in Thayer's voice.

"I'm okay. I'm trying not to be sick," he moaned as he swallowed the bile back down. "I can't throw up here."

"What will happen?"

"I don't know, I've never had this problem before." He retched once into the corner on his knees, still trying to hold the little bit of breakfast down. "I have to go. I'll be right back."

He focused on the hotel room until he returned. Falling out of his chair onto his knees in the room, he grabbed the nearest trash can, emptying what little breakfast he had had into it.

"What the fuck!" Knox exclaimed, jumping up from the bed where he and Murphy had curled up to watch a movie. "What's happened?" Falling to his knees next to Memphis, he laid his hand on the man's back as he continued to throw up.

"I have to get back." Memphis was pasty as he reached for the rabbit on the floor.

Knox tried to stop him, wrapping his arms around his thighs, pulling him back, but Memphis was already gone.

Memphis landed back in his dark corner, collapsing against the wall. Thayer looked at the corner in concern but couldn't call out to him. They could hear the men talking as they walked down the tunnel. She stiffened her spine, prepared to do whatever had to be done to put their plan in motion. Memphis willed her to feel his support even though she couldn't see him. She had to know he was there, giving her the courage she needed.

"Hi, baby." The man with her breakfast greeted her with a malicious tone.

"Hey, yourself." Taking a deep breath, she arched her back, sticking her breasts out. "What's for breakfast this morning?"

She took a seductive step toward him. She had to get him to open the door, then distract him long enough to shove the piece of her pants she had ripped off earlier into the lock.

Thayer had told Memphis she would do whatever she had to help in her escape. As much as it killed him, all he could do was wait and pray she didn't get hurt in the process.

Running his hand down the front of her shirt, she just managed to school her features into a smile instead of showing the repulsion she had to feel for the man. Using his key, the man opened the door to get closer.

When he grabbed her hair, pulling her head to the side, Thayer backed against the door, hurriedly stuffing the small piece of cloth in the hole. He licked the side of her neck while pinching one of her nipples painfully.

Hearing his buddies calling him, he shoved her back inside, swinging the gate closed behind him. With a nasty laugh, he stalked out of the room.

Thayer just managed to grab the door as it banged closed, the cloth preventing the lock from catching, before it swung back open. When she heard the door close down the tunnel, she threw open the cage door, rushing to Memphis.

"Memphis! Are you okay? I can't see you in the dark."

"You can stop trying to feel for me too. You're digging around in my abdomen."

She laughed, sitting back on her heels at his words.

"Thank God. I was freaking out."

"Yeah, that was unpleasant. I'm fine now though. Are you okay?"

She nodded at him.

"Go eat, then we'll look around the tunnel to see what we can find."

Thayer sat still for a minute.

"I'm coming. Go eat, you need your strength."

With a quick nod, she stood up, moving back to the

cell. She left the door wide open, however. Looking up, she flinched at Memphis's pale face and dark rings under his eyes as he walked toward her from the dark corner of the room. He knew this was taking a toll on both of them now.

"Sit with me while I finish." She watched him as he slumped onto the cot. "Do you have to do anything special to make something solid?" she asked between bites of her cold breakfast.

"Not really, I just have to focus on it being solid. I just can't do it with people or animals, I don't know why. I also have to have something personal in my hand to focus on, and I can't really bring anything extra with me, like a lockpick or baseball bat."

Thayer nodded, eating the sausage biscuit they had left in the McDonald's wrapper. She took a small sip from a bottle of water, knowing it would have to last the day.

"Is this all they feed you?"

Thayer nodded again.

"No wonder I could see your hip bones. I wish I could bring you more to eat."

"I thought you said you weren't paying attention?" she asked, a small smile playing at her lips. "You know, when you stripped me?"

With a deep sigh, he looked over at her. "I'm a man, of course I paid attention." He smiled when she laughed, shaking her finger.

"And I thought you were a gentleman!" She grinned back at him. "I promise not to tell Knox about it."

"I already did. So far, he's tased me, tied me to a chair, punched me in the face, and threatened to feed my testicles to my dog. I think we're getting along pretty well all in all."

Thayer burst into laughter. When she finally caught her breath, she looked over at Memphis. "Thank you."

"For what?"

"For making me laugh in the middle of this horrible situation. If I could hug you right now, I would." She tried to bump his shoulder, forgetting she would pass through him. She started giggling again. "That's the second time I've been inside you. Next time it's your turn." Turning pink, she clamped her hand over her mouth. "I can't believe I said that."

"We'd better go check the tunnel out. If you make me hard again, Knox really will chop it off." Memphis stood, crossing through the bars.

"Again?"

He just turned, winking at her before stepping to the doorway. "Follow behind me. When we get to the end, I'll try to pop outside to see what I can see. Wait for me, but if you hear anything, run back for the cell. I'll just fade away."

Thayer looked at him, her eyebrows knit in concern as she followed him slowly. "I don't like the idea of you just fading away."

"I'll just go back to the hotel room. It's fine. Come on." Memphis led the way down the tunnel, slowly following the light from the bulb halfway down. At the end, there was a set of stairs leading up. "Wait here a second."

Climbing the stairs, he passed through the door, finding himself outside. A quick look around confirmed that the door was chained shut with a padlock, preventing anyone without a key from entering or leaving. There was an old rusting shed next to the door with old equipment lying around. The roof had partially collapsed years ago. The whole thing lay in the middle of the woods on the side of a mountain.

He could hear muffled yelling coming from the cellar door. Walking back through it, he climbed down in front of Thayer.

"Is everything okay? I tried pushing on the door, but it won't open," she said, concern lacing her words.

He was standing as close to her as he could without touching her. He desperately tried to control his heart rate, certain she would hear the hammering. She had climbed the stairs, hoping to get out.

"It's fine, but I need to look around some more. Will you be okay alone for a few minutes?"

She nodded with wide eyes.

"There's no one up there, so you're safe. Do you trust me?" he asked.

"Yes," she said without hesitation.

"Then trust me to come back to you in a few minutes. I have to get all the information I can for Knox."

When she nodded again, he pushed back out through the door.

Looking at the foliage around him, he memorized every variety he recognized. There was a rough dirt road to the location, which was good. He thought he could hear water running in the distance but couldn't see its source.

He walked as far as he could before starting to fade. When he had all of the information he could, he returned to Thayer.

"Anything?" she asked the second he reentered the tunnel.

She reached out, trying to touch him for reassurance, her hand passing through his arm. Soon he would come for her for real, then Memphis would be happy for her to hold on to him for all she was worth.

"I think so. I need to get the information back to Knox. He's brought in drones and the FBI. He'll rip this entire country apart hunting for you if he has to."

She nodded slowly, but the fear was still hovering in her eyes.

"Let's get you back so I can report in."

When she shook her head furiously, he stooped down until he could look into her eyes. They were still standing on the old cement steps leading out of her dungeon.

"Please don't make me go back in that cage," she whispered in terror at him.

It broke his heart seeing her this scared, knowing he could do nothing about it.

"Thayer," he growled out. He had to get her calmed back down. Taking the hem of her shirt in his hands, careful not to touch her, he jerked on it, getting her attention. "We're going to find you. You can survive until I come for you. I need you to stay strong for me. Understand?"

She just stared at him with those big blue eyes.

"You are the most amazing woman I've ever met. I refuse to give up, so you can't give up either. Tell me you can wait for me."

She nodded her head this time as he watched the steel come back into her eyes.

"Come on, I have to put you back," he said after a

few minutes. It broke his heart apart to see her trying to fight the fear bubbling so close to the surface. Leading her back down the tunnel, he watched as she climbed back on the cot, pulling the blanket over herself.

"When will you come back?" she asked quietly.

"Just as soon as I can. We're going to head out to find you as soon as I get back. Whatever happens, I'll be back tonight."

She nodded again as a tear slipped down her face. Memphis backed slowly into the corner until he was shrouded in the shadows.

"Thayer?"

She didn't answer, so he continued anyway.

"Just so you know. The next time I enter you. It won't be as a hologram." He smiled in the dark as he watched her mouth fall open in shock, temporarily forgetting her fear.

CHAPTER SIX

"I wish you came with a warning system on reentry," Knox grumbled when Memphis sat up suddenly on the bed. His eyes wide, he looked over at Knox sitting in the chair before stumbling toward the bathroom.

Knox listened as Memphis threw up again. He wasn't sure what he possibly had left in his stomach, but he knew something was wrong. This was obviously harder on the man than he originally let on. Crossing to the bathroom, he pulled Memphis off the floor.

"Come on, you need something to eat. Then you'll at least have something to puke up. Drink this." Knox placed a bottle of water in the man's hand before dragging him through the room.

They walked back over to the diner, finding a corner booth open. It was a little early, but Knox ordered them both a large cheeseburger, a plate of fries, and one of onion rings to share. He also had the waitress bring Memphis a ginger ale, hoping the soda would help settle his stomach.

When the food arrived, Memphis told him everything he had learned. He listed the plants he could remember on a napkin, along with drawing a rough draft of the area around the cellar.

"We don't have long, Knox. The men are getting too brave."

The big man just nodded his head, a scowl crossing over his face.

"If they hurt her, I will rip every one of them apart," Knox growled, matching Memphis's thoughts exactly.

"The senator can only stall so long."

Knox frowned at Memphis's words. He knew they were running out of time.

"Are you feeling better?" When Memphis nodded his head, Knox threw some money on the table. "Okay. I'm taking you back to the room before taking this information to the feds and our people. You need to get some sleep while we begin the search."

"No, I'm going with you."

Knox would have argued, but the look on Memphis's face made him reconsider. With a quick nod, the men separated at the hotel.

Knox went to the room set up as a command center to update everyone on the new information. He worried that the feds were becoming a little too interested in where he was getting his information. He had understood Memphis, not wanting to make his abilities known to the FBI, but they weren't stupid. The look of disbelief on Agent Tanaka's face said that he didn't buy the story Knox had spun about Memphis being just another hired tracker.

Memphis went to the room to lie down until Knox returned to get him. Knox watched as the feds worked, using the little bit of information Knox could provide to whittle down the area to search for Thayer.

After agreeing on an area of the mountains she was most likely being held in, he walked back to their room to get Memphis. Knox found him sacked out on the bed with Murphy draped over his legs. Running a hand over the dog's head, he shook Memphis awake.

"We have satellite images we need you to come look at. Don't worry, I gave the feds an alias for you. I know you're nervous about them finding out too much about who you are."

Knox grinned into his face as Memphis tried to clear his mind. Getting up, he slipped his glasses back on before following Knox out the door.

"Mr. Calipari, it's nice to meet you. I'm Special Agent Dex Tanaka. If you'll step in here, we have the enlarged aerials of West Virginia. We thought you might help us search for anything that might give us an idea of where to search." The agent gave them both a smirk before he turned, expecting the men to follow him through the door.

Putting his arm across the doorway, Memphis stopped Knox.

"Did you give me the name of the Kentucky basketball coach as an alias? You know I went to the University of Tennessee, right?"

With a smirk, Knox leaned into him. "That's for the hillbilly crack from earlier. Could be worse, you could be Coach K." With a shove, Knox pushed Memphis through the door.

Covering one table was a stack of maps showing, in remarkable detail, the mountains of the Appalachians.

It took two hours before Memphis found what he was looking for.

"This is it!" he said excitedly, looking around the room. "That's the shed that's next to the door."

"Are you sure?" Knox asked, crossing the room to where Memphis sat on the bed, hunched over a map.

"As sure as I can be."

The men locked eyes as Knox debated.

"Knox, this is it. I know it is."

Knox nodded at him once before turning to start organizing the rescue.

When he got tired of watching the feds argue over proper procedure, Memphis slipped out the door to return to his room. After taking Murphy for a quick walk, he sat down, picking up the stuffed rabbit.

SCREAMING. Phasing into the cellar, Memphis could hear muffled screaming.

"No!" he roared out when he saw the man fighting to wrestle Thayer's pants down.

Her shirt had been torn off, and he could tell one of her eyes was already swelling from being hit.

"I'll fucking kill you with my bare hands!" he yelled, walking toward the man.

He was barely more than a kid, really. She had managed to pull off the hood hiding his face. The kid jumped up when he saw Memphis, running out the door of the room, holding his pants up.

Sliding onto his knees inside the cell, Memphis jerked the blanket over her. "Thayer! Are you okay?

Thayer!" He would give anything to be able to pick her up and carry her away from this nightmare.

"Please answer me, baby."

He laid his forehead down on the side of the cot she had curled up on. He sat on his knees in silence as his chest heaved in and out. Thayer's hand smoothed the air next to his head.

"I hoped you were real. You looked so real charging out of the corner," she whispered.

Looking up at her, he watched as she turned toward the wall, curling back into a ball. Memphis felt a sudden sharp pain in the back of his head.

"Oww! Thayer, I think I've found you. Ahh!" A second pain shot through his head. He started to fade slowly. "Thayer, I'm coming for you. Don't give up on me!" he shouted as he faded away from her.

Memphis came back to the room, standing against the wall. He was actually being banged against the wall by Knox.

"Wake up, you stupid fucker!" Knox yelled, banging Memphis's head against the wall again.

Murphy was keeping up a steady cacophony of barking while dancing around their feet. Memphis couldn't tell if he was trying to stop Knox or urge him on.

"Stop! What is wrong with you?" he asked, pushing against Knox. It was like trying to move a cinder-block wall.

"We heard you scream at the other end of the hotel. What's wrong? I barely kept the feds from barging in here."

Memphis's eyes grew wide as he remembered why he was screaming. "We have to get to her now, Knox!

She's in trouble. One of the men was trying to rape her, but I managed to scare him away. I don't think it'll be long before he returns with his buddies."

Knox nodded once, then grabbed his bag, stuffing the bunny in it. Memphis was right behind him as he jerked open the door, running for the SUV.

"We'll get a location on the way. They're trying to pinpoint the exact coordinates. My guys just left with the drones to scout it out." Knox threw his bag in the back seat, then waited for Murphy to jump in.

With wheels squealing, they headed out of the parking lot toward the hills. Knox talked to his team on the phone while Memphis watched out the window for anything he recognized. Murphy quickly lost interest, curling up in the back seat. The men paused in their searching to look at the back seat when they heard snoring.

"You've been a bad influence on him," Memphis stated when Knox ended his call.

"I don't snore," he responded somewhat indignantly.

"Then what the hell was that noise coming from your side of the room last night?"

"I'm surprised you could hear it over all your farting."

"Hey! You can't say a word."

They sat in silence for a minute. Memphis stared out the window, trying hard not to let Knox see him grinning.

"What the hell did we eat last night anyway?"

With Knox's question, Memphis finally let out a burst of laughter. If Knox hadn't lightened the mood, Memphis was positive his head would have exploded from the frustration of it taking so long to get to Thayer.

"I don't know, but it damn near killed me." He laughed.

"Me too, brother, me too." Knox shook his head with a smile.

They both sobered up when his phone pinged with a text. Handing it to Memphis, he motioned for him to check it.

"It's coordinates. They found the shack, and it's only about five miles from us." Memphis gave Knox directions down the winding roads as they climbed farther into the wood-shrouded hills. When the road finally ended, both men jumped out of the SUV with Murphy at their heels.

"Here's what we're going to do," Knox said, reaching in the back for an AR-15. "You're going to focus on finding Thayer. I'm going to have your back while you do it. The feds are behind us, and my guys are using the drones to watch our six." Knox jumped out of the SUV, pulling on body armor.

Without saying a word, Memphis started farther up the hill. It took him about half an hour of searching before he finally caught sight of the shack.

"That's it," he said to Knox, crouching down.

"Okay, the feds are about fifteen minutes out. Go slow. Don't do anything stupid, just get Thayer and get out."

The men eased forward, looking for threats. They couldn't be certain if there were any traps though Memphis hadn't found any earlier.

It seemed like hours before they finally reached the door to the cellar, although it was probably only a few minutes. Murphy crept along next to Memphis, seeming to understand the need for patience as he waited for a command from his master. Knox swept the woods with his eyes as Memphis tried the door.

"Look, he left it unlocked. I'll need something to pick the cell door." Knox handed the gun to Memphis while he dug through his vest, pulling out a kit.

Slowly easing the door open, Memphis froze when he heard the hinges squeak. Knox pulled out a small can of lithium, soaking the hinges. With a nod, Memphis laid the door back against the ground before stopping above the steps to listen. Hearing nothing, he slowly stepped into the cellar.

"Be careful. I'll be up here watching for unwanted guests." Knox hoisted himself onto the sturdiest looking part of the roof of the shack, taking up the best vantage to see anyone coming.

At Memphis's quiet command, Murphy shot down the steps in front of him to scope out the cellar. He waited, hunkered down on the steps, until the dog came back around the corner to pull on his sleeve. When Memphis finally made it to the main room, he didn't see Thayer at first.

"Thayer?" he whispered. He saw the small ball on the cot move slightly, breathing a sigh she was still here.

Kneeling, he began to work on the lock. At least the Army had taught him to pick locks. He technically had a rank and was assigned to a Green Beret unit, but it was all classified. He had picked up some random skills from the other men that came in handy on occasion.

When he finally got the door open, he carefully crossed to Thayer on his knees until he reached the edge of the bed.

"Come here, baby. Let me help you." When she didn't respond, he gently laid his hand on what he guessed was her hip.

"No!" she cried, spinning in the bed as she swung a fist at him.

He grunted when it connected to his shoulder. Screaming, she kicked out at him, barely missing his face.

"Thayer, it's me, sweetheart. It's Memphis," he said calmly.

She fought him with everything her weakened body had. Finally grabbing her wrist, he pulled her flush against his chest. Wrapping his arms around her, he held on as she pushed against him.

"Open your eyes, Thayer. I'm here, I found you." He rubbed her naked back slowly as she started to settle.

"Memphis?"

He sighed when she finally relaxed in his arms. She only stayed that way for a few seconds, though, before she began to panic, clawing at Memphis like she was drowning. Wrapping her legs around him, she clung to him as great sobs escaped her. Murphy crawled over to them, pushing on Thayer's body with his nose, trying to help.

"It's okay, Murph. I've got her."

She slowly relaxed her grip on him, and he set her back on the cot. Shaking his arms out of his coat, he took off his heavy flannel shirt, sliding Thayer's arms into it. It swallowed her up, but at least it was warm.

As he finished the last button, they heard shouting outside, followed by a volley of gunshots. With a scream, Thayer threw herself tight against him.

Holding her in his arms, Memphis stood before crossing into the darkness in the corner where he used to materialize. Crouching down, he turned them against the corner, setting her on his thighs as he squatted. With one hand holding her against him, he used the other to pull her head against his chest. He could feel her shaking against him.

He wasn't worried about Knox holding off whoever was outside, but there was always the possibility of a stray bullet finding them. He had seen it happen one too many times to take a chance. With Thayer snug against him and Murphy sandwiching his body next to hers, Memphis waited for the all-clear signal.

After a few more minutes of gunfire, everything grew quiet. Memphis stood with her in his arms, preparing to fight whoever came through the door if necessary.

Whistling quietly, he sent his dog outside to find out what the threat was. He hated putting Murphy in harm's way, but he knew the dog was a master at sneaking around. It was better he had an idea of what he was about to find instead of facing it blind. Soon his dog ran back downstairs, barking. Jumping up, he placed both paws on Memphis's arms with a woof.

"Memphis?" he heard Knox yell at the opening to the tunnel. "It's all clear. Did you find her? Tell me she's okay."

Making sure her legs were securely wrapped around his waist, Memphis pulled his coat around her as she snuggled closer to him.

"We're going up, okay?"

She nodded her head before burying it into his

neck. With a last look around, he headed down the tunnel.

How COULD they be so incompetent that they couldn't keep a twenty-year-old woman hidden in a cellar?

Curtis Floyd pushed the red button on his phone, angrily ending the call. What he wouldn't give for an old landline phone that he could slam the receiver down on. He should never have left the job of securing the senator's daughter to the local idiots. At least two of the morons he had hired were dead. He would send one of his men to eliminate the remaining one. There could be no loose ends.

It would be fine. He simply needed a new plan. With his brilliance, it should be no problem to finish the job he had been assigned. He would need patience to wait until the media circus he was certain would surround the rescue quieted down before issuing the order to finish the job.

Knowing that big fucker who hovered around her, security would be impenetrable at both her home and on campus for quite some time. He would have to wait for his opportunity to pounce.

He flinched slightly when the buzzer went off on his intercom. His employer still preferred the old way of summoning his people to his office.

"Yes, sir?" Curtis said, pressing the talk button.

"I need a status report."

"Of course, sir. I'll be right in." Curtis stood, buttoning his jacket. He felt a smile cross his face as he checked his reflection in the mirror hanging near the door.

He would bide his time and wait for the perfect moment, but in the end, he would bring the Kents to heel. Thayer Kent just thought she had gotten away. She had merely seen the tip of the iceberg of what he was capable of. He wasn't head of special projects for the Lehman Group because of his inability to get a job done. As long as he met their goals in the allotted time, they never asked how he did it.

He had first met his current employer, Mr. Roberts, the chief operating officer, when he worked his bodyguard detail in Los Angeles two years ago.

It would have just been another job had Mr. Roberts not been threatened with extortion when he dumped his latest mistress. As her threats escalated to the point of informing his wife of their affair, Curtis calmly stepped forward and offered to "take care" of the problem.

Mr. Roberts never asked how Curtis had made the problem suddenly disappear, and Curtis never told him, but it culminated in an offer as acting head of "special projects."

His latest project was to ensure that in just two weeks, the Lehman Group was awarded one of the largest military contracts the SASC had ever awarded. It would guarantee one of their companies would be the sole supplier of a new missile tracking and defense system.

Curtis wasn't sure what it meant other than it stood to make his bosses close to twenty-eight billion. The bonus Mr. Roberts would make alone would guarantee him a nice new mansion in the Caymans with a shiny new yacht moored outside.

As it stood now, Senator Kent was the main deciding vote. That alone wouldn't mean much except he was not only the head of the SASC, but he also held sway over the majority of the senators on the committee. If Senator Kent voted no, it was almost certain the contract would fall through. Mr. Roberts had tasked Curtis with the job of ensuring that never happened.

Curtis's plan had been simple. Kidnap the senator's daughter, force him to divulge military secrets, then use extortion to get him to vote in favor of the Lehman Group.

When that fell through, due to the senator's unwavering morality, Curtis adjusted the plan to pull the senator away by revealing the location of his daughter at the time of the vote. The senator would be away on a wild-goose chase, and the contract would be approved. Simple.

Or it should have been a simple operation. However, thanks to the two men who had tracked her to the cage in the cellar, the plan had turned into an operational nightmare. Watching the news coverage from the hospital the girl was at had made Curtis furious. Failure did not sit well with him.

Realizing he had already kept his boss waiting too long, Curtis pulled open his office door. He was doing pretty well in life to go from a shithole apartment and babysitting rich, spoiled debutantes to an office on the executive floor of a major corporation and a condo with a doorman.

Walking across the reception area, he got a perverse pleasure out of watching the secretaries lower their eyes in apprehension. Just as it should be. Chances were good they knew what he did for the company. Rumors always ran wild in an office this size.

Knocking once on the door, he opened it to find his boss sitting behind his desk.

"Ah, Curtis. Sit."

Curtis took a seat across the desk from Mr. Roberts. He had grown used to waiting until his boss was ready for his report. Finally, Mr. Roberts put down the paperwork he had been studying and turned his cold gray eyes on Curtis.

"I shouldn't have to explain to you how important this assignment is. I won't tolerate another failure on your part."

There was no need for Curtis to answer, his boss wasn't expecting one. All the man expected was the successful completion of Curtis's assignment.

He listened for a few more minutes as Mr. Roberts reminded him of the potential windfall if they won the contract before being dismissed.

Returning to his office, he picked up the phone, calling his best man in the field. He ordered a twenty-four-hour watch put on all of the parties involved. It would be expensive, but nothing like losing out on twenty-eight billion dollars.

Now to catch the senator's daughter alone again.

CHAPTER SEVEN

Thayer squinted in the light when they emerged out of the cellar before burying her face back in Memphis's shoulder. Knox was waiting with an offer to help carry her down to the ambulance. When Knox placed his large hand gently on her shoulder, Memphis felt her cling even tighter to his neck. Flinching, Knox withdrew, leveling Memphis with a stern gaze.

"Keep her turned away," Knox growled with a swipe of his hand toward the two bodies that lay on the ground.

Memphis moved one of his hands from her back up to cradle her head.

He fought his way back down the hill to where the emergency vehicles, police vehicles, and a handful of nondescript black SUVs were parked. He shook his head slightly at the EMT, who rushed forward to help him. Understanding dawned on the man choosing instead to take Memphis's arm to help him into the waiting ambulance.

In a panic, Thayer whimpered at the change of motion, digging her nails into his back.

"Easy," Memphis said softly. "We're in an ambulance. I need to set you down so they can look at you." He set her on the gurney, kneeling in front of her with his hands holding her arms until she opened her eyes.

"I'm right here," he said as she stared at him with wide eyes. "You're okay."

Slowly, Memphis sat back across from her as the doors closed. Two EMTs surrounded her, gently hooking up an IV as they checked her for injuries.

"Can you tell me your name?" one of the EMTs asked her.

"Thayer Kent."

"How old are you?"

"I'm twenty-one now. My birthday was two days ago, I think."

"How about a little harder one. Where do you go to school?"

"Amherst."

"Perfect. Just try and relax. We'll be at the hospital soon." The two attendants laid warmed blankets on her before they found seats where they could easily monitor what was going on but weren't in her face.

"I'm sorry," Memphis said. Thayer's eyes found his again.

"For what?" she asked, watching him.

"For not knowing it was your birthday. For not finding you sooner. For not being able to protect you from them." Memphis watched as her eyes slowly closed. He assumed they put something in her IV to make her sleep. Or maybe she was just so tired she couldn't fight it anymore.

"Memphis," she slurred, reaching out her hand. Memphis leaned forward, taking hers. "You found me. You kept your promise." Thayer opened her eyes again, desperately fighting the obvious fatigue that threatened to pull her under. "Your eyes are so green. I've seen them somewhere before."

"We gave her something to help her rest. It can make her a little loopy," the EMT said with a laugh when Memphis raised an eyebrow at her in question.

"Memphis?" The slur had turned into a whisper this time.

"Yeah? I'm here."

"I want to run my hands through your hair," was the only drunken sounding thought she said aloud before sliding into a deep sleep.

"Did she say she wanted to touch my hair?" Memphis's hair was a rich deep-brown with traces of blond and red running through it. It was usually too long, not because of style but because he never got around to getting a haircut. It laid in soft waves a little past his collar. Usually, he was trying to push it out of his face.

"No, she said she wanted to run her hands through your hair. That's completely different." The woman EMT winked at him before he turned away from them, red running quickly up his face. "Can't say that I blame her. She's right, you do have unusually bright-green eyes and soft looking hair." She chuckled softly when she saw even his ears turn red.

Senator Kent was already at the hospital by the

time they wheeled Thayer in, having been notified immediately when they left the hotel to find her.

Memphis was joined by Knox in the waiting room, where Murphy curled up to sleep at their feet. They had been ushered in there when Thayer disappeared into the back. Her father had been allowed to follow her, leaving them both to wait. They both stood when the senator entered the private waiting room later, followed by a bodyguard.

"Gentlemen, I can't thank you enough." He shook Memphis's hand. "Dr. Prescott, there is a jet waiting for you at the airport to take you home. I had one of the men bring your things from the hotel. They are already on the plane. I'll have my accountant contact you about payment."

"You don't owe me anything," Memphis answered, confused. He was being dismissed before he could even check on Thayer. Why would he be chased off so quickly?

"Knox, I'll be with my daughter if you need me." Turning on his heel, he walked out of the room.

"What the fuck?" Memphis was pissed. "Can I not even tell her goodbye?"

"Apparently not. Come on, I'll walk you out."

"Don't fucking bother." Memphis walked out of the room to head to the airport.

Pushing through the door into the hallway, Knox yelled at him. "If you ever need anything, you have my number."

"Fuck you," he shouted back as he walked toward the door.

What was the harm of letting him see Thayer before he left? He had promised he would be there, and he hated breaking a promise. He guessed it really didn't matter in the end. It wasn't like he would ever see her again.

Thayer woke up slowly. Looking around, she desperately tried to get her bearings. She could tell she was lying in a hospital bed with an IV running into her arm. It came back to her in a rush when she noticed the plaid shirt she was wearing. With a soft laugh, she studied the warm shirt that could wrap around her at least twice.

"You wouldn't let them take it off."

With a start, Thayer looked over her shoulder to where Knox sat in a chair reading a newspaper.

"The nurse said you fought like a wildcat every time they tried to remove it, so they finally just gave up."

She slowly rolled over to face him, feeling the painful scream of every sore muscle.

"Your father had to go work for a while at the hotel. He asked me to keep an eye on you until he got back. I guess he doesn't trust the cop sitting in the hallway." Knox set the paper down when she remained silent. "Doing okay? Want me to get you anything?"

"I'm hungry."

He nodded, standing up. Opening the door, he let it shut behind him as he went hunting for a nurse. Returning to the room, he helped her sit up before emptying his pockets onto the small table.

"The kitchen is already closed, but they let me raid

the small fridge they have. Let's see...it looks like you get Cheerios, Jell-O, crackers, juice, and milk."

"Thank you, Knox. It all looks amazing right now." Thayer sipped on the juice as Knox fixed her cereal.

Pushing the table up to her, Knox returned to his seat as Thayer dug into the cereal.

"Memphis kept telling me to eat whatever they gave me to keep my strength up. Some of it was disgusting, but I ate it. If I never see McDonald's food again, it'll be too soon." She smiled slightly at him before turning to one of the Jell-Os.

"Where is Memphis?" she asked.

"He had to go home, Thayer."

She tried not to show the disappointment radiating through her. Why did the thought of not seeing him again make her want to curl up and cry for a week?

She had to be careful not to let Knox see what she was thinking, or he might think there was something more than just gratefulness for Memphis's help. He had once gone so far as running a background check on a guy she mentioned in passing she was casually dating at college. Knox did occasionally turn in on big brother mode where she was concerned.

"Of course. I'm sure he had people waiting on him. He said something about being the local vet in some rural area in Minnesota. I just wish I could have thanked him is all." She looked back down at her sad buffet, suddenly losing her appetite. Thayer was almost positive it was just because she wasn't used to eating much, not because Memphis had left without even saying goodbye.

"Thayer?" When she looked up at him, Knox just shook his head. "Nothing."

"What, Knox?"

He looked up at the ceiling, a move she knew meant he was debating if he wanted to ask a question or not. "You've never had a problem asking me anything before. Do you remember when you thought my prom date had rented a hotel room for us? You held him by his throat outside the ballroom while you interrogated both of us. I thought I'd die of embarrassment, but I answered all of your questions."

"Thayer, why do you have on Memphis's shirt? What happened when he went into the cellar? I mean, the rape kit came back negative, so your father feels better about that," Knox quickly added when she flinched like he had slapped her.

Between clenched teeth, she answered him. "When he showed up the last time as a hologram, I was being attacked by one of the men Memphis had been worried about. Memphis managed to scare him off, but not until the man had torn my shirt off. When he came to get me, all I had on were my pajama pants and the filthy blanket they gave me. He helped me put on his shirt before picking me up to carry me out."

"Okay." Knox held up his hands as if he could stop the anger radiating from her. "I'm just trying to get a full picture of everything that happened."

"He never stopped trying to find a way to get me out. I trust him with my life. It's just too bad you can't believe in him as well." She stared at him hard until the big man actually started to squirm. Thayer had always been taught by this very man never to back down. He had also taught her to call bullshit when she saw it. "Did my father send him home?"

"Thayer, he's just concerned about you."

"I get that, but you, Mr. Monroe, should have stuck up for him." Knox sighed in relief when Mr. Kent took that moment to enter the room. As her glare cut to her father, Knox ducked out of the room.

"I'm exhausted," she said, turning over to place her back to her father. She loved him and knew he was only concerned for her well-being, but this time he had gone too far.

There was the sound of chair legs scraping on the floor as her father took up his post next to her. She knew he would still be there in the morning, offering her all the support he could. Knox would also be there in the same way.

Unfortunately, the one person she wanted, who would understand what she had been through, was back in Minnesota.

CHAPTER EIGHT

Memphis had blown off the text from Knox. Like the man cared how the fuck he was doing. He did wonder how Thayer was, though. He had dug through his bags, hoping the stupid pink bunny was still there, but everything of hers had been carefully removed. He couldn't just simply jump to where she was. That's simply not how this ability worked. Or at least, it never had in the past.

His staff at the clinic, which just consisted of the high school vet tech and the receptionist, had gone from looking at him with concern to shaking their heads with sadness whenever they caught him staring into space thinking about her.

He would put her behind him eventually. It's not like there was any other choice. He didn't have her cell number, and he wasn't pathetic enough to hunt for her on social media. Not yet anyway. It had already been two weeks since he carried her out of that hole. He knew time was the only thing that could help him now. He could survive this.

Shaking his head, he bent back over his desk to finish the prescriptions he was writing for one of the local cattlemen. He had promised to get them done before the end of today so the man could buy the mineral for his cattle he needed tomorrow. He would email them to the feed store as soon as he had them done, so there would be no hold-up on his part.

He had already told his staff they could leave for the day. Murphy slept on his dog bed across his office, contentedly waiting until Memphis had his work finished.

"All right, boy. I think I've got everything done. Let me get these sent, then we can go home."

The dog thumped his tail but didn't open his eyes.

With a sigh, Memphis scanned and emailed the prescriptions. He had some billing he needed to work on, but he was tired. He had been on his feet all day between an emergency surgery and a full day of appointments. Tomorrow, he had three farm visits before he even saw the office.

Turning off the lights, he whistled for Murphy as he headed out the door.

The dog happily trotted to his truck as he locked the back door. Murphy always rode in the front seat next to Memphis when he came to the office. On farm visit days, the dog would just laze around the house for the day.

The one time Memphis had taken him on a visit, he had spent the entire time herding the man's sheep around. The dog would herd anything if given the chance. There had been more than one incident at the office of him herding kids into an empty exam room.

The kids thought it was great fun, the parents, not so much.

"I would suggest we stop by the grocery store to get a movie, but I think I'm too tired tonight. What do you say we read for a while after supper, then hit the hay?" He rubbed his hand down the dog's back.

Sure, Memphis, that sounds great, he answered himself in a goofy voice. Good God, he must be pathetic if he was expecting his dog to answer him.

Turning onto the narrow road leading up to his cabin, Memphis caught a glimpse of someone sitting on his front porch steps.

"Oh, come on!" he grumbled, not looking forward to whatever vet emergency was waiting for him.

Pulling closer, he slowed to a stop in front of a woman. She had stood at hearing his approach. Holding her hand up to shade her eyes from his headlights, she waited for him to get out.

Throwing the truck in park, he quickly turned it off, cutting the lights off as well. She lowered her hands, wrapping her arms around her middle. Murphy started jumping around in the truck, barking. Memphis just sat completely still, staring at her until he was hit in the face by a tail, breaking him out of his stupor.

"What in the hell..."

Murphy responded by barking even harder.

"Dog!" he shouted, reaching for the door handle.

When he wrenched it open, Murphy bounded over his lap out the door. Reaching the woman, the dog jumped up, knocking her back down onto the steps. Memphis jumped out to rush to her but saw her laughing as the dog bathed her in kisses.

"Murphy!" Memphis shouted, crossing to the dog.

Catching his collar, he pulled the straining dog back. "Inside," he said, turning the dog loose.

With one last lick, he raced around the cabin to use the dog door.

"I like him!"

"Thayer, what are you doing here? How did you even find me?" Memphis stood over her, staring down for a minute, wondering if he had actually dreamed enough about her that he was starting to hallucinate.

"I brought your shirt back." She smiled shyly up at him.

He couldn't stop the grin that spread across his face. Reaching a hand down, he wrapped it around hers, pulling her off the step into his arms. Her arms quickly reached around his waist, holding on to him like she might drown. She was cold enough that it was obvious she had been waiting for him for hours.

"Christ, you're shivering. What am I thinking? Let's get inside, you can sit in front of the fire while I make us some supper." Memphis fished the key out of his pocket, opening the door. With a grand gesture, he motioned for Thayer to enter, making her laugh.

"Supper sounds amazing. I can help."

"Just make yourself comfortable, I got this." He quickly made a fire in the small fireplace on one side of his living room. "How did you get here? Better question, how did you ever get Knox to let you come? How long do you think I have before Knox strings me up by my ankles? I bet he has a cattle prod with my name on it."

Memphis grinned at her when she sat down in front of the fire, laughing. Murphy sat down next to her, laying his head in her lap. For Memphis, it was like she had always been here. Like they had never spent a day apart since meeting in that cold cellar.

"I needed a change of scenery for a little while," she said, petting the dog absently.

Memphis looked at her from the door of the fridge with his eyebrows knitted in confusion.

"Don't worry. I'm just taking the rest of the semester off. I've already missed too many classes to catch up anyway."

"Why did you decide to come here? Don't get me wrong, it's great to see you. But Massachusetts is a long way from here." He carried the meat he had put into a marinade to the island. "Stir-fry okay?"

"Sounds amazing." She bent down to hug Murphy, talking to him in that way all women seemed to talk to his dog. He waited a few minutes for her to speak as he began to brown the meat.

"You didn't answer my question."

The question hadn't been asked just out of idle curiosity. He had no doubt that Knox would show up on his door soon to get her back. Memphis needed to know what to expect. Did he need to hand her over to return to her life or fight to keep her here? As much as he was willing to go toe-to-toe with the giant to keep her, he wanted for her to be happy and safe even more. If that meant sending her home, then that's what he would do.

"I didn't like how things ended. I couldn't believe you would leave without so much as a goodbye, like I meant nothing." She had said it so softly, Memphis had to strain to hear her.

"Thayer, I tried to see you. You have to believe you mean more to me than that. I was strong-armed out of the hospital, so I did what I thought was best." Memphis added the vegetables to the wok as if on autopilot.

"I know. Knox explained why Dad wanted you gone. It's just...you're the only one who was there, who knows everything that happened."

"What are you talking about? Why did your father want me gone?"

"Can I have something to drink? A beer if you have one." Memphis opened them both a beer, bringing hers over. "He thought something more happened between us in the cellar. He decided that's why I had on your shirt and wouldn't let them take it off."

"Why would he think that?" Memphis asked as he reached the kitchen. "Where would he get that idea?" His voice trailed off as a thought occurred to him. They must have gotten their hands on more than just his military file.

He had been assured that the records from his childhood were sealed, but if it were possible for someone as powerful as the senator to get his hands on redacted military files, it wouldn't be a huge leap to get sealed juvenile records. It made him angry that they would judge him as a man based on what had happened to him as a boy. He was pulled from his thoughts by Thayer, clearing her throat.

"I think it's my fault. Apparently, I also talked a lot in my sleep about you. I don't remember anything after getting in the ambulance until I woke up with Knox sitting in the room. I explained what happened."

"Huh," he grunted, staring at the wok for a minute as he angrily stirred the vegetables and meat.

"I wanted to tell you in person how thankful I am

for you. Without you, Knox said they would never have found me. I know words are not adequate, but I just want to say thank you, Memphis, for everything you did."

He looked up to find her beautiful blue eyes shimmering with tears. She was so beautiful and strong that it took his breath away. It didn't matter what had happened, as long as Thayer was here now, he was happy. He could feel the irritation slip from his face as he looked at her.

"Well, I'm sorry it took so long to figure out where you were. I'm just glad you're okay." They stood staring at each other before Memphis turned back to the stove. He needed to change the conversation before it got too heavy.

"Okay, that has to cook for a little longer. I'm going to go throw on a different shirt. Preferably one that doesn't smell like I've wrestled bears in a pigsty all day." Thayer laughed as he headed around the counter toward the bedroom, pulling his shirt over his head on the way. Thayer sucked in a quick breath.

"You might be more comfortable on the couch. Make yourself at home. I'll be right back."

Something sounding like, "Hummf," was all the answer he got. It didn't slip his notice, though, when her eyes ran down his hard pecs to the muscled abs. He would be lying if he said it hadn't been a calculated move on his part. Just because he hadn't been the monster they assumed he was in that cellar didn't mean he wasn't insanely attracted to her. It just meant he would take the slow route most men did to get a woman's attention.

He gave her a smirk when her eyes snapped back up to his before walking into the bedroom.

Memphis took the time he had in private while changing to shoot Knox a text. The fact the man hadn't already picked her up was baffling to him. Knox had to have had an eye on her since she got home.

Memphis
She's here. She's safe.

The reply came back instantly.

Knox
Thank God, we've been frantic. You'd better keep your hands off of her.

Memphis
Damn it. To think I had her tied up so nicely face down on my table with her ass in the air. Seriously, what do you people think I am?

Knox
You're not very attached to those testicles after all, I see.

Memphis
You sure seem to be fascinated by them. She's safe with me. I think she needs some space from what happened.

Knox
Understandable. I'm trying to chase down any leads on who masterminded the ordeal. I can't come get her for a couple of days.

Memphis
I'll make sure she's fed and gets some rest. She'll be fine. I give you my word.

Knox
Make sure she is. Contact me if anything happens. Until we find who did this, it's important that you keep her with you. I'm trusting you to keep her safe.

Thayer was still standing in front of the fire when Memphis returned. Not only had he slipped on a fresh T-shirt making his biceps look huge, he had also changed out his contacts in favor of his glasses.

As if they had a mind of their own, her eyes slowly slipped down until they took in the gray sweatpants that hung low on his hips, leaving a hint of what lay beneath the material. Being an English major, she had a very vivid imagination that instantly went to work filling in the picture. It was saying this was no ordinary country vet.

"My god," Thayer whispered to herself.

"Everything good?" he asked, raising one eyebrow.

She nodded, wondering if that had come out louder than intended. Walking into the kitchen, he pulled down two bowls, filling them with their dinner. Balancing the hot bowls in one hand, he reached into the fridge, grabbing two fresh beers.

"Come on, I usually eat over here."

Thayer followed him the short distance, flopping

down on the couch. Taking the other end, he set the beer down before handing her a bowl.

"It's nothing great, but I have ice cream in the freezer for later."

"Thank you," she said, taking the offered bowl. Thayer hadn't realized how hungry she was until she started eating. She had been living off vending machines and snack bars for several days getting here. Reaching the bottom of the bowl, she suddenly became aware of being watched. Looking up, she found Memphis with his bowl still half full watching her.

"I'll take the couch so you can have the bedroom. I can put fresh sheets on the bed," he said with a smile as he took her bowl. Standing, he refilled it before taking his seat again next to her.

"I'll be fine at the hotel. I don't want to put you out of your bed," she answered, taking her time with her second helping of stir-fry.

"I'd feel better if you stayed here. The hotel can be a little sketchy. Do you want to go on a couple of farm calls with me tomorrow? I can find you some boots at the office."

"That sounds amazing!" Thayer answered with an enthusiastic nod.

She had needed to get away from all of the press, the psychiatrist, and her smothering father. He had waved at her as he pulled away from the dorm, leaving a bodyguard behind, thinking everything was fine. How could he not? She had said all the right things and smiled at all the right times. He just didn't realize the self-defense lessons Knox had given her also included how to evade someone tailing you.

She had spent one night in the room before

temporarily withdrawing from school to catch a train west. It had taken some work to locate him, but she figured there could only be so many Dr. Memphis Prescotts in rural Minnesota.

When a Google search turned up the town his vet clinic was in, she mapped out her route. One train and two buses brought her to the town closest to him. She found the address of his vet office online at a local coffee shop before some well-meaning waitress provided her with directions to his house.

She just wanted to be around someone for a little while, someone who was there with her as the ordeal was unfolding but didn't expect anything from her. No more questions from doctors, no more sympathetic looks from well-meaning neighbors, no more awkward pats from school professors. She jumped when Memphis interrupted her train of thought.

"Would you like more?"

Looking down, she didn't even realize that she had plowed through every bite of her second bowl. "I think I'll hold out for the ice cream later."

With a nod, he stood, taking their bowls to the kitchen. Murphy took the opportunity to jump on the couch next to her, giving her a wet kiss across her face.

"Murphy!" Memphis growled at him.

Thayer pulled the dog against her, giving him a big hug. Memphis leaned against the sink, watching.

"You helped find me too, didn't you? You're a good boy."

He barked and gave her one more sloppy kiss before jumping off the couch to curl back up on his dog bed. Murphy had stayed by their side after checking the cellar first. He had stood watch, pressed against her, as Knox had opened fire, then raced down the stairs to bring them out. The dog would always hold a special place in her heart.

Standing, she walked over to Memphis. "Let me help clean up."

He just stood against the counter, looking down at her. She loved looking into his bright-green eyes, he never seemed to be able to hide his emotions behind them. He looked at her with soft concern instead of pity, like everyone else. Well, everyone but Knox, maybe it was impossible to hide anything behind his green eyes too. Though his eyes usually just blazed with anger or irritation.

"I can get this. You look exhausted."

With a deep sigh, she smiled up at him. "Do you have a bathtub? I would kill to soak in a tub. Or are you a shower-only guy?"

"Well," he said, taking her hand. Pulling her toward the bathroom, he continued, "I am usually a shower-only guy, but I put in a soaker tub anyway when I remodeled the bathroom. I occasionally have to soak bruises out."

He led her into a beautiful bathroom finished in masculine grays with a river stone shower, granite counter and a deep soaker tub at one end.

"I don't have anything to make the water smell fancy except Epsom salt."

"It's fine, I don't have to have fancy-smelling water." Thayer laughed as he pulled a towel off a shelf running under the counter.

"Wait!" Memphis reached into a small closet next to the door, pulling out a pink bag. "All they had was

Himalayan pink salt last time I was at the store. It smells pretty good."

Thayer just smirked at him.

"Okay, I'll be in the living room if you need anything. Take as long as you want." He backed out of the room, closing the door behind him.

Thayer started the water before she slid her clothes off. Sinking into the hot, salty water, she sighed as the stress of the last month eased out of her body. Yeah, running away to Memphis had been a very good decision.

CHAPTER NINE

Memphis did his best to clean up, but knowing Thayer was sitting in his tub with water lapping around her naked body made it very hard to stay focused. He had never met another woman he wanted as badly as Thayer Kent.

In no way did he want to take the chance she was suffering from some need to get close to him because he had rescued her, though. It would be unforgivable for him to take advantage of the situation. But how would he know the difference between want and obligation?

Adjusting his painfully swollen erection, he concentrated on finishing the dishes. Twenty minutes later, he was reading his newest library book when Thayer emerged from the bathroom.

"Fuck me," he growled as his gaze worked up her body from her bare feet to the wet hair brushed straight down her back. Her face was scrubbed clean of any makeup, her soft blue eyes watching him.

She had on the flannel shirt he had wrapped her in when he found her in that cellar. It hit mid-thigh, showing off her long brown legs to perfection. His thoughts waffled between hoping she had on shorts under it and praying she had on nothing.

"Um. Do you have a hair dryer?" she asked.

"Yeah. I'll get it for you." Memphis jumped off the couch, wishing he had put on jeans to help hide his straining cock. He couldn't seem to control it when she was around.

Fishing the hair dryer out of a drawer in the small cabinet in the bathroom, he turned to take it to her. He ran right into her, where she had followed him on quiet feet.

"Thanks," she said, reaching for the hair dryer.

"Let me help you," he rumbled with the dryer in a death grip. Wasn't he just giving himself a talk about why he should leave her alone not half an hour ago? "Here, hop on the counter." With strong hands wrapped around her waist, he picked her up.

Plugging it in, Memphis began to hold out strands of hair as he worked down them with the dryer. How had something so trivial as blow-drying her soft blonde hair become such a turn-on? Maybe it was the fact he was standing between her long tan legs, close enough he could feel her breath on his neck.

His heart began to race when he felt her slowly ease her hands beneath his shirt, finding his tight stomach with her fingertips. Memphis froze as she ran her hands higher to his pecs, making his breath hitch. He knew he should step back. As much as he ached to touch her, it was too soon. Nothing good would come from this. But as hard as he tried, he couldn't turn her loose.

Pushing his shirt up, he heard a possessive growl come from deep inside him as she ran her tongue over his chest. Turning the hair dryer off, he set it on the counter before wrapping his fist in her hair, pulling her head back. For just a moment, he took in the raw look of lust on her face before pressing his mouth against hers. His tongue pushed into her mouth as he took what he wanted, capturing her moan as it escaped her lips.

She tasted like innocence. What was he doing? He needed to get away from her before he pressed her against the door and took everything he wanted from her. She had run to him looking for comfort, and he was taking advantage of her.

"Goddammit!" he growled out before stomping out of the room. If he could just get some fresh air, maybe his brain could catch up.

She found him standing on his front porch, his hands on top of his head, his fingers interlocked in his hair. Memphis turned to look at her. If he was going to put the brakes on this, he could at least have the balls to look in her eyes when he did it.

"You should go back inside. It's cold out here."

Turns out, pulling the brake was much harder than he thought. He stared up at the stars for a minute before looking back down at her.

"Look, I'm sorry. I shouldn't have kissed you. I don't want you to think I would take advantage of..."

"Blah, blah, blah. Cut the bullshit speech, Memphis. I've listened to enough of them by now."

He jerked his head back at her words in momentary shock. He crossed his arms over his chest, waiting for her to continue.

"Dad, Knox, the doctors, now you? Everyone thinks they know what's best for me. Well, what if what's best for me is you?" Thayer said, poking him in the chest with her finger. "Just tell me you don't want me. I'll pack my shit and go home tomorrow. I won't bother you again." She shivered when she looked up at him. Memphis had lowered his arms while she spoke, fisting his hands at his sides.

"Thayer," he growled out, watching her shiver.

What was he thinking, letting her stand outside in the cold in nothing more than his shirt? He had never had the primal need to protect someone rise up in him like it did when he was around her. Not even when he was still doing search and rescues in the military.

She was standing inches away, her beautiful face turned up to him in defiance. Taking her arm, he pushed open the door, pulling her inside.

"Message received," she said, pulling away from him.

Everything in his soul told him he should let her go, but he somehow couldn't fool himself into believing that. Wrapping an arm around her waist, he pushed her back against the door.

Bracing her against the door with his body, he bent down, taking her mouth with his. His tongue swept in, exploring as she melted against him. When neither of them could survive on the air left in their lungs, he pulled back.

"Am I just something you need to work out of your system to move on?" he asked. He had been a part of several one-night stands before, but this was different. He watched as she considered his question.

"I don't know. I hope not, but I honestly don't know," she answered.

"Then please don't ask me to do this. Once I bury

myself in you, I won't be able to let you go. You deserve better, Thayer."

She pushed him back with her palms on his chest. She studied him closely, running her gaze down his body until she stopped on his hard erection, straining unhampered in the sweats.

"Don't ever question if I want you, though. I've wanted you from the moment I saw you curled up on that cot," he said, reaching out to brush a stray piece of her hair behind her ear.

"What if we just go forward slowly until we see where this takes us?" she asked, looking up at him. "We can promise to tell the other one if we don't feel like it should continue."

He nodded his head once, letting her step past him toward the fire.

"I know I'm hiding from everything right now," she continued. "But would you let me hide just a little longer, here, in your arms?"

He leaned against the front door, staring down at the floor for a few minutes before raising his head to look over at her.

"Yeah, we can do that," he answered her after a few minutes, pushing off the door.

Thayer was adding whipped cream to the ice cream sundaes she'd made when he walked out of the bedroom wearing flannel pajama pants. That was all, just pants and glasses. Did he do it on purpose, or did he really have no idea how sexy she found him? His hair was still damp from the shower and sticking out at different angles. She had never wanted to run her hands through someone's hair as much as she wanted to Memphis's. Maybe while it was between her thighs.

"Please stop looking at me like that. I'll have to go change again. I already have a pair of compression shorts on under these."

Thayer laughed as she handed him his bowl of ice cream. "I guess if you don't want me ogling you, you should remember to put on a shirt," she teased him.

"Apparently," he answered, starting to rise from the couch where they had settled to work on their ice cream.

"Not now," she said, pulling him back down. "Later. Much, much later."

Thayer liked being with Memphis. Even pinned against a door or being devoured on the bathroom counter, she always felt safe with him. She wondered if it was because he had always kept his word.

When she had been doused with water, he had taken care of her. He was even still sitting in the doorway when she woke up later. She understood what he meant earlier. If he ever did bury himself in her, she knew she would never be able to leave him.

"You're deep in thought. Anything you'd like to share?"

She smiled over at him. "Do you know why I've never had sex before?"

Memphis spat his mouthful of ice cream out, causing Murphy to jump to his feet where he lay on his dog bed. With one big leap, he landed in Memphis's lap, licking the treat off his mouth. Sputtering, Memphis finally managed to fight the dog off while Thayer roared in laughter.

"Wow, that was an impressive share," he said, trying to regain control of both himself and his dog. "Murphy! Get on your bed."

"Sorry, I just assumed Knox had told you that," she said, laughing.

"Jesus, why would he share that information with me? No wonder he wants me far away from you."

Sliding her cold feet under him, she snuggled deeper into the blanket he had covered her with earlier. "Okay, this is going to make you laugh. It's really stupid." Memphis watched her as she began her story.

CHAPTER TEN

"My mother died when I was just entering middle school," Thayer began. "At the time, my father was a commander on a submarine. He had taken a leave of absence to be with her at the end but had to return to service soon after the funeral. He didn't like being gone all the time and leaving me in the care of nannies, so he put in for a desk job. That's how I met Knox. He served on the sub under Dad, and when he was transferred to the office, he took Knox with him."

"I still don't understand how he fit on a sub," Memphis said, shaking his head.

"Dad said he was pretty good at adapting to his surroundings, and he can sleep pretty much anywhere." Thayer laughed. "Anyway, during that period between Dad working on the sub and running for senator, he worked really hard at taking on the role of both mom and dad.

"One night, after I was supposed to be asleep instead of reading, I heard a voice downstairs. Sneaking down the stairs, I noticed the door to Dad's office open a crack. He was sitting at his desk telling the picture of Mom everything that had happened that day."

Memphis watched her as she stared at the far wall, lost in thought, before turning her smile on him again.

"Mom told me that she knew from the moment she met Dad he was special. They met at a social held by one of the families my grandparents were friends with. Their son had just graduated from Annapolis with Dad, so he was invited to attend as well.

"She said the moment he walked in the door, there was this force that drew them together. He asked her out that night, and they were together until her death. Even when I was little, I could tell just by the way he looked at her that she was everything to him. Do you know I've never seen him even look twice at another woman? He's still in love with her."

"That's amazing," Memphis said when Thayer became quiet again.

"Yeah, well," she finally said. "It might just be the pipe dream of a naïve girl, but I want that. I want the kind of man who crosses a roomful of people to get to me as if no one else exists. I want the kind of love that lives on into the next life. I don't want someone just looking to get his rocks off in a dorm room that smells like stale beer, socks, and Cheetos."

Red began to creep up Thayer's neck when he remained silent, staring at her. "See, I told you it was stupid," she said, standing to gather the bowls of melted ice cream that Murphy had discovered on the floor and licked clean.

"It's not stupid," Memphis said to her back as she walked into the kitchen. He hadn't meant to give her that impression. He had been wondering how many of the girls he had had casual sex with in the back of cars, dorm room beds, and under bleachers had felt the same way. "As a matter of fact, I think you should hold out for that man. You deserve that kind of love."

"Yeah, well, pipe dream," she said, breezing past him toward the bathroom.

"Shit," he said quietly when he heard the bathroom door close. He didn't just think she deserved that kind of man. He knew he wanted to be the one to be that for her. How could he not want to spend the rest of his life slaying dragons for her? Problem was, he had no idea how to do that.

So here he stood, trying to figure out what to do next. He knew exactly how Senator Kent had felt when he saw Thayer's mother across the room because he felt the same way every time he looked at Thayer. Like the wind had been knocked out of him and she was his saving breath.

With a sigh, Memphis walked to the front door, checking the lock to make sure they were secure. When he crossed into the bedroom, Thayer was already curled up in his bed, facing the wall. He slipped quietly into the bathroom to get ready for bed. Finishing quickly, he opened the door, turning off the light before taking a moment to let his eyes grow accustomed to the dark before making his way to the couch in the living room.

"Can you leave the light on please?" Thayer asked from his bed.

"Sure, no problem." He reached over, turning the light back on. "Do you want me to crack the door some?"

"No, it's fine. Can you also leave the door between the bedroom and living room open?"

"Are you having problems with nightmares?" Memphis asked, stopping next to the bed. It was a subject he was well acquainted with, having suffered from them for years. They had begun shortly after his mother passed and still showed up from time to time.

"Yeah. The doctors said they will fade eventually. I just don't like feeling closed in when it's dark."

He nodded his head at her, brushing her hair back from her face, cascading it over his pillow.

"They will fade, I promise. It just takes a while."

"Do you have nightmares? Knox told me you searched for people in the Army," she whispered at him.

"Sometimes. They've kicked up a little more lately, but they'll slowly fade back to a manageable level again. Did you want to tell me about your nightmares? Sometimes it helps to voice them out loud. It makes them less real somehow."

He wiped away the tear that slowly rolled out of her eyes. "Jesus, Thayer, I can't seem to say anything right. Please don't cry."

"I think you are the only person who does say everything right. Would you tell me about your nightmares if I tell you about mine?"

Memphis ran a hand through his hair, considering. It had taken him years to gain control of the nightmares that had plagued him since his youth. If he could help her in any way, he knew he had to try.

"Yeah. Hold on, I'll be right back. Murphy, go do your business."

The dog ran past him, disappearing through the dog

door in the bedroom. Memphis walked into the living room, checking the front door once more before turning off the lights.

"Scoot over," he said when he returned.

When Thayer quickly complied, he slid into the bed next to her on his back.

"Murphy is really good at waking me up from a nightmare. I'm sure he'll do the same for you."

"The worst one always begins with someone putting a hood over my head," she began.

Memphis rolled onto his side when she began telling him about the nightmares. Not once did he interrupt her as she talked about what had happened in that dark cellar. When she cried, he didn't try to tell her not to, he just held her in his arms until she stopped.

They talked a little about a few of the tamer nightmares he had, but he wouldn't share everything he went through.

When Thayer started to slur her words, Memphis knew she needed to get some sleep.

Snuggling into his arms with her back against his chest, he felt her relax. He had said he would head to the couch when they were finished talking, but he couldn't bring himself to disturb her.

Slowly feeling himself start to drift off, he was suddenly jerked back awake by her wiggling against him. By the third time she did it, he was at full mast.

"You have to quit grinding against me," he growled into her ear, making her jump. He hated to wake her, but he couldn't take much more. "I already have a full mental list of ways to fuck you. I don't need your ass added to it." He felt a shiver run through her, making his problem worse.

"Sorry," she mumbled, taking a deep breath, trying to relax. "Am I making you too hot?"

Memphis let out a snort of laughter.

"Yeah, you're making me entirely too hot." Thayer let out a giggle. "Just lie still." She settled back against him with a promise to lie still.

THAYER FELL INTO A RESTLESS SLEEP. She was back in her dorm room again, but instead of men in black balaclavas, it was Memphis who stole into her room. Even though it was dark, she knew it was him when his green eyes glowed in the moonlight seeping through the curtains in her window.

He stalked toward her, those green eyes never leaving hers until he joined her on the bed. She could feel his weight pressing her into the bed as he roamed his lips down her neck. As if by magic, they were suddenly both nude as he worked his way along her body, leaving nothing untouched.

She was woken by a grunt from Memphis before a strong arm clamped around her waist, pulling her tight to him. Had she been grinding her hips against him again? Feeling his hard cock pressing against her cheeks, she couldn't stop the moan escaping her lips. He hadn't been the only one who had felt an instant connection in that cellar.

He had been so beautiful appearing from the dark corner that, for a moment, she was convinced he was just a dream. They were just fooling themselves if they thought they could fight their need to be with each other.

"Thayer," Memphis groaned, rolling away from her.

She held her breath, waiting to see if he would climb out of bed.

Instead, she felt the bed buck slightly before he rolled back against her. Her breath caught in a gasp as he ran his hand up her leg, pulling her shirt above her waist. He had taken off the pants, leaving on nothing but the compression shorts.

"Would you like me to help you fall asleep?" he whispered into her ear.

"Yes," she answered in a breathy moan.

"Do you trust me?"

"Yes." She wasn't sure she had actually spoken the word out loud until Memphis ran his hand down her body, pulling her leg back over his.

"Then relax."

She felt her heart race when he pulled her earlobe into his mouth, gently nipping it with his teeth. He slid his bicep under her head, pushing her pillow off the edge of the bed. "Tell me if I do anything you don't like. I'll stop." Thayer could barely focus on the words as his hand made its lazy trip back up, brushing across her panties that now lay soaked against her skin. "Thayer?"

"O-okay," she managed to wheeze out. His hand continued up her body, skimming over her breast until it landed near her throat. She could feel him slowly unhooking buttons until her shirt lay open.

Goose flesh rose up on her skin as his rough hand traveled up over her stomach, gently cupping her breast. He kneaded it until she felt her nipples stick out like diamonds. When he pinched one between his finger and thumb, she arched her back in a moan.

"You're so beautiful." He pushed her hair aside so

he could kiss the sensitive spot where her neck connected to her shoulder. She could feel the ache between her legs building like an inferno reaching out to caress her.

"Memphis, please."

"Shh, I've got you." Thayer knew why the attempts she had made to produce her own orgasm had always ended with disappointing results. She had never had his deep voice in her ear. The sound alone could quite possibly send her crashing into her climax.

Memphis wrapped the arm her head was resting on around her upper body, holding her close to him. With his other arm, he worked his way down her body, touching every inch of skin.

"Memphis!" she cried out when his fingers slid inside her panties to the v between her legs.

"You're soaked," he growled as his fingers began to explore. "Next time come to bed without these." She bucked against his hand when he moved her panties aside, sliding two fingers down her wet folds. Circling her clit, he eased the two fingers slightly inside her heat. Thayer arched up into his hand, trying to get more of him, but he pulled out, rubbing her clit again. "Not yet."

She knew she should probably feel indignant, but instead it made her desperate for him to continue. Why hadn't any of the boys she had dated in the past known how to do this? There couldn't possibly be just one man in the universe who could set her on fire like this one could.

She could hear her voice begging him to make her come, but it seemed like she wasn't connected to it. She was simply floating.

"Come for me, Thayer," she heard Memphis growl in her ear as he slid his two fingers into her heat again.

He pressed his palm against her clit, fucking her with his fingers as she felt her sight narrow. When he pinched her nipple hard with his other hand, she exploded.

"Are you okay?" was the first thing she could comprehend when her ears stopped ringing. Memphis still held her close but was pressing against her clit every time she tensed with an aftershock. That had to be what they were called because she was positive she just experienced her first earthquake.

"Yeah," she managed to get out. As she lay against Memphis, she could feel a heartbeat racing but couldn't decide if it was his or her own. "Holy shit." She felt him chuckle. "Are you always this good?"

"My ego thanks you for that. I'd like to think I'm better with less material restricting me."

"I once had a guy try through our jeans, but it just resulted in him coming, not me."

"Ahh." They sat in silence as their heart rates finally returned to normal. "I could make you come in your jeans," he said.

"I think you could make me come from the other room!" she agreed. Thayer began to shake as Memphis, still holding her tightly in his arms, burst out in laughter.

"Wait here, I have to go get something to clean you up." He held her still when she tried to roll over. "Stop, we don't want to have to sleep in sticky sheets."

"Why are the sheets sticky?" she asked when he eased out of bed. He walked into the bathroom, returning a few moments later. Pulling back the sheets, he wiped a wet washcloth over her ass, easing her panties off in the process.

"Because, baby, I came all over your ass like a high school boy." He pulled her shirt off, rolling her onto her back, dragging the covers over her.

"Even through the shorts?"

"Even through the shorts."

"Sorry," she mumbled, feeling the red burn up her cheeks.

Returning to the bed in a clean pair of shorts, Memphis slid into bed next to her.

"Why are you sorry? I don't think any man in his right mind could keep from blowing, feeling you clamp around his fingers. I suspect I should keep a towel handy when I eat your pussy. I'll destroy the sheets for sure."

Burning with embarrassment at the thought of having Memphis's face between her thighs, she buried her head in his chest.

"What?" he said, laughing as he pulled her close. "Does the fact I can't stop from dry humping your ass or that I'm planning to eat you out like a piece of watermelon embarrass you?"

"Oh my god!" Thayer snorted in laughter.

She quickly fell asleep, still in Memphis's arms, while he lazily rubbed his hand on her bare back. For the first night since being carried off to that dungeon, she didn't have a single nightmare.

Curtis Floyd disconnected the call in a much calmer frame of mind this time. His man had informed him that the senator's daughter had left the safety of her bodyguard to join Memphis Prescott at his cabin.

He had been furious when he was informed that she had managed to slip past his man unnoticed. Obviously, Knox Monroe had taught her more than even he had realized. The only reason his man was still breathing was his skill at picking up her trail again.

He had wondered why she didn't just hop on a plane, but he quickly realized she was making sure no one, including her father's office, could easily trace her movements. Yes, she was quite a clever mark.

Now she was happily ensconced in a false sense of security at the veterinarian's house. It was the opportunity he had been looking for. He could now move his new plan forward. No one could ever say he wasn't a man of his convictions. Right now, his only conviction was getting his hands on Thayer Kent.

His men would be in the air within the hour, heading toward the unsecured cabin among the Minnesota trees. Their only objective was to bring her back, what they did with Dr. Prescott was of no concern to him. Curtis had suggested to his second-in-command that one less man trying to protect her could only be advantageous to them. There was no reason to spell it out, his man knew exactly what he needed to do.

Curtis pressed the number two on his speed dial. "Is everything ready?" he asked when a man on the other end answered.

"Yes, sir. Everything has been arranged." Curtis pressed end to sever the call.

He had sent one of his men to a company safe house in Minneapolis to prepare everything for Thayer's arrival. He knew the house would never be traced back to his employer based on the number of shell corporations its deed passed through.

He already had one of the smaller company jets fueled and waiting for him. It would be in and back out of one of the small airports in Minnesota before anyone noticed it was missing.

He checked his watch again, trying not to grow impatient. Pushing this contract through the committee now rested squarely on his shoulders.

Mr. Roberts had already made it clear that the senator could not be touched, but Curtis thought the sudden discovery of the death of his daughter in Minneapolis from an overdose might be enough. If her death didn't keep him away from the committee vote, Curtis was positive the ensuing scandal would.

Sun Tzu wrote in *The Art of War* that quickness is the essence of the war. There was no reason why his men shouldn't have the cabin secured within the first few moments, making her extraction as unnoticeable as possible. No reason to call out the locals to a gunfight. His men would be far away by the time anyone noticed.

Curtis smiled again. All he had to do now was wait for the phone call.

CHAPTER ELEVEN

Thayer woke to the amazing smell of bacon frying the next morning. Stretching with a moan, she rolled out of bed, pulling on another one of Memphis's flannel shirts he had left next to the bed for her.

Wandering into the kitchen, she stopped to give Murphy a quick pat on the head before hopping onto a barstool. Turning, Memphis sat a plate heaping with eggs, bacon, potatoes, and a buttered English muffin in front of her.

"Holy cow, is this the last meal for today?" Thayer asked, smirking at him.

"I never know with farm calls. Sometimes I get lunch, sometimes not. I don't want you going hungry."

"You're saying I'm still too scrawny."

"I'm saying you're perfect however you look, but I worry about you." Memphis plopped down on the stool next to her, digging into his breakfast. After a moment, he set down his fork, looking over at her. "How could you think I see you as anything but beautiful and always will whatever size you are?"

Thayer laughed. "You won't think that when I reach my original weight again. My thighs are too thick, and I always seem to have this slight tummy roll that no number of sit-ups can get rid of."

"So, what I'm hearing is that you'll still be just as stunning. Now," he said, carrying their empty plates to the sink. "If we're done with this insane conversation, we need to stop by the office on the way out."

Hopping up, Thayer quickly headed to the bathroom to brush her teeth. When she returned to the living room, Memphis had packed up his truck with a thermos, food cooler, and extra coveralls for her.

"I thought you said we won't get lunch," she said, eyeing the cooler when they reached the truck.

"What? This is backup, just in case. Just snacks really."

Rolling her eyes, she hopped inside for the short drive.

At the office, he picked up a pair of muck boots his receptionist brought for her to borrow. They were a little big, but she could still wear them comfortably.

The morning went smoothly as they worked their way through two routine wellness calls. Thayer stood fascinated as he pregnancy tested a small herd of cows using ultrasound. The machine not only told him if the cow was having a calf, but how far along it was. The rancher ran a chute that held the cow still so Memphis didn't get kicked standing behind it.

For her part, she managed to pet every single one of their heads as they stood there waiting to be released.

She was positive it made the process slower, but neither one of the men seemed to mind.

Memphis also had her help corral a new litter of puppies so he could give them their first shots. He explained to her that if the farmer was going to pay for a farm call, he tried to do as much as he could while he was there.

Quite often, he treated as many as five or six different animal species at a visit. If there was just one animal that needed tending to, they usually were brought to his office for treatment. It explained why his office had a complete set of pens, several stalls, and a working chute in the back of the clinic.

They were between calls at lunchtime, so Memphis parked near a pond so they could sit on the tailgate to watch the geese. He pulled out bags of cut sausage, cheese, crackers, and grapes out of the cooler. Wrapping a blanket over her legs so she wouldn't get cold, he poured her a mug of the hot chocolate he had brought.

"I can't believe how much there is to do on these calls. It's barely noon, and I'm already wiped out," Thayer said between bites. "Is it like this all the time?"

"Mostly. Sometimes it's not as busy as others. It all depends on what time of the season it is. When everything starts having babies, it can get really hectic. But in the middle of summer, it's not too bad."

"So, what do you do when it slows down?" she asked.

"Not much," Memphis answered with a laugh. "You saw the town on the way here, right? There's a post office, diner, small library, hair salon, grocery store, a bar, several churches, and the schools. Not too much else around here. Sometimes I go watch the little league games in the summer just to have something to do."

"After everything that's happened, that sounds like a perfect day," Thayer said, smiling at him.

By the end of the afternoon, Thayer had managed to fall in the mud twice while trying to catch piglets on a farm. It had rained overnight making the pen they were in the equivalent of a muddy skating rink. The farmer had laughed as hard as she had as they chased down the pigs before sliding inside the barn to hand them off to Memphis.

She was covered in mud and smelled a little funny but was ridiculously happy. She understood what appealed to Memphis about living as a rural farm vet. Carrying the last of the piglets into the barn after being checked, they said their goodbyes before heading back to his truck.

"Stand here by the truck so I can help you take off your coveralls," Memphis said. Using the water hose attached to his truck, he wet a washcloth to remove most of the mud from her face. "I don't think I can do much about what's in your hair. It's only about a half-hour drive home though."

He unzipped the coveralls, pulling them down to her knees before picking her up by the waist to sit on the passenger seat. When he had pulled her boots off along with the coveralls, she spun in her seat, sliding her legs under her. At least she had worn a pair of yoga pants under them.

It was already dark when they made it back to the cabin. "Stay there. I'll come around and help you," Memphis said, parking the truck in front of the steps to the porch. Hopping out, he walked around the front of the truck as she opened her door. Scooping her into his arms, he deposited her on the porch. "The door should be open. I'll grab our stuff then be in."

"I'm heading for the shower," Thayer said as she bounded to the door.

Quickly giving Murphy a pat on the head, she walked inside. The mess that greeted her in the mirror was right out of a horror movie. Memphis had made a valiant effort to remove most of the mud, but a lot of it was still spread across her face. Her braided hair was matted with it, making it hard to separate.

Dropping her clothes on the floor, she turned on the water to near scalding before climbing into the shower. When the water finally ran clean, she turned off the taps. Opening the clear glass door, she stepped out to find Memphis standing just inside the door, his eyes grew wide as he froze to stare at her.

"Sorry," he said with a shake of his head. "I...shirt?" He laid one of his flannel shirts on the counter before turning around. "Sorry," he mumbled, walking out of the bathroom. She grinned when she heard him add, "Not really that sorry."

Quickly pulling the shirt over her head, she gathered up her dirty clothes, dropping them in the hamper before walking into the kitchen. Memphis was bent over the stove, madly stirring something in a pot.

"What are you cooking?" Thayer asked, looking into the pot.

Startled, he spun toward her with a wooden spoon dripping with chili.

Narrowly escaping being smeared with dinner, she laughed, jumping back. "Whoa! I almost had to take another shower. How about if I go sit at the bar?"

"Sorry. I was heating some chili. It's almost ready."

"Why don't I keep an eye on it so you can go shower? We can sit on the couch and watch a movie while we eat."

"That's probably a good idea." Memphis crossed to the bedroom in a few quick strides.

PLACING both hands on the counter in the bathroom, he leaned in close to the mirror. "You have got to get your shit together. Last night was a one-time thing."

Stripping off his clothes, he turned the taps on, barely past freezing. Maybe a cold shower would help. When he felt close to normal, he flipped the water to hot, reaching for his shampoo.

"Do you always mumble to yourself in the shower?"

Memphis jumped, opening his eyes. "Thayer!" He quickly shut his eyes again as shampoo ran into them, causing them to burn. Sticking his head under the showerhead, he worked at rinsing the shampoo out.

Sputtering, he tried to open his eyes again. Thayer was leaning against the wall with her arms crossed.

"What are you doing?" Memphis growled, feeling his erection growing hard again already. He had almost gotten it under control before she strolled in.

"It seemed fair. You were ogling me. I figured it was my turn."

"I said I was sorry."

"Then you said you weren't really sorry. I heard you, Dr. Prescott. So, were you really sorry?" She stood staring through the shower door before adding, "Has anyone ever told you that your ass is amazing?"

"Yes...I mean about the sorry thing, not the ass thing. I really meant sorry, but mostly just because I got caught. Are you going to leave so I can finish?"

"Nope."

"Did you at least turn the chili off?"

"Yep."

Memphis sighed loudly before reaching for the soap. Even with the steam from the shower frosting the glass, she could watch as he ran the soap over his body.

Before he realized what was happening, Thayer pulled her flannel shirt off and stepped out of her panties. She quickly opened the shower door, stepping inside to meet him.

Now that she was here, however, she suddenly seemed unsure of what to do. Her face heated up when Memphis let his eyes make their lazy path down her naked body.

"Is there something you need?" Memphis growled at her, winding his hand in her wet hair as he pulled her closer.

"I don't know what I was thinking."

"Do you want to get back out?" He pulled her head back, tightening his fist in her hair. Bending, Memphis brushed his lips lightly across hers before taking a small step back and turning her hair loose. He watched as a myriad of emotions swept through her eyes. "Thayer?"

"I don't know. My brain tells me I shouldn't be here." Looking up at him, she took a deep breath before continuing. "I'm supposed to leave tomorrow, you're twelve years older than me, and you have a lot more experience at all of this. I don't think we are supposed to be together, but so help me, I can't seem to stay away."

Cupping his face in her hands, she searched him as if looking for answers. "Why can't I get enough of you? Why does my heart skip a beat every time you look at me?" she whispered.

"Maybe..." he began, watching as the water ran down her face. Clearing his throat, he started again. "I don't know, Thayer. When they were throwing water on you in that cell, I knew I had to do something. But you waved me off. You held your head high, never giving in to your fear. It was the most courageous thing I've ever seen, and I've seen a lot. I haven't been able to get you out of my mind since."

He gave her one of his lazy grins. "I know I was in junior high when you were born, and that we might never see each other after tonight. By the way, I'm not quite the manwhore you just alluded to."

"Memphis, I didn't mean—"

"Shh, let me finish," Memphis said, placing a finger against her lips. "I don't think society gets to decide what's right for us, we do. So how I see it is you have three options. Option one, we dry off, dress, eat some chili while watching a movie, stay up half the night talking, then get a little sleep before Knox shows up."

Taking a step toward Thayer, he ran his hand back into her hair, wrapping it around his fist. "Option two, we stay in here, I drop to my knees and see how many times I can make you scream my name before you pass out."

Memphis watched as Thayer's nipples beaded to a hard point as her breath hitched. Dropping his mouth to her neck, he ran his tongue up to her ear, gently nipping at her earlobe.

"Option three," he said, standing back up. "I turn

the water off, carry you to my bed, hunt around desperately for wherever I left the condoms I bought a while back, pray they haven't expired, then spread your legs so I can make love to you all night.

"But think about this option very carefully because once I bury myself in you, you're not walking away from me tomorrow. I won't agree to just a one-night stand with you."

Thayer stood quietly, looking at Memphis as he waited for her answer. He knew this was the woman he was meant to be with, even if she didn't yet.

She was the one he would protect at any cost, love without question, and be by her side through every hardship. For him, she was everything strong in this world. He would fight to give her the ability to trust in someone again, to be vulnerable knowing he would be there beside her.

"Do I still get chili regardless of what option I choose?" She smiled when she saw him laugh.

"Yes, chili is always on the table. Unless Murphy found it. He does love chili." Turning loose her hair again, he waited patiently for her to make the first move.

CHAPTER TWELVE

Thayer thought carefully about her options for a moment before answering. "I don't think I'm ready for option three yet," she said, looking up at him shyly. She watched as a look of relief crossed Memphis's face.

"That's probably a good choice. Thinking about those condoms, I'm pretty sure they've expired. So, no explosive sex ending in a panicky trip to the drugstore for the morning-after pill.

"Besides, I'm not sure that a few ghost hauntings and one day rolling in the mud together constitute a relationship on that level. What else?"

Thayer threw her head back with a burst of laughter.

"See, I didn't know you snorted when you laugh really hard. That's fucking adorable." Memphis leaned in, brushing his lips against hers.

"Stop!" Thayer said, making him flinch back against the shower wall. "Sorry, I didn't mean it to come out like that. I think that I'm going to choose option four."

"I don't remember there being an option four, but I'm open-minded. What did you have in mind?"

"Since you've been in charge every time we've been together, it's my turn. This time, I get to touch you." She smiled when he closed his eyes with a moan. Taking his hand, she positioned him so the water hit his shoulders, splashing down the front of his body. "Put your hands on the shower walls out to the side." When he complied, she stepped back, looking at him. "Now don't move unless I tell you."

Thayer decided she could stand forever just staring at the man staring back at her. She slowly ran her eyes down his body, taking in every inch of him.

Marveling at his lean muscles, she slowly let her hands roam over them as they made their way down to his rippling abs. She ran her hands over the soft smattering of hair on his chest, marveling at how soft it was as she followed it down his happy trail.

Finding herself staring at two powerful thighs, she couldn't help but measure them with her hands, forcing his feet wider. She shook her head in wonder when her hands wouldn't even wrap halfway around one.

Feeling her way around his hips, she grabbed his ass, giving it a squeeze. When he growled, she felt powerful knowing she was being allowed to control this man who could do anything he wanted as she helplessly let him.

Looking up at him, she wrapped a hand around his cock, feeling him twitch in her hand. She met his eyes as they turned a deep storm green, watching her do what she wanted with his body.

Before it registered what she was doing, she bent her knees until she was on the floor in front of him, drawing his erection into her mouth. Taking it to the back of her throat, she sucked hard as she drew it back out.

"Fuck, Thayer! Wait!" Memphis growled out, stepping back. Reaching down, he quickly grasped the base of his cock hard as he worked to catch his breath.

"I'm sorry. What did I do wrong? Did I hurt you?" Thayer asked, standing.

"No, hang on." When Memphis finally managed to regain some control, he looked up, meeting her worried gaze. "I just don't do blow jobs. It's nothing you did." Stepping back into the water, he settled his hands on the wall of the shower again. "All right, I'm ready."

Thayer stood staring at him, not sure what she should do.

"Really, it's good. I just don't want to come in your mouth. Keep going. I'm sure I'll come soon anyway, the way you're touching me." He grinned at her, making her sigh in relief.

Laying her hands on his chest, she reached up on tiptoes, kissing him softly on the corner of his mouth. She was trying to decide where she wanted to explore next when something caught her eye. Leaning closer, she ran her hand over a small tattoo high on his ribcage that she hadn't noticed before. It was in the shape of Tennessee with the word "always" in script and coordinates under it.

"What does this mean?" she asked, running a finger over it.

"Can I tell you later? I'm struggling to remember my own name right now." Memphis ducked his head, trying to catch a kiss, but Thayer pulled her head back.

Narrowing his eyes in challenge, Memphis slowly lowered his arms. "I think playtime is over."

Before she could take a breath, Thayer found herself pinned against the back wall of the shower. With one easy movement, Memphis had picked her up around his waist as his mouth crashed into hers. She closed her eyes, giving herself over to the possessive probing of his tongue.

"No sex, remember?" she managed to whisper when he let her come up for air. Thayer knew it would be so easy to rock herself down on him, surrendering herself to her need. She was hell-bent, however, to know him better before she let that happen.

"I'm not going to fuck you unprotected standing in the shower for your first time, so don't worry about it."

"Oh," she breathed out as he kissed down her neck, sucking gently on the space where her shoulder connected to it. "Why?" Thayer asked, laying her head back against the wall as his hand came up to cup her breast, his thumb rubbing over her hard nipple.

"Because if I'm taking your virginity, it's going to be in a bed, where I can take my time without tearing you apart."

She gasped when he pinched her nipple, sending a round of spasms through her core. Hiking her higher up his body, he pulled one into his mouth, flicking his tongue over it as she arched toward him.

"Do you think you can have an orgasm just from having your nipples sucked?" she asked with a gasp.

"I don't know. I guess it's possible," Memphis said before moving his focus to the other one.

"I think so. I mean, last night was really good when you were just playing with them, but this is so much better." At Thayer's words, Memphis snorted a laugh, releasing her.

Wrapping his hands around her waist, he set her back on her feet. There was a moment of worry that crossed her mind she had done something stupid again. Everything was wiped from her mind a moment later, though, when his hand gently wrapped around the front of her neck, his large palm resting on her collarbone.

"You like when I play with your nipples."

It was more of a statement than a question, but Thayer nodded her head anyway.

"You like it when I do this."

She gasped when he gently pinched one between his fingers.

"But you really like when I do this." Lowering his head, he lightly flicked his tongue over one as he sank to his knees.

"What are you doing?" she whispered when he pushed her back against the wall.

"The next thing on my list. Hold on to me if you need to."

"There's a list?" was all she managed to get out before Memphis pulled one of her legs over his shoulder. Leaning in, he growled when he ran his tongue through her folds. "Oh my god, Memphis."

She knew he could work magic with his fingers, but this was something so much better. He wasn't timid in his exploration of her. He devoured her. In minutes, she could feel her orgasm building. When he sucked her clit into his mouth, her orgasm raced through her with a vengeance. Somewhere in the distance, she heard a scream but couldn't tell if it was her.

She would have issued a fervent thanks when she finally stopped panting, but he didn't give her a chance. Sliding his finger into her heat, he amped up his efforts. When she felt another orgasm barrel through her, she couldn't decide if it was a new one or just the continuation of the first one.

Her heart was pounding so hard she thought it would actually tear its way out of her chest. Even with Memphis's hand pressing her thigh against the wall, she simply couldn't remain standing.

As she melted down the wall, he caught her, pulling her into his lap on the floor. Adjusting until his back was against the wall, he held her to him as she recovered.

Sitting up suddenly, Thayer reached between his legs. "I'm sorry, I can finish you."

He laughed, catching her hands before pulling her back into his chest. "Don't worry about me. I came again just like I did last night. It's a wonder I didn't blow a hole in the shower wall."

She grinned up at him, meeting his bright-green eyes.

With a shrug of his shoulders, he added, "You came on my tongue. What was I supposed to do? I don't have that kind of control."

"I think you melted me."

"I melted you? That was just two."

"Oh my god. I can't feel my bones. You think I can do more?"

"I'd like to find out," he said with a wicked grin.

Levering off the floor with her in his arms, he shut off the water before stepping out. Pulling a towel from the rack, he set her on her feet, wrapping it around her.

Pulling two more towels from the cabinet, he wrapped one around his waist before handing her the other one for her hair.

When she was dry, she pulled the flannel shirt back over her head while Memphis slid on a pair of sweatpants. He scooped her up, depositing her on the couch with a blanket.

Moving to the kitchen, he relit the stove, moving the chili back over the flame, ladling out two bowlfuls when it was hot. Popping open two beers, he crossed back into the living room.

"What movie?" Memphis asked, handing Thayer a beer.

"*Magic Mike*," Thayer said with a grin.

"Pretty sure I heard *Deadpool*," Memphis answered, looking through the DVDs.

"*10 Things I Hate About You*?"

"I'm not fifteen or full of teenage angst. *Avengers*?"

"Yes! Lots of hot male flesh. Is Tom Hiddleston in this one? Love me some tall, lanky bad boy." Thayer was trying hard to keep the laugh trying to bubble up from escaping.

"Nope," Memphis said, turning back to the movies, tossing the box back on the shelf as Thayer gave up a giggle. "We're watching *A Knight's Tale*. It's got Heath Ledger, jousting, and classic rock. I can't believe you would think I have a copy of *Magic Mike*," he grumbled in disgust, flopping down on the couch next to her.

Thayer dug into her dinner, not realizing she was so hungry until her first bite. She watched Memphis out of the corner of her eye as he sat with his eyebrows knit in concentration.

Finally, he turned to look at her. "I don't think I'm pretty enough to pull off Loki."

Thayer couldn't hold back this time as she burst into laughter. When she had regained control, she looked at Memphis, hoping she hadn't hurt his ego, but he sat grinning at her.

"Actually, I developed a crush on him watching *Wallender* with my dad. You'd have to dye your hair blond."

"Oh no. I look stupid with blond hair. One of my foster sisters decided I should have the surfer dude look when I was sixteen, so she bleached my hair out with a bottle of peroxide. I thought our foster mom was going to kill us." Memphis laughed. "I had these black eyebrows and platinum blond hair. I looked like an idiot."

"I didn't know you were in the foster system," Thayer said, forgetting about the movie.

"Yeah, since I was seven, when my mom died. My dad had long since taken off, so they had to do something with me. That's where I got this tattoo. The foster home I lived in through high school started with four of us boys and two girls. I don't know why they never moved us, but Jay, the oldest, decided we should all get matching tattoos. He said that no matter how old we got or how lost, we could always find our way home."

Rolling his eyes at Thayer, he added, "I know it's cheesy, but we were teenagers."

"I don't think it's cheesy. I think it's pretty cool. My question is, how did you get a tattoo while still in high school?"

"No idea. I never asked. Based on the place we got

them, I guess I should be thankful I didn't contract a raging case of hepatitis."

Memphis took her empty bowl, placing them both on the coffee table. Turning, he braced his back against the arm of the couch, pulling her to his chest. Arranging the blanket over both of them, he motioned toward the TV.

"We should probably watch the movie."

She laughed to herself, wondering how he thought she was supposed to focus on a movie when she was pressed against his naked chest, feeling every muscle when he shifted into a more comfortable position.

Memphis eased a little farther down the couch, slowly running his hand idly up and down Thayer's back until she had to fight to stay awake. She knew they should move to the bed so they could both get some sleep, but she couldn't resist staying there for a few more minutes being held against him.

Knox had texted earlier to let them know he made it to the hotel in town. Tomorrow he would show up early to take her back. Thayer wasn't exactly sure what they were going to do, but she decided to think about it tomorrow.

Right now, she was happy just listening to his heartbeat.

CHAPTER THIRTEEN

Knox lay on the bed in the same room he had stayed in the last time he was in Minnesota. Lately, every time Thayer had disappeared, this is where he had wound up.

He understood why she had run to Memphis. Her father didn't understand that a chapter in her story had been left unfinished when he sent Memphis home from the hospital. He had given her the time he thought she needed to heal some before reporting to her father that she had run away. It took some quick talk to convince him that she was safe.

He had observed how Memphis looked at her when he brought her out of that cellar, how tightly he had held on to her. Knox understood the need to protect her, but with him, it was more of an older brother feeling. With Memphis, he wasn't so sure.

Her father hadn't asked Knox where she had gone. When he had informed the senator that she had run off this time, he had simply sent Knox to retrieve her.

Knox had argued for better security, but she had been furious at being shadowed by a guard every moment. Naturally, she had used the evasive maneuvers he had taught her when she was young to sneak away from her bodyguard. He wasn't sure if he should be pissed or impressed.

Rolling over, Knox grumbled at the double bed the hotel insisted was all they had left. Was there that big of a rush for hotel rooms in this tiny town? Even turned diagonally, his feet still hung off the end.

He had spent most nights awake since Thayer had been kidnapped trying to come up with any lead on who would want to hurt her. He was still no closer to figuring it out than he had been before. Whoever it was simply left no trace of himself.

The first thing he had done when he had returned to Washington, DC was to pull files on everyone staffed by the senator. He had combed through the household staff in Connecticut, office staff in Washington, campaign staff, he had even put together dossiers on her college friends and professors, to no avail. There was simply no one who stuck out as a threat to her that he could find.

With a sigh, he tried once more to find a more comfortable position. At least he had the feeling that, for a couple of days at least, Thayer had felt safe.

Knox had met Thayer while she was still in middle school. She would come to her father's office after school to work on her homework until they went home for the day. Knox had served under her father in the office, so he had a front-row seat to her struggle with math. When he couldn't stand it any longer, he began to tutor her.

After he left the Navy, he decided to stay in Connecticut while he searched for a job.

The senator helped him get hired as a math teacher at the private college preparatory school she attended. Her father quickly employed Knox to continue tutoring a very math-challenged Thayer.

The year she entered his math class in high school, her father won the race for the Senate. Not wanting to uproot Thayer from her life, the senator started splitting his time between Washington, DC, and Connecticut. He had hated leaving her behind with the household staff when he had to be away.

Soon, Knox was offered a very generous salary to play babysitter to Thayer. He moved into the basement of the house, taught at her school during the day and watched over her during the evenings and weekends when her father wasn't able to come home.

It had seemed odd to be an older single man spending most days with a young high school girl, but he tried not to smother her constantly. Besides, with the rest of the household staff constantly around, he was rarely alone with her. It only took a month together before the big brother/little sister relationship set in.

When the senator had insisted that Knox shadow Thayer at college, he had refused. She was going to Amherst, for Christ's sake, not some university in the middle of the gangs of Los Angeles. No college student should have to put up with a babysitter, especially a giant, terrifying one. Besides, the idea of suffering through even one sorority party made him physically ill.

But that was before she had been kidnapped out of a seemingly safe dorm room. He had personally checked out the campus before she started there, it should have been safe. The dorm had the latest safety practices in effect, the campus police were competent, and she was rarely alone. He had even given her lessons in self-defense.

Rolling onto his back, Knox scowled up at the ceiling. So, what had happened? He knew he was missing something, but he couldn't quite put his finger on it. He had to figure it out soon. Thayer wouldn't be truly safe until he found the fucker who had turned her over to a team of rapists to be disposed of.

"What am I missing?" he asked no one.

Looking at the clock beside the bed, he growled, seeing it only read three fifteen. He had laid here most of the night trying to figure it out. He had to get at least a few hours of sleep if he hoped to function tomorrow. His eyes had finally started to drop closed when his phone on the nightstand rang.

"Are you fucking kidding me?" Grabbing it, he stared at the display, panic lacing through him when he saw it was Thayer. "Thayer?" he barked into the phone, springing off the bed.

"Knox!" He jumped when he heard a gunshot.

"Thayer!" he yelled into the phone while pulling on his pants with one hand. Quickly tying his boots, he listened to a confusing concoction of noises coming through the phone. Thayer had obviously dropped the phone with it still connected.

Running out to the car, Knox slid sideways out of the parking lot, heading for Memphis's cabin.

"See if you can flush them out the back. Kill the man, but don't hurt the girl. She's going with us," was the last thing Knox heard before her phone went dead.

It had sounded like whoever it was had made it into the house.

Sliding the car to a stop next to the driveway leading to Memphis's cabin, Knox grabbed his sidearm, pocketing the extra clip. He cursed himself for not bringing more firepower, but he hadn't expected to face an unfriendly welcoming committee when he left that morning.

After quickly creeping through the woods next to the driveway, Knox crouched behind a tree, where he could see the cabin. The front door was open, so he could see three or four men inside the living room. He also saw one that lay on the front porch not moving.

He took a couple of minutes to assess the situation. If they had already made it in the front door, chances were good Memphis had moved them into the bedroom at the back of the house.

Knox remembered there being a door in the back with a dog door in it. It made the most sense that the back bedroom door would be their best escape route.

Moving through the trees to the side of the cabin, Knox saw his first target waiting on the side in the trees with his gun pointed at the back door. So, they had thought of the same thing. He knew he had to clear the way out if Memphis and Thayer had even a slim prayer of making it out of the cabin alive.

With a quick pull of the trigger, Knox put the man on the ground right before he had to dive behind the trees, dodging a second man's bullets.

Suddenly Murphy burst out of the dog door running for the trees. Knox sprang up, shooting the other man in the chest as he took aim at the dog. He managed to hit the man in the head with the second shot as he fell back. They were all wearing Kevlar, so a bullet to the chest wasn't going to do it. He would have to adjust his aim.

Knox would have loved to get at least one of the automatics from the men he shot, but he simply didn't have time. He moved quickly to station himself at the back of the house. If Memphis was trying to bring them out this way, he needed to be in place.

With a sharp whistle, he brought Murphy over to him. "When I tell you to, dog, I need you to go get them."

The dog looked at him quickly before crouching down on his haunches to face the cabin, letting out a bark.

"Ready," he whispered. Murphy stood, his muscles quivering. "Go!"

CHAPTER FOURTEEN

Earlier, Memphis woke up still holding Thayer on the couch. The movie had ended a while back, he guessed, based on the black screen of his TV.

He was starting to drift back off when Murphy crawled off the end of the couch with a growl. That was odd, Murphy never growled. When he heard steps on the front porch, he sat up, shaking Thayer.

"Thayer, wake up," he whispered.

Though groggy, she sat up to let Memphis stand.

"What is it?" she whispered, her eyes going wide when she saw the concerned look on his face.

"I don't know. Get your phone and come to me."

He had crossed the room to a small coat closet. Reaching in, he pulled out a shotgun and a box of shells, emptying them into his pockets.

"Call Knox. I think we might need his help. Murphy. Come."

With trembling fingers, Thayer hit the speed dial for Knox, getting him almost immediately. Memphis checked that the gun was loaded before pulling Thayer behind him as they backed slowly toward the bedroom.

When the front door crashed in, she screamed, dropping the phone.

Pointing the shotgun at the door, Memphis emptied the first barrel. When a head popped in the door shooting, he emptied the second barrel at it. With a grunt, Memphis pushed them into the bedroom. He kicked the door closed as they both fell to the floor. Cracking the gun open, he fished two more shells out, reloading.

"Quick, help me shove the dresser against the door," he yelled, cocking the gun.

Scrambling out from under him, Thayer helped him push at the dresser, maneuvering it in place. Memphis pushed her to the floor again in the corner behind him.

"When I tell you, I need you to run out the back door into the woods. Don't look back, just keep running. You'll come to a neighbor's house in about a quarter mile. You can call for help from there."

Memphis gritted his teeth watching Thayer look down at her bloody shirt as she tried to understand where it was coming from. Pulling up her shirt, she found nothing until she looked at her hands. They were covered in blood. Her eyes wide, her gaze darted to him as he shook his head, trying to clear his vision.

"Memphis! You're bleeding!" she whispered as she started frantically feeling around his body.

He grunted when she found the wound on his side.

"My god, what do we do?"

"Thayer!" he barked at her to get her attention. "It doesn't matter. Did you hear what I said? I need you to run when I say."

She shook her head vigorously. “I don’t want to leave you.”

“I know, sweetheart,” Memphis said calmly. “But they’re not getting their hands on you again. I’ll keep them here so you can get away.” Taking his eyes off the door briefly, he turned to look at her. “Please, Thayer. I need you to do this.”

Leaning forward, she placed her forehead against his.

“I’ll go, but I’ll be back with help. Okay?”

He nodded his head before turning back around. The men were crashing against the door, forcing it open a little at a time. Memphis set the shotgun against his shoulder, ready to unload it on the first person through the door.

“Murphy. Scout,” Memphis said to the dog, who immediately shot out of the dog door.

Thayer sent up a quick prayer, begging that the dog would be okay.

When an arm with a gun slid through the slit in the door, Memphis unloaded the gun at it. He quickly reloaded, looking up only when he heard Murphy bark.

“Okay, here we go,” Memphis said, shooting once more at the door to the living room as he gently opened the back door, looking out. He closed his eyes for a second when he saw Knox in the trees across from him, clearing the back. “Knox is out there. Run past him deep into the woods, he’ll come get you. Understand?”

“Yes.” Thayer nodded as tears streamed down her face.

The men in the living area continued to shoot at them, slowly forcing their way in. Memphis brushed his hand down her cheek, trying to wipe away her tears.

"Stay low." With a quick kiss, he shoved her out the door. "Run!"

Turning back to the living room door, he emptied the other barrel at it, hoping he could hold them off long enough for her to get away. He was reloading when the door crashed open, letting two shooters in.

Falling out the back door that was still hanging open, he managed to get two more shells loaded as he landed on his back. He couldn't figure out why his left arm wasn't working right anymore, but he aimed as best he could with his right, firing through the doorway.

When the gun was empty, he knew he was done. His bloody left arm was no longer capable of helping him break the big gun open anymore.

He had begun trying to push himself toward the trees when he felt teeth clamp onto his pants. Since he had never put on a shirt, Murphy was doing his best to use whatever he could to pull him toward the trees.

"Murphy. Go!" he yelled as a man stepped onto the back stoop, aiming his gun at Memphis.

Suddenly, the back of his house exploded into flames as a large ball of fire hit it. Memphis could only throw his good arm over his face as the fireball was followed by a second.

Soon the entire cabin had gone up in flames. The scene had gone completely silent except for the sound of the flames consuming his cabin and screaming from inside.

"Come on, we need to get out of here." Memphis heard behind him as he felt himself pulled off the ground in one mighty heave.

"Knox, where's Thayer? You need to find her. She has to be kept safe," he said, trying to wrestle out of the big man's grip. The large arm around his waist was pulling him toward the front of the house as he fought to get away. He had to find Thayer.

"I'm here, Memphis," he heard her say from behind him. He finally managed to break free of Knox's grip, pulling her against him in a one-armed hug when she ran over sobbing.

"Thayer. Thank God," he said, squeezing her tight. With a sudden scowl, he used his good arm to hold her away from him so he could look in her eyes. "You were supposed to keep running."

"Come on, we'll have enough time for tearful reunions, or whatever this is, later. We need to be gone when the cops arrive. There's going to be a lot of bodies in that house to account for."

Knox pulled Memphis's good arm over his shoulder, heading toward his car. Thayer followed them with Murphy and the shotgun. Easing him into the back seat, Knox shot a concerned glance at Thayer.

"We have to get him patched up, but we can't risk a hospital. Any suggestions?"

"My vet tech can do it. Take me to my office."

As Knox drove, Memphis recited both the tech's and the receptionist's numbers to Thayer. When they pulled up to the back door, Jonathon met them to help carry a barely conscious Memphis into the surgery room.

"You understand I've only watched this, right? I've never been allowed to suture something myself. He's losing a lot of blood, you need to drive him to the hospital," the high school student said, looking around at the group gathered in the room.

"Just do what you can," Knox growled.

Turning, the tech began gathering what he would need to clean the wounds before sewing them up.

After twenty minutes, Knox studied the kid's handiwork. "Well, I'm not sure it'll win any awards, but it should do the job. Got any horse tranquilizers we can give him for pain?"

"Or, instead of killing him, how about some antibiotics and ibuprofen?" Jon asked with a smirk.

Thayer saw a slight twitch at the corner of Knox's mouth. She agreed with him, she liked this kid too. "I don't think the bone is broken in his arm, but it will take me a little while to get the X-ray machine warmed up."

"I don't know what you've got him into, but I brought everything you asked for," the receptionist said, bustling through the door, giving Knox a steely stare. She had rounded up some fresh scrubs for Memphis and Thayer, food, more twelve-gauge shells and even another pair of boots.

When Knox opened his mouth to speak, she held up her hand. "We know, if asked, we know nothing. He called in with the flu yesterday."

Knox gave a full smile this time. "We have one more favor to ask," he said, looking at the woman with a glint in his eye.

When he had Memphis loaded into the receptionist's Bronco, he turned to Thayer. "You have to disappear until I can find out who is after you. You're not safe here. Hell, I shouldn't even know where you're headed until you're tucked away somewhere."

"Where do we go?" she asked.

Knox was deep in thought when he heard Memphis croak out an answer from the passenger seat.

"We go home, Thayer. Do you remember where I said my home would always be?" he asked, looking over at her with his brilliant green eyes.

She nodded her head.

Turning back to Knox, she wrapped her arms around him, hugging him fiercely. At first the big man stood stiffly, but she felt when he finally pulled her into him, lightly kissing the top of her head. Gently easing her into the driver's seat, he fished out a fistful of cash, handing it to her along with his credit card.

Looking over, he leveled a stare at Memphis. "You'd better guard her with your life. Do you understand me? If anything happens to her, I'll rip your fucking heart out."

Memphis nodded once. "You won't have to. If anything happens to her, it won't exist any longer to rip out."

Knox tapped the top of the SUV twice as Thayer pulled away. He watched them disappear from sight before walking back to his car. He had to track these fuckers down, and he was running out of time.

Fishing his phone out of his pants pocket, he searched his contacts until he found what he was looking for.

"Agent Dex Tanaka," said the voice on the other end of the line.

"Agent Tanaka, it's Knox. We have a situation," Knox continued, telling Dex everything that had happened in the last couple of hours.

Hanging up the phone, Knox knew Dex would find out everything he could about who the men were when he showed up here in a couple of hours. They had agreed it was best for Knox to limit the amount of exposure he had to the incident.

After securing promises from both Jon and the receptionist to leave his involvement out of what happened tonight, he pointed his rental car back toward the hotel room. It only took him a few moments to gather up his bag before heading to the small airport several towns over. He had one more phone call he had to make after touching base with the pilot, but he was dreading it.

Pushing the speed dial on his phone, he sighed deeply when the sleepy voice of Senator Kent answered.

CHAPTER FIFTEEN

Thayer drove for hours before she dared to stop for gas. She was still shaking from what had happened earlier as she replaced the dressings on Memphis's arm and side in a parking space by the back of the convenience store. He didn't say anything, but she could hear him hiss through his teeth as she pressed the bandages in place. Jon had done a good job, but the wound in his side had started bleeding again.

She debated ignoring the instructions Knox had given her and taking Memphis to a hospital, but she was terrified whoever had traced her to the cabin would simply find them there.

Somewhere in Missouri, she realized Memphis had slipped into unconsciousness when his hand dropped from the barrel of the shotgun he had been holding.

Pulling over, she set the gun on the back seat before trying to wake him. It was no use, he was pale and sweaty, even with the air conditioning on. She was lucky that the Bronco had a GPS system on the dashboard. Consulting the coordinates on Memphis's ribs, that evening she pulled up in front of a nice two-story house in Tennessee.

"I don't guess you can tell me if this is the right house?" She looked at Memphis, he was still out cold, and his bandages were bloody again. "Okay, I'll be right back." Leaping out of the car, she ran up to the front porch.

With a deep breath, she rang the doorbell. When no one answered immediately, she began banging on the door with her hand, calling out to anyone inside.

The foster house Memphis had spent his high school years in was a large two-story home typical of the South. It was painted a cool yellow with white trim and looked well cared for. A large front porch contained several rocking chairs and large pots filled with flowers. The ceiling under the porch was painted a sky blue to encourage the birds to build their nest somewhere else.

"Can I help you?" an older woman asked, opening the door. She was at least a couple inches taller than Thayer, with the most beautiful caramel-colored skin.

"Um, do you know a man named Memphis Prescott?" Thayer stood awkwardly for a moment, rocking nervously from foot to foot before the woman responded.

"Of course, I know Memphis. He's one of my boys. What do you want with him?"

Thayer breathed a sigh of relief.

"We need help. He's been hurt and told me to come here. He's in the Bronco," she said, pointing behind her. "Please, can you help us? I'm sorry just to show up, but I don't know where else to go." Thayer waited anxiously, hoping this beautiful woman would help them.

"Boys!" she called over her shoulder. "He's in the car?" she asked Thayer, heading toward it with a quick clip. She gently opened the passenger door, holding Memphis up. "Oh my good lord. That's more than a little hurt. Boys, help me get him inside. Jordan, go call Jay and tell him to get over here."

They eased Memphis out of the car, carrying him into the house.

"Girl, that's a big gun in the back seat. Can I expect trouble?"

"I hope not," Thayer answered.

The woman nodded at her before instructing one of the young men to bring the gun into the house before parking the car in the garage on the side of the house.

When Thayer made it inside, Memphis had been laid out on one of the beds. They had eased his shirt off and pulled the covers up to his waist, pressing fresh gauze against his gunshot wounds. Looking at his pale face, Thayer felt herself start to gasp for breath uncontrollably.

"Slow down before you hyperventilate. Go bring me some tea," the woman said to one of the kids.

The young girl scooted off into another room as Thayer was eased into a chair.

"You tell me what happened. Did Memphis get himself shot up doing something stupid?"

Thayer shook her head, trying to focus on slowing her breathing down. She didn't want to pass out in a houseful of strangers before she could make sure Memphis was taken care of.

"Are you his girlfriend? I don't see a wedding ring. What kind of trouble are y'all in?"

"I don't know," Thayer said uncertainly as a mug of

tea was placed in her hand. She realized that this was the first time she had had time to really think about the situation they found themselves in. If she didn't fight against it, the enormity of everything that had happened would overwhelm her.

"You don't know if you're his girlfriend, or you don't know what trouble you're in?"

Thayer just shrugged her shoulders.

"Why does that not surprise me either." The woman laughed, shaking her head.

"Now you just sit here and drink your tea. His foster brother will be here in a minute to see to him. You're safe now. You understand?"

Thayer nodded, looking up into the woman's kind face.

"You can call me Miss Beulah. What do I call you?"

"Thayer," she said quietly. "Thank you, Miss Beulah. I didn't know where else to go. Memphis just told me to go home."

They sat quietly, watching Memphis, until she heard the front door open.

"Jay, we're in here." Miss Beulah stood, sticking her head into the hall.

Thayer watched as a tall, handsome man entered the room with a doctor's bag. He gave the older woman a quick peck on the cheek before nodding to Thayer.

"What has the kid done to himself now?" he asked in a booming voice, stepping to the bed. Gently, he peeled back the bandage on Memphis's side to assess it. "Did you sew him up?" he asked, looking over at Thayer.

"His vet tech did."

"Humph," he grunted, turning back to Memphis.

"Miss Beulah, can you get Ben to bring the portable X-ray machine over here? He should have one in his rig. Tell him to park in the back with no lights. We don't want to invite anyone to come snooping around who doesn't need to."

When she left to make the call, Thayer stood, walking to the other side of the bed.

"Is it bad? We couldn't take him to the hospital." Thayer took Memphis's hand, holding it in hers as she brushed his hair back with the other one. Not receiving an answer, she looked up at Jay, who was studying her intently.

"I think it missed everything important, but we need an X-ray to confirm that," he finally said, looking back down at Memphis. "Let's look at this arm." Gently removing the bandages from his arm, he moved it while feeling for damage. "I don't think it's broken, but I'll need an X-ray of that as well."

Laying the arm down carefully on the bed, Jay stood straight, glaring at her. When she finally swung her eyes up to meet his, he asked, "What the fuck happened? Why couldn't you take him to the hospital?"

"Jay! You are not too old for me to scrub that dirty mouth out with soap," Miss Beulah exclaimed, walking into the room with a heavyset man who kept trying to sweep his hair out of his face.

He had a grin plastered on his face behind her back.

"Sorry, Miss Beulah. But I would like an answer on why, after all these years, Memphis shows up on your doorstep with two gunshot wounds. I'm pretty sure this woman has something to do with it. I, for one, would like to hear what story she tries to sell us." He crossed his arms over his muscled chest as he glared at her.

Thayer shrank back, overwhelmed at the man's anger.

"We'll learn what happened only when Memphis is out of trouble. Now, we are going to the kitchen to wait for you to finish tending to him." Reaching out, Miss Beulah gently took Thayer's hand, pulling her out of the room. "Let's find you something else to wear."

Looking down, Thayer noticed the dried blood on her scrub shirt for the first time.

"I'm bound to have something that will fit you. Probably still have a couple of Memphis's old T-shirts if truth be told." Digging through a closet in the hallway, she pulled out a T-shirt with a blue tiger on it. "There's a bathroom at the end of the hall you can change in. Should be fresh hand towels on the rack too."

Closing herself in the bathroom, Thayer took in her appearance in the mirror. No wonder they didn't trust her, she was a mess. Her hair looked like she had been through a windstorm, she had dirt still on her face where Knox had basically clotheslined her as she ran past him, and there was also crusted blood on her shirt and arms. She even still had on a pair of Memphis's scrub pants that she had to belt with a piece of rope after rolling them up. She looked like a prison escapee.

Pulling her shirt over her head, she groaned, remembering she didn't have a bra on. They had barely made it out of the cabin with their lives, undergarments hadn't seemed like a big deal.

Finding a washcloth, she scrubbed it on her face and arms until she had all of the grime off. Searching around, she finally found a hair tie, pulling her hair up into some semblance of a ponytail.

When she felt at least somewhat clean, she pulled

the clean T-shirt over her head. It fit a bit snug, but at least it wasn't covered in Memphis's blood. Looking in the mirror, however, she realized it left little to the imagination. She was going to have to pick up some new underwear at some point.

"Miss Beulah?" she called quietly from the door of the bathroom.

Walking down the hall past the bedroom where the men were working on Memphis, Thayer turned the corner into a large kitchen. She had just a moment to take in the room, marveling at the large modern appliances, commercial mixer sitting on a gleaming granite counter, and an island large enough to accommodate six cooks at one time.

"Oh, my! We'd better find you a shirt to put over that. Although Jay would probably be a lot more patient sitting across from those. I would hate to see Memphis pull his stitches out fighting with his brother." She dug back through the closet until she found a long-sleeved flannel shirt for her.

Sliding it on, Thayer looked up with a questioning shrug.

"Better." Miss Beulah grinned at her. "Let's go see how Memphis is."

Thayer followed her back into the bedroom, relieved to see a little color returning to Memphis's face.

"The X-ray of his stomach shows a through-and-through, which is lucky," Ben said, smiling shyly at her. "The bullet that went through his arm, however, chipped part of the bone off. We had to cut it out, but he should be okay. We put it in a sling to keep it still. I'm Ben."

Thayer shook his hand before looking over at Jay.

"I've given him a round of antibiotics and hooked up an IV," Jay continued. "I'll give him another shot tomorrow. I also added some painkillers to help him sleep. He should be pretty sore, but he'll be fine. Now, I'd like a cup of coffee while we hear what happened."

Thayer nodded to him before he turned toward the kitchen. When everyone had filed out, she walked over to the bed. Holding his hand for a moment, she finally bent down, kissing his forehead. With a sigh, she turned to the door. She knew they needed an explanation, she just hoped they didn't kick her out when they heard it.

With a deep breath, she walked into the dining room that sat right off the kitchen. It was decorated in light green paint with wainscotting wrapping around the bottom of the walls. The large bay windows on one side looked out into the backyard at a crepe myrtle tree that lay dormant for the winter. There were two large buffets gracing the wall opposite the windows that Thayer assumed housed all of the dinnerware needed to feed a large foster home family.

The rest of the house was quiet. She supposed the younger kids had been chased to bed already. She could barely remember what it felt like to sleep. Thayer stood looking at the large table with Miss Beulah, Jay, Ben, and another young man who introduced himself as Shaun. Sliding a cup of coffee across, Miss Beulah pointed at an empty chair across from Jay.

"It started about a month ago," Thayer began her story, sinking into the seat. She proceeded to tell them everything. Though she skirted around Memphis appearing to her as a hologram until Jay brought it up. "I didn't know if you knew about that."

"We do, but we've never shared it with anyone else.

He used to get into so much trouble over that," Ben said, laughing softly. "He landed in the middle of the girls' locker room once. He was grounded forever, but he said it was worth it," he added with a grin.

Thayer laughed. "Yeah, he has a tendency to pop in at the worst times." She continued her story until the end. "I'm so sorry to bring this to your doorstep."

"There's a garage apartment you are both welcome to stay in as long as you need. When he's well enough, we can help you get him up there. I'll have Hettie come over tomorrow to go pick you up what you need. Tonight, I think we've all had enough excitement. There's an extra toothbrush in the drawer in that bathroom. I'll set you up in one of the upstairs bedrooms." With a nod, Miss Beulah stood up, bringing everyone else to their feet as well.

"I'm going to check on Memphis one more time, then I'll be back tomorrow," Jay announced, leaving the kitchen. "You need to let Randall know," he told Miss Beulah.

Ben and Shaun followed him, leaving Thayer alone in the kitchen.

When the front door finally closed, she moved back into Memphis's room. Pulling a chair next to the bed, she watched his chest rise and fall with each breath. Slowly she felt the fatigue overcome her until her head slowly rested on the side of the bed. Before she realized it, she had fallen asleep slumped over on the edge of the bed.

MEMPHIS FELT himself come out of the darkness sometime in the night. When he finally convinced his eyes to open, he took a moment to look around. He vaguely recognized the room, but it had been rearranged since the last time he saw it.

Raising his right hand, he found it was connected to an IV that hung above his head, so he assumed Jay and possibly Ben had been here. Looking over his left arm, it felt like it was on fire. He noticed the blonde head by his thigh. He tried to touch her hair, but the best he could manage was brushing it with his fingertips.

The light brush was all it took for Thayer to come instantly awake. With eyes that looked like they ached from fatigue, she gazed at him.

He couldn't describe the relief he felt when she gave him a small smile. Memphis could feel his eyes burn as they stared at each other in the quiet. It was as if they had somehow walked through the fires of hell and had made it out the other side.

"Why are you crying? Are you hurt?" Memphis somehow rasped out in concern as tears started to roll down her face.

"I was so scared I had killed you," she whispered.

"Come here," he responded, carefully holding the blanket open for her.

"I don't want to hurt your side."

"Then climb in carefully. I promise to be a gentleman," he said with a slight chuckle before groaning.

Thayer stood, climbing in slowly until her head lay on his good shoulder. She was careful not to brush his injured side. "Close your eyes, beautiful. I've got you."

Memphis knew they should be worrying about what tomorrow would bring. They should be talking to

Knox about how they were going to lure the man who had ordered him shot out from the shadows. He heard her sigh deeply as he held her tighter. There were a lot of things they should do, but for right now, all he knew was that they were both alive and together. Everything else could wait.

He gently kissed the top of her head as she drifted off. Yes, it could all wait for tonight. But tomorrow, there would be hell to pay.

CHAPTER SIXTEEN

The next morning, Thayer woke slowly to the sound of whispering. "I have to move her to check your side."

"You can move her when she wakes up."

"She told us what happened last night. Memphis, you finally got out of finding bodies. What the fuck were you thinking? Not even good pussy is worth this."

"Fuck you, Jay! You don't know anything about us."

"Guys!" Thayer said, sitting up. "I'm going to go get some air so you can finish your pissing contest in peace." She stalked out of the room, passing Miss Beulah in the kitchen. With a nod, she pushed out through the front door, walking over to the curb.

Turning around, she leaned up against one of the cars to wait for Jay. He might be an ass, but she needed his help. Closing her eyes, she tried breathing exercises to calm down. She had almost fallen asleep on her feet when she was startled by a deep voice in front of her.

"I apologize for what I said. It was crass."

Opening her eyes, she found Jay standing in front of her.

"In my defense, Memphis is the closest thing I have to family. I don't like patching him together because of some shit he shouldn't have gotten involved with in the first place." He stood with his arms crossed against his broad chest, watching her. "But for what it's worth, I don't think this shit is your fault either."

"Look, it doesn't matter if you like me or not. I don't know why I've been targeted by some lunatic, but it ends now. Memphis has already taken two bullets for me. They won't get another chance at a third. I need you to help me." Thayer stood in front of Jay with a look of determination on her face.

After a few minutes of studying her, he nodded once. "Good. I'm calling in reinforcements. We'll meet back here tomorrow morning."

"Anyone I know?" he asked, scowling when Thayer ignored his question.

"I also need your help to find us a secure place to stay away from this house. There are children living here, and I won't bring the devil to their front door. I need it by tonight so you can help me move Memphis out later. Can you do that?"

"He shouldn't be moved yet..." He held up a hand when she started to argue with him. "But I don't want trouble brought here either. I think I know somewhere. I'll get Ben to help us move him."

Slumping in relief, Thayer fought to hold back the tears threatening. "Thank you." She stepped aside so Jay could get in his car. After closing the door, he rolled down the window, leaning out.

"By the way, the idiot tore the stitches in his side,

taking a swing at me for my comments. I stapled him together this time. Tell the dumbass he screams like a girl, will ya?" With the hint of a smile, Jay pulled away from the curb.

Walking back into the house, Thayer stopped in the doorway to watch a very left-handed Memphis in bed trying to eat scrambled eggs with his right hand.

"Here," she said, taking his fork away. "You look ridiculous." Plopping a generous portion of egg into his mouth, she took the opportunity to catch him off guard. "So, I understand you tore your stitches out acting like a dick."

"Huh-uh," he said around his mouthful of food. When he had successfully swallowed it, he added, "No, no. It wasn't me being a dick. Look what he did." Pulling down the sheet, Memphis showed her not just the staples now holding his wounds together but two farther up on his pectoral muscle. Thayer laughed at the extra staples. "It's not funny. They hurt like hell. Fucking asshole," he grumbled.

"Yeah, he's an asshole. But I like him."

"Yeah, me too," Memphis agreed with a grin.

The day crept by as Memphis rested. Thayer kept herself entertained as long as she could, but by the hundredth round of solitaire even she became restless watching him sleep. They both agreed if they stayed here much longer, with Miss Beulah feeding them continually, neither one would fit through the door soon.

One of his foster sisters, Hettie, breezed into the house that afternoon. She hugged Memphis until he finally grunted in pain. Making a note of their sizes, she blew out again with the remaining cash Knox had given them to find them some clothes, promising to return for dinner. After school, the house filled up with kids of different ages running around. This time, when Jay walked through the door, they both welcomed him with relief.

"I talked to your friend. He has something he is following up, but he said he would be here tomorrow morning. He had me pick up two burner phones for you." He tossed the phones at Memphis. "I made arrangements for you to use Randall's loft as long as you need it. It has steel doors and security cameras, so it's as secure as I can find. I can take you there after dinner." Jay examined Memphis's gunshot wounds. "I see you got the extra staples out."

"If I wanted a nipple pierced, I would find a professional. Not some quack calling himself a doctor." Memphis smirked at Jay. "I'm thinking about filing a malpractice suit."

Jay turned to Thayer. "You know I will happily staple that mouth shut for no extra charge."

"But that mouth is so talented," Thayer popped off without thinking.

The men stared at her for a minute. "Ohhhh!" they both shouted with a high five.

Thayer could feel the red race up her face. They were both looking at her, laughing, when Miss Beulah breezed into the room.

"Boys, are you ready for dinner? Come on, sweetie," she said, taking Thayer's hand. "I don't know what they're carrying on about, but you don't want any part of it."

"Too late, Miss Beulah. Sounds like she's already had a big part of it," Jay hollered as she was led out the door. She grew even redder hearing them laugh behind her as Jay helped Memphis get out of bed. There was a large group of people assembled around the table by the time Memphis gently slid into the seat next to her.

"Just so you know," he whispered into her ear. "I'm really looking forward to using those talents again real soon." He ran his tongue up the side of her neck, making her both blush and wet simultaneously.

"Memphis! Is that appropriate at the dinner table?" Miss Beulah yelled at him from the head of the table.

Thayer looked up in time to see Jay fighting a grin. Leaning over, he whispered something in Ben's ear before he broke out in a grin, too.

"No, ma'am," Memphis answered, slowly pulling Thayer's hand under the table. Resting it on his lap, he rubbed her hand against his cock. She could tell he was hard as a rock. With a smirk, he looked at her in mock exasperation. Thayer couldn't tell if it was the painkillers Jay had him on, but she was happy to see Memphis looking a little better.

"Miss Beulah, they don't have their hands ready to pray," a small voice next to Ben said. Memphis and Thayer immediately brought their hands above the table.

Ben grinned at Jay as Memphis tried to adjust in his seat.

"Hey, Miss Beulah. I'm sorry that I'm late. Did I miss anything?" Shaun said, coming in the door.

"Just Memphis trying to get a dry rub under the table," Jay snickered.

"Oh my god," Thayer whispered, staring down at her empty plate.

"But don't you have to have a big piece of meat to

dry rub it?" another small voice asked. A strange keening sound started to come out of Ben as he desperately tried not to laugh.

"Yeah, Memphis, don't you have to have a big piece of meat for a good rub? We'd hate to waste a perfectly good rub," Shaun asked, joining in with a smirk.

Memphis answered by flipping them all off.

There was a gasp from one of the younger girls. "Miss Beulah! He's not supposed to do that."

"I know, sweetheart. After dinner, we'll line them all up for a bar of soap," she answered calmly.

"Oh, come on, Miss Beulah. When has Memphis ever shown up with a girlfriend? You know we have to bust his chops a little," Jay said with a wink.

"You know, Jay, you're right. I don't remember Memphis ever having a girlfriend to speak of," Hettie said.

"See, not a manwhore," Memphis quipped at Thayer.

"Oh, you were a complete manwhore, you just never brought one home," Hettie added.

Thayer looked up at Ben in concern. His keening had now turned into what appeared a shaking fit.

"Hey, at least I didn't do that band kid with the buck teeth behind the school," Memphis growled back at her.

"Are you sure? You did everyone else."

"Girlfriend!" Memphis shouted back at her, motioning with his head to Thayer. When Thayer looked up at him in shock, he blurted out, "What?"

"When did I become your girlfriend?" Thayer asked. The table went silent as everyone focused on them, even the younger children.

He looked at her with a scowl on his face. "I thought...I mean...I don't know." His words drifted off for a minute. "Do you think I'd take up with just anyone?"

"Apparently so," she said with a smirk, gesturing at Hettie.

"Oh, snap," Hettie said quietly, reaching over for a high five from Thayer.

"That's enough now," Miss Beulah said, interrupting the silence. "Jay, say the prayer so we can eat while it's still hot."

The conversation turned to more mundane topics through dinner. Thayer learned a little more about the people who had raised Memphis as they good-naturedly bantered across the table at each other. She smiled, thinking about how different this chaos was from her quiet dinners with her parents when her mom was still living.

Soon, she noticed Memphis starting to favor his side more and more. Standing, she looked over at the woman who had obviously meant so much to the rest of those sitting around the table.

"Thank you so much for dinner, Miss Beulah. If you don't mind, I think it might be time for us to head out. I think I'm still exhausted, and I know Memphis has to be as well." With a nod, Miss Beulah rallied the younger kids to help with cleanup while Thayer walked into the bedroom to gather their things.

When Memphis walked in a few minutes later, he found her staring out the window into the night.

"I'm sorry about the crap at dinner," he said quietly, stopping behind her.

Looking at their reflection in the dark window, she

was shocked at how weary they looked. Taking a tentative step toward her, Memphis wrapped his good arm around her waist, pulling her against him. He breathed a sigh of relief when she relaxed against him.

"I'm really sorry," he started again. "They were just teasing you. I was pretty screwed up when I was young, but somewhere along the way, I got my act together. I haven't been with anyone since I moved to Minnesota." He gently spun her in his arms, pulling her chin up until her eyes met his. "I sure as hell have never cared enough about someone as much as I do for you."

She smiled up at him. "I don't care who you've been with, and I know they were just trying to get a rise out of us." She rose up on her toes so she could kiss him gently. "So, I'm your girlfriend now? Is that what I understand?" she asked, giving him her best smirk. She had to admit she didn't hate the idea. As a matter of fact, the more she was with him, the more promising their future seemed.

"I have no idea what we are," he answered, grinning back. "But I think for right now, we're stuck together. I've got to say, though, I'm not opposed to the idea."

They reluctantly turned when there was a knock at the door. "Yeah," Memphis answered, holding Thayer against him.

"Hey, guys. We came to apologize," Jay said, sticking his head in.

"I'm really sorry, Thayer," Hettie added, slipping into the room. "I should never have said what I did. I was just teasing though."

"It's fine, really. I love that you have such an amazing relationship with each other. I really loved getting to know everyone better," Thayer answered with a yawn.

"I think we should get you two on your way. Thayer looks like she could fall asleep standing." Jay nodded to the others, prompting them to start gathering up stuff.

Ben drove Memphis and Thayer over in their SUV while Jay followed behind with Hettie and Shaun. The twenty minutes it took to drive across town were just long enough for Thayer to fall asleep.

THEY WERE ALL INCOMPETENT, every single one of them!

Curtis had read the news reports from Minnesota. He had even managed to get his hands on the preliminary report the FBI agent had filed.

The papers had failed to report the two bodies found dead in the trees dressed in night combat gear. He assumed Agent Tanaka had his own reasons for covering that up. The report also stated that none of the burned bodies were female.

The veterinarian was also a question. They had found blood on the ground behind the cabin that matched the doctor's blood type, but a DNA match was still pending.

When the staff at his clinic was questioned, they claimed he called in sick, but no one had heard from him since. For now, Curtis had to operate under the assumption they were both alive.

It was his fault, really. How many times has the old adage *if you want something done right, do it yourself* proven to be true? This time, he would take care of the problem personally.

The fact he had no idea where they were was only a minor inconvenience to him. It was a reasonable assumption that the math teacher would eventually lead him to her if he was patient. Well, he was not a patient person, but just this one time, he would have to make an exception.

CHAPTER SEVENTEEN

Even though the loft was in a questionable area of town, it was quite nice inside. It had two bedrooms at the back, each with en suite bathrooms. The rest of the apartment was open, revealing a living room, kitchen, and dining area. It was industrial, but comfortable at the same time.

The worst part was trying to drag himself up the stairs into the second floor of the converted warehouse with one arm in a sling and a bullet hole in his side. He tried to hide it, but he could tell Thayer was aware he was well past when he should have had more painkillers.

Jay had swung through an all-night grocery store, grabbing them enough food to last a couple of days, showing up a half hour later. He checked Memphis's staples one last time before heading out the door.

After the last person had filed out, Thayer bolted the door, sighing in relief. Sitting down on the couch next to Memphis, she rested her head on the cushion.

"Don't fall asleep here," Memphis said gently.

"There's a huge bed calling our name. Can you do me a favor first, though?" he asked.

"Of course," she said, smiling at him.

"I could really, really use a shower, but I don't think I can wash my hair with my gimp arm. Could you lean in to help me with the shampoo?"

"I'll do you one better," she answered, standing up. Pulling him up, they walked into the bathroom. Thayer gently eased the clothes off of Memphis, carefully taking off his bandages.

Jay had told them earlier that a shower would be fine, they would just have to make sure the areas with the staples were dried well before reapplying the bandages. He had left an entire bag of supplies for that reason. When she had him undressed, she slid out of her clothes before turning on the water.

"Oh shit, I forgot you didn't have a bra on," he exclaimed, staring at her with a glint in his eye. "I can't believe Ben didn't mention it. No wonder he's been staring at you like a lost puppy all night." Shaking his head, he stepped into the shower with Thayer.

He held his bad arm tightly to his side with his other hand as he bent over for her to rub shampoo in his hair. After he rinsed the shampoo out, she rubbed her hands together, creating suds from the soap before running her hands down his body.

"Can I ask you a question?" Thayer asked, rubbing shampoo into her hair. She had helped Memphis rinse the soap off before trading positions with him.

"Okay," he answered warily.

"Why don't you like blow jobs? I thought all guys loved them." She picked up the soap, lathering it in her hands. She was trying to act casual as she waited to see if he would answer. When he didn't, she asked, "Did something happen?"

"Yeah, but it was a long time ago. It's not worth talking about."

Opening the door, he slipped out, grabbing a towel off the rack. Turning off the water, Thayer stepped out behind him, taking the towel from his hand. She worked her way down his body, drying him.

"Turn around," she said, working down his back to his feet when he did what she asked. When she was satisfied that he was dry enough, she quickly dried herself before ordering him to stand at the sink so she could replace his bandages. "So, is it a hard no?"

"I don't know, Thayer. Maybe. It has been in the past." Memphis closed his eyes when Thayer wrapped her arms around him, laying her head against his back. He had worked hard to forget what happened in that foster home before they moved him to Miss Beulah's.

His mother died when he was only seven, leaving him devastated but not destroyed. She had raised him with love, teaching him to be a good person. He had trusted the adults in charge of him, since she had never taught him not to.

At first, he had been placed in a group home, but eventually, they found what they thought was a suitable foster home. He had been an excellent student, so his caseworker had fought to keep him in the same schools he had started in.

The next several years had been torture. By the time he learned that not all adults could be trusted, he was entering puberty. The torture finally ended one day when a teacher discovered him cutting himself in the school bathroom.

When the smoke had cleared, the adults in that house had been arrested, and he had been placed in a children's psychiatric hospital. It took his caseworker six long months to get him out. She placed him with Miss Beulah, which moved him to a new school district.

Everyone had thought it was too late to save him. His grades dropped, he snuck out of the house constantly, he started drinking when he could get it, and he had sex with anyone who'd give him the time of day. The one thing he never allowed again, though, was a blow job. They represented everything bad that had happened in that house.

Fortunately, Miss Beulah had welcomed him into her home with love, patience, and discipline. She started by simply listening to him when he flew out of control in frustration, which eventually taught him to communicate calmly.

Tutors were hired to catch his schooling up, which made him believe she saw something in him worth saving. She was liberal with praise when deserved and meted out punishment that matched the crime only when absolutely necessary.

In essence, she had picked him up, straightened him out, and taught him to trust again. It was still a work in progress, but he had come a long way from that scared little boy who had been brought to her doorstep.

"I can try," he said when their eyes met in the mirror. "They just bring back some bad memories."

With a nod, she gently turned him to face her. Standing on her toes, Thayer pulled him down into a kiss. It wasn't a carnal one that begged him to pin her against the wall. It was one full of longing, his lips lightly pressed against hers.

"Let's get you ready for bed," she said, pulling away.

Helping him pull on a pair of shorts, she carefully eased his sling back on. Once she had finished in the bathroom, Thayer joined him in the large bed.

Logically, he knew she should sleep in the other room, so she didn't accidentally hurt him. But Memphis also knew in his heart that without him holding her, the darkness would overwhelm them both.

Taking her hand, Memphis pulled her into bed with him. Thayer snuggled up to him, careful not to push against his side. With her head on his shoulder and his arm draped around her, pulling her closer, it didn't take long before he felt himself drift off.

ON THE EAST coast of the country, while Thayer and Memphis slept, Knox tried to follow the thin trail to her abductor. He had no doubt it was someone who knew her, even though his investigation had turned up nothing so far.

Dex had passed on everything they found at the fire, which wasn't much. The men had been thugs with impressive firepower that traced to no one. The mystery person had been smart enough to pay them with cash, probably through a common postal drop. Dex had promised to continue working that side of the case, but Knox wasn't holding his breath that anything would turn up.

Knox thumped the desk in frustration. There had to be something he kept overlooking, he just couldn't understand what it was. So far, he had called in every favor he had in the search, only to turn up nothing.

He had combed through Senator Kent's life a dozen times, at least. If there had been any questions about the man's honesty before, there certainly weren't now. His financial records were so clean they actually squeaked. There were no infidelities, bribes, special favors or questionable endorsements in his history.

"What am I missing, Murphy?" He stared at Memphis's dog sleeping in the corner of the senator's office. It was the question that kept playing on repeat in his mind.

Murphy thumped his tail once on the floor, offering little in the way of help.

"Really? You have nothing more to add?"

The dog answered with a soft bark that sounded more like a bored snort. Knox shook his head. He had refused to leave Murphy behind at the vet clinic. The dog belonged with Memphis, and he was going to make sure he got him back sooner rather than later.

He had never been all that enamored with owning a dog before, but this one was different. When all of this was over, he might have to think about getting one. As if Murphy could read his thoughts, the dog got up to wander over to Knox, nuzzling his hand to be petted. Knox sighed, rising to his feet.

"I guess we'd better go if we're going to make it tomorrow. I just wish I could figure out what I'm missing." Knox had insisted on adding extra security to the senator's staff while he was on the campaign trail.

Senator Kent had not been happy when Knox had explained why Thayer was still with Memphis. As a matter of fact, he had taken a pretty good ass-reaming from the man.

Details of the firefight at Memphis's house hadn't helped either until Knox finally reminded him that Thayer was the reason the mercenaries were there in the first place. He's pretty sure he saw a small spark of grudging respect for Memphis in the senator's eyes when he heard about him taking two bullets trying to protect her. Maybe there was hope for Memphis yet, since Knox was pretty sure he was completely taken by Thayer.

"Get in," Knox said to Murphy when they got to the parking garage. He had had to make a few adjustments to his transportation for the dog, mainly adding a sidecar. Knox had driven a Harley-Davidson since he was sixteen.

His first one had been an old, worn-out piece of crap that he spent more time repairing than riding, but he had loved it. His newest ride he hadn't had long. It was a stunning Softail Deluxe in midnight blue. The sidecar didn't really match, but he had been in a hurry trying to find one. He could always have it repainted later.

With a roar, the engine started in one smooth move. Grinning over at the dog, Knox swore he saw the dog grin back at him. They were expected at Reagan National soon for the flight to Tennessee.

He had spoken briefly to Memphis's foster brother earlier. He had agreed to be at his old foster house tomorrow afternoon. It was time for them to go on the offensive to draw this man out. The sooner they had a plan to do that, the sooner this could all be over.

It was time for him to get back in the classroom.

This security detail had taken a toll on him. It was time for them all to get on with life.

THAYER WOKE up to the sound of soft snoring. Her head lay on a strong arm that wrapped around her, holding her in place. One of his legs was flush up against her but the other one had twined itself around hers, pulling it back. Somehow, Memphis had managed to engulf her without hurting himself.

She loved the feeling of waking up completely surrounded by him. It felt safe. She smiled when he ground himself against her with a moan before resuming his snoring. It appeared that at least something was awake.

Barely suppressing a giggle, she moved slightly, freeing his erection from digging into her hip. Slowly, so she didn't disturb him, she eased her hand between them, sliding inside his shorts. She closed her hand over his throbbing cock, making him moan again.

"What are you doing?" he growled into her hair. In the past, she was pretty sure she would have frozen before asking herself that very question.

But that was before she met Memphis, now she simply continued her journey back up, circling the head with her thumb. When she heard him hiss out a breath, she gently pulled her hand out, rolling over in his arms. Wrapping his hand in her hair, Memphis pulled her to him in a kiss.

Thayer rolled him flat onto his back as she kissed him. It wasn't a sweet, gentle good morning kiss. This one attempted to melt the paint from the walls in its intensity. Her hand worked feverishly to push his shorts down as his mouth battled for control of hers, taking his fill.

"Lift your hips," she moaned when he released her. "Gently."

When he complied, Thayer pulled his shorts off his legs and threw the covers back. Her hand wrapped back around his shaft as she crashed her mouth back down on his. She could hear his breath hitch as she worked her fist down with a twist before running it back up.

"Christ, Thayer," Memphis growled out.

Squeezing harder, Thayer picked up her pace, causing him to push his head back into the pillow. Fearing she had hurt him, she froze, not sure what to do next.

"Don't stop."

Looking into his face, she saw deep-green eyes looking back. With a small smile teasing at the edges of his mouth, he wrapped his hand around hers as she started running her hand down him again. With his hand guiding her, she squeezed even tighter, rubbing harder.

Leaning down, Thayer kissed his jaw, running her tongue down his neck until she stopped at his chest. Nipping a light bite against his skin, she heard him growl. Licking over the bite, she made her way farther until she flicked her tongue over his nipple, drawing a hissed curse from his lips.

She could feel his legs shake and marveled at how she could bring this man to the edge so quickly. Grabbing her hair again with his one mobile hand, he pulled her up to his mouth as she felt him spill over her hand in one last thrust.

Thayer lay on his chest, listening to his heart hammer as he caught his breath.

"Holy shit," he groaned, looking up at the ceiling.

With a grin, Thayer leaned up on her elbow so she could see his face.

"Did I do okay? I just thought I'd say good morning," she said, trying for her best sultry voice. "I didn't hurt you, did I?"

His bright-green eyes caught hers as a smile slowly spread over his face. "You can say good morning like that any time you want." When Memphis tried to sit up, he flopped back with a groan. "I need to go clean up. I think I might have pulled a staple out."

"No, Memphis! I'm so sorry, I didn't think."

Memphis cupped her concerned face with his hand. "So worth it," he said with a grin. "But I think you're going to have to help me."

"No, stay there. It's my turn to clean you up." She hopped out of bed, crossing quickly to the bathroom. "What are you laughing at?" she asked, walking out of the bathroom carrying a wet washcloth.

"Because we're living on the run, my side feels like it's on fire, I can't use my dominant arm, and I'm completely covered in cum. This relationship is about as far from normal as you can get. What's not to laugh about?"

"I think it's me," Thayer continued quickly when he knitted his eyebrows together, looking at her. "Think about it. If it wasn't for me, you'd still be living a quiet existence in the woods. Because of me, you've been tased, shot, and your house set on fire."

"Just think how bored I'd have been if you hadn't come along. I can tell you this though, this is definitely the hardest I've ever pursued a woman." His laugh sounded painful as Thayer cleaned his stomach before inspecting his side. She helped him sit up on the edge of the bed.

"I think we could both stand a little more boredom," she said, leaning down for a quick kiss. "Jay and Knox are meeting us this morning at Miss Beulah's. I'll get Jay to check your staples, then. Go do your thing in the bathroom so I can help you get dressed. I think Knox is already over there waiting."

"You want to have some fun with Knox?" Memphis asked with a wicked grin. "Watch."

Thayer watched Memphis as he went into some kind of trance. After a few minutes, he seemed to pop back into his body.

"We'd better go. He's hopping mad now." He laughed, telling Thayer what he had just done.

"Wait," Thayer said. "I thought you had to have something personal belonging to the person you're trying to find. Do you have something of Knox's?"

"No, that's the weird thing. It's like I can just feel where he is. I've never had that happen before. I don't know, I've learned not to try to understand it. Now, come on, before he hunts us down."

Thayer had a suspicion she knew what it was about, but this was something Knox needed to tell Memphis about. In the end, the relationship between them was none of her business.

CHAPTER EIGHTEEN

Knox had shown up at the house where Memphis had spent his high school years half an hour ago. He greeted Miss Beulah, taking her up on her offer of coffee while they waited for everyone else.

Sitting in the dining room sipping on his coffee, he watched as kids of different ages came to a screeching stop outside the door to stare at him. Though he tried nodding at them, they just stood with their mouths open, watching him until Miss Beulah finally pushed them out the door for school.

"Sorry about that, they don't see many giant white guys sitting at the table," a deep voice announced from behind him.

Holding his hand out, Jay shook Knox's hand before sitting down.

"It's been what, around thirteen years?" Jay added, watching the big man over the rim of his coffee. "I would never have talked to you that first time you showed up on the doorstep looking for him if I had known you'd bring him into this shit show." Leaning over, he rubbed Murphy's head where he was snoozing at Knox's feet.

"Yeah, you would've. I had to get him out of the previous shitshow."

They sat in silence for a while, waiting until Ben showed up. Introducing himself, Ben plopped down into the chair next to Jay, immediately petting Murphy as the dog thumped his tail. They all jumped when Memphis suddenly appeared at the end of the table.

"Hey guys, we're on our way. Just as soon as I get dressed from tapping your student, Mr. Monroe." Memphis laughed, slowly fading away when Knox made a grab for him. Ben giggled as Jay just shook his head, watching Knox set his chair back up where he had knocked it over.

If they looked close enough, Knox was positive they could see actual steam coming out of his ears as he ran his hands through his hair.

"Don't let him get to you. He's always been a little ass," Jay said with a smile at Knox. "You should have been around him in his teens."

"I'm going to kill him when he gets here," Knox growled with a scowl on his face, slamming back down into his chair.

"You KNOW he's going to kill you," Thayer stated as they pulled the Bronco into the driveway of the house.

They spotted Jay and Ben's cars, as well as what they assumed was Knox's rental already here. Miss

Beulah waved, walking down the steps to take the younger kids to the bus stop.

"I figured it's just a matter of time anyway," Memphis said with a shrug. Opening the passenger door, he walked around the hood to open Thayer's door.

Sliding out, Thayer found herself suddenly pushed against the SUV.

"You'd better kiss me now. You might not get another chance."

With a smile, Thayer pushed up on her toes, meeting Memphis's mouth so he didn't have to bend too far. When he finally stepped back, he winked at her.

"Dead man walking!" he announced, taking her hand to pull her up the steps.

Opening the door, Memphis was greeted by two paws placed firmly on his chest. "Murphy! Where did you come from, boy?" He painfully squatted down to rub on the dog as Murphy danced around him barking. "Did the big, scary man bring you with him?" Standing, Memphis pulled Thayer by the hand through the house as the dog pranced after them.

Memphis managed to make it into the kitchen before Knox grabbed him by the throat, pushing him against the wall, sending a jolt of pain through his body. Thayer pulled on Knox's muscled bicep, trying to free Memphis from his grip to no avail.

"He was just kidding. Turn him loose, Knox," Thayer pleaded with the big man.

It probably would have helped her case if Memphis hadn't been laughing. Actually, it was more of a rasping gurgle coming from his throat, but the grin on his face spoke volumes.

Lowering his face to within inches of Memphis's,

Knox growled out. "Don't make me kill you. They'll never get a conviction." With one more light thump of Memphis's head against the wall, Knox turned him loose.

"At least you didn't have to live with him." Jay smirked, using his hand to push Memphis in the face.

"They probably would have had to have the same mom then, too." Ben laughed, looking between Memphis and Knox.

The room grew immediately quiet as Ben's words registered. The words weren't lost on Memphis as he looked back at Knox, his eyebrows pulled together in a look of confusion. When no one spoke, Memphis turned to his foster brother.

"What are you talking about, Ben?" he asked with a forced laugh.

Ben's eyes got wide as they slid over to Jay. "I'm sorry," he mumbled. "I thought you told him when you told me. I'm sorry."

"What the fuck is Ben talking about, Jay?" Memphis asked again, his voice growing deathly calm this time as the remnants of his smile disappeared. "Told me what?" He looked around the room before his eyes settled on Knox, the man's bright-green eyes staring back at him. "What?"

"I'm sorry, Memphis. I should have told you Knox is your half brother." Jay flinched when Memphis scowled at him. "He came to me years ago looking for you. He had proof..." Jay drifted off when Memphis spun back around to Knox, who was leaning up against the jamb of the screen door leading into the backyard with his arms crossed.

"Years? What the fuck is he talking about?" he

yelled at the big man. "What the fuck are you talking about?" Looking around the room, he took in the tension as everyone tried to look anywhere but at him.

With a shrug, Knox finally answered. "I've known about you for at least twenty years. Mom told me I had a half brother when I turned fifteen. She helped me search for you. I finally tracked you here right after you left for college."

Memphis shook his head, trying to digest what the big man was saying. If he had an actual blood brother, why hadn't anyone told him? Why didn't Knox just tell him the first time they met? Suddenly, his eyes grew wide in understanding.

"It's why you knew so much about me, isn't it? Why didn't you just tell me instead of knocking me out then tying me to a chair? You already knew I could project, didn't you?" Memphis stood looking at Knox with his fist clenched at his side.

"Not officially. At least, not until I saw you do it that first time. But, yeah, I did have my suspicions. I decided to leave you alone until I started hearing rumors about a guy in the Army who had an unreasonably high recovery rate finding missing soldiers. I thought about telling you then, but once you were out and accepted into vet school, it just didn't make sense anymore."

"Did you ever think I had a right to know? Maybe I deserved to know, or that I would want to?"

"You were finally settled. It seemed like the right choice to leave you alone. Until Thayer was kidnapped, anyway."

"Why would you suspect I had some weird-ass

ability in the first place?" Memphis narrowed his eyes at Knox, waiting for the man to answer.

Knox stood silently, looking around the room until his eyes resettled back on Memphis. "Because I can create fire with my hands, so I figured you could do something. I made an educated guess what your gift was, and Jay filled in the rest," he said quietly.

"Motherfucker. You burned down my house. That's where those fireballs came from." Memphis's voice was controlled, but he could feel the rage course through him as he took a step forward. "You threw a fucking fireball at my house!"

Suddenly he was moving fast at the big man. Knox only had a second to stand up straight before Memphis barreled into him, sending them both crashing through the back screen door into the yard. With a satisfying crunch, Memphis heard his first punch connect with Knox's jaw.

It only took Knox a second to recover, though, before he threw Memphis over his head onto his back. Spinning, Knox found his little brother crouching as he ripped the sling over his head, throwing it into the grass. Memphis rushed him, but with his bad arm, it didn't take long for Knox to roll him over onto his back. Knox straddled his thighs, careful to avoid the stitches in Memphis's side.

"For fuck's sake, stop!" Knox yelled at the struggling Memphis.

After a minute, Memphis finally relaxed.

"If I get off of you, will you quit pitching a fit?"

"Fuck you," Memphis growled out.

Knox waited patiently until he finally nodded at

him. Carefully climbing off to the side, Knox motioned for help. "Jay, I think he ripped his staples out again."

Thayer rushed over to kneel in the grass on the other side of Memphis. They carefully eased Memphis's shirt off, looking at his wounds.

"Ben, go get the staple gun and antiseptic out of my car," Jay said, hurrying down the steps into the backyard.

"Hardheaded jackass," Jay mumbled, looking at Memphis. "Help me get him back in the house. By the way, dumbass, you owe Miss Beulah a new screen door," he added, looking at Knox.

"Why do I owe her a door? Memphis tackled me," Knox said with a growl.

"Because you should have come clean a long time ago, so this is your fault," Jay responded. Looking down at Memphis, he shook his head. "Let's get you patched back up so we can figure out what to do about the psycho chasing Thayer instead of you bitch-slapping each other in the backyard because you share the same father."

Pulling him off the ground, Knox wrapped an arm around Memphis, holding on to him until he regained his balance. Feeling a little light-headed, he let Knox help him up the steps into a chair in the kitchen. Miss Beulah chose that moment to return from making sure the kids were safely on the bus.

"What happened to my screen door?" she asked, looking around. When Ben slowly pointed at Knox, the big man rolled his eyes. Memphis agreed with Jay though, Knox created this mess, he could clean it up.

"I'm sorry, ma'am. I'll make sure it's fixed," Knox mumbled when no one else answered.

"Memphis, what have you done to yourself this time?" she asked.

Memphis looked at his shoes when she placed her fists on her hips standing in front of him. The woman could still strike the fear of God into all of them, if necessary.

"Accident?" he mumbled.

With a snort of disbelief, she cleared off the end of the island. "Climb up here so Jay can look at you. I swear, you boys will be the death of me yet."

Memphis obediently sat on the end of the island with his feet dangling.

With Knox's help, he leaned back so he was lying down. Ben came back carrying the supplies Jay had requested, as well as new bandages. Thayer had collected his sling from the backyard so Memphis could put it back on when Jay was done.

After more staples, an antibiotic shot, several confusing strings of curse words, and his sling back on, Memphis was back in a chair staring at the dining room table.

KNOX COULD TELL Memphis was trying desperately to wrap his head around the fact that not only did he have an older brother, but one with a special gift as well. He watched as Thayer leaned over to whisper something in his ear while squeezing his hand in hers. Knox could remember the shock he felt when his mother had first mentioned he had a little half brother out there somewhere.

"I started hunting for you when I was still in high

school in Kentucky." Knox began breaking into the cacophony around him. The room grew silent as he took a moment to gather his thoughts.

"My mother helped me as much as she could, she just didn't know that much about you beyond your name and where you were. She received a call from your mother one evening asking if Mom knew where our dad was. They didn't talk for very long, and I have no idea how she got our phone number," he continued when Memphis opened his mouth to ask the obvious question.

"It wasn't until I entered the Navy after college that I finally learned how to access the personnel records I needed. After finding out about that first foster home, I took my next furlough to head to Tennessee. I guess I assumed you wound up in the pen or something. But when I finally tracked you here, one of the kids still living in this house informed me that you had left the year before on a baseball scholarship for college. He filled me in on what he knew about you after I promised to keep the information to myself."

He looked up at Memphis, who was staring at him with an unreadable expression. "I did manage to catch one of your games before returning to base. You looked like you were doing okay, so I didn't see any reason to approach you. I even came back for graduation."

Knox had watched proudly when Memphis graduated with honors. He had left as Memphis's foster family cheered from the stands.

"By then, I was working under Commander Kent on the base. I became involved in tutoring Thayer and lost track of where you were. I knew you had entered the Army, I assume to use the GI Bill for vet school.

"One day, I got bored and decided to see what your current assignment was. When I couldn't find any information except for your recruitment record, I became concerned, but then Thayer's mother passed away, and I didn't have time to pursue where you were stationed." Knox cleared his throat when he glanced at Thayer, seeing the sadness in her eyes. He knew her mother's death still affected her deeply.

"The commander took early retirement when his wife died to be with Thayer more. When he decided to run for the Senate, he offered me a job if I would chapter out. I would teach at Thayer's private school while doubling as her caretaker when he was gone. I agreed if he would help me with one last thing before I left.

"When he was elected, he called in several markers to help me locate you. By then, you had been on active deployment for five years, and they had decided you were simply too valuable to send home. We did whatever it took to get you released.

"Once you were safely in vet school, I left the Navy, as agreed, and focused on my new career as a math teacher/security guard/babysitter. I swore when I watched you receive your DVM degree, I would leave you alone to start your new life."

That was, until everything changed. When Thayer was snatched from her dorm room, the senator called in every agency he could to hunt for her. As the first forty-eight hours turned into two weeks, he knew they were out of time.

So here he sat across from the brother he swore he would leave alone. He had been tased, tied up, his house burned down, and two bullet holes shot through him, but he still sat here willing to do whatever it took to protect Thayer. He was so fucking proud of his little brother it took everything he had not to swoop him into a bear hug.

But Knox wasn't the bear-hugging type. He was the badass, long-haired, bearded, Harley-riding giant with a head for numbers type.

"So, what are we going to do, Knox, to keep Thayer safe?" Jay asked when everyone had finally settled around the table.

Knox was exhausted, he didn't remember ever talking that much about anything, much less his feelings. Memphis had remained quiet at the end of the story, which Knox couldn't decide if that was good or bad. He knew it was a lot to take in.

Miss Beulah sat down at the head of the table after passing coffee around to everyone.

"I do know one thing," Knox answered. "This was no ordinary kidnap for ransom. Whoever this is, they have a bigger agenda than just easy money, and until we figure out what that is, we're always going to be trying to counter their attacks."

"So how do we get ahead of this?"

"Unfortunately," Knox said, looking at Memphis. "I think it's time to take the fight to him."

CHAPTER NINETEEN

"Everything all right in there?" Thayer called from the door to the bathroom, hearing Memphis moan as the hot water hit his body.

"I haven't been this sore since being kicked in the chest by a horse on a farm call. Thayer?"

"I'm still here," she answered.

"If you knew Knox and I were related, why didn't you tell me?"

Thayer remained silent for a moment, thinking about how to answer. She heard him hiss, turning in the shower. She could only imagine how it felt when the water hit his wounds.

"I wanted to," she finally answered. "At first, in the cellar, I didn't make the connection, though I should have. Knox never talked about his gift, but I knew it existed and should have realized his brother might have one too. Then in the cabin, I almost did tell you. But in the end, it wasn't my secret to tell."

"I guess I just don't understand why he would keep

something like that to himself. It wasn't just his secret to keep. It was mine as well."

"So, does this change us? I don't think I can stand you not trusting me any longer," Thayer asked.

The water turned off, and Memphis pushed open the door of the shower. Even covered in bruises and staples, he still took her breath away.

"Look at me," he said, stepping out.

She was looking at him. As a matter of fact, she was slowly taking in every glorious inch of him.

"No, look up here where my eyes are," he added, picking her chin up with his hand until her eyes met his. "This changes nothing. Do you understand? Nothing. This is on Knox, not you. Thayer, you trusted me to save you when you had no reason to. Nothing could ever alter how I feel about you. Nothing. Now, if you're done admiring the view, help me get dressed."

Thayer matched the smile that Memphis had on his face. She knew that if anyone in the future asked her when she knew she was in love with Memphis Prescott, she could honestly say it was at that moment. Standing in front of her, bruised, stapled, and dripping water with that laid-back smile on his face, he had won her heart forever.

Taking one of the towels, she carefully helped him dry off. Once he was in a pair of sweatpants and his staples were rebandaged, he followed her out to the living room. Knox was sitting on the couch with Murphy curled up at his side. Shifting the dog onto the floor, Memphis eased down on the opposite end of the couch.

"Reading anything good?" Thayer asked, pulling

Knox's ponytail on the way into the kitchen to start dinner.

It was decided that he would stay with them for extra protection. Memphis had put up a weak argument, but he was the first to admit he could use the extra help in the end. Knox grunted at her before turning back to his paper.

"Your jaw has a bruise on it," she stated, looking back over her shoulder.

"Well, if he hadn't coldcocked me after shoving me through a screen door, I would have been able to avoid it," Knox growled.

"Well, maybe if you hadn't kept something that monumental from him, he wouldn't have felt the need to shove you through a door. I told you this would bite you in the ass in the end. I didn't even recognize him when he first appeared in that cellar." Knox scowled over his paper at her before mumbling something incoherent as he refocused on his reading.

"Speaking of asses—" Memphis began when Knox slammed down his paper.

"For the love of God, let it go," Knox said. "I didn't tell you we were brothers, now you know, blah, blah, blah, get the fuck over it."

Thayer bent farther over the broccoli she was cutting up, trying desperately not to laugh. She had learned long ago that Knox had a nasty bark, and yes, he could bite, but when it came to family, he actually had more patience than any one man should.

"Okay, before your tantrum gets any worse, I was going to ask what the plan is for tomorrow," Memphis said. Looking over at Thayer, he rolled his eyes, causing her to bark out a snort.

"We did exactly what we agreed on today. Thayer used her new credit card to buy groceries and clothes. I ordered replacement contacts at one of the places downtown. We ate lunch at one of the places popular with tourists. There should be an impressive paper trail laid down. I still don't like this plan."

"I don't like it any better than you do," Knox responded. "But we can't just continue to sit around and wait for the next attack. We have to lure them out from the shadows. If you have a better plan, please, inspire me with your brilliance."

Memphis blew out a frustrated sounding breath. He picked up a section of the paper Knox was working on, burying his face behind it. To be honest, Thayer was as frustrated by the situation as they were.

Neither man had said another word by the time Thayer had finished dinner. "Ready to eat?" she asked, setting the main course on the table.

"You're not sitting at the table without a shirt," Knox growled at Memphis, not bothering to look up from his paper.

With a derisive snort, Memphis eased off the couch, heading back into the bedroom. After a few minutes, he threw a shirt at Knox as he returned.

"Help me put it on," he groused. Knox stood, helping Memphis ease his sling back off before slipping his injured arm into the sleeve carefully.

Thayer shook her head, watching them wrestle with the buttons. She wondered if they realized how much they already acted like brothers after just a few short weeks. Both would deny it, of course, if she dared to point it out.

Memphis crossed into the kitchen, wrapping his arm around Thayer.

"It smells amazing," he said, placing a kiss on her cheek.

Handing him a basket of bread, she shooed him toward the table. Knox added bottles of water to the table from the refrigerator, and they all sat down to eat.

Taking her first bite, Thayer had to admit it was better than even she expected. At least not bad for someone who'd had a cook since high school.

"Is your mother still alive?" Memphis asked seemingly out of the blue.

"Yes," Knox said without looking up. "She lives in a retirement village in Louisville. I thought she would want to move to Florida, but apparently, she doesn't want to leave Kentucky. It took me a while to convince her to retire after I left the Navy."

"Stubborn?" Memphis asked around bites.

Thayer smiled. She had spent one summer with Knox's mom while his mother was recuperating from a broken leg she had acquired repelling off a mountain to save a baby goat. She had argued with Knox until she was blue in the face when he happened to point out that the goat wasn't really in need of rescuing. It was a mountain goat after all, and she was in the Rocky Mountains. She countered his argument, claiming the goat's bleating was obviously an anguished cry for help.

"More like she's a free spirit. She was afraid a retirement community would hold her back until I found one with residents just as crazy as her.

"She worked at the PX on base as long as I can remember until moving to Louisville. I always just assumed our father was one of the soldiers stationed there until I was around ten. She told me he had been a government contractor on base for a brief period. He moved on before I was even born. Mom told me she knew he had another son out there, just didn't know where. She never explained how she knew about you. It took me another couple of years to find that out," Knox answered.

"You would love Sunny Monroe," Thayer added enthusiastically. "I did from the moment she moved into the big house with Knox. For one summer, it felt like I had a mother again or at least an awesome aunt. Mrs. Monroe regaled me with stories of adventure and mayhem. I never really knew what was real and what was made up, but it didn't matter. I would listen to them for hours."

It also had been obvious that summer that Knox adored his mother, treating her with constant respect and love. It's part of the reason Thayer had never been scared of him. No one could be fearful of the giant man once they witnessed him fluffing pillows to make his mother more comfortable.

"Yeah, well, I do love my mom. However, her life has been a cautionary tale of what happens if you have too wild a weekend of sex, drugs, and rock and roll," Knox said.

"Is she an Amazon like you?" Memphis asked with a smirk at Knox.

Knox simply returned the smirk with a scowl.

"Seriously, I'd like to meet her sometime, if that's okay. My mom was amazing. She was so stubborn, though. She would never tell me anything about our dad. I don't even know his name," Memphis added, shaking his head.

"Mom worked at a diner near St. Jude's while taking college courses one night a week at the University of Memphis when she was diagnosed with cancer. We would sit at the kitchen table while we did our homework together."

"I can arrange for you to meet her," Knox said before returning to his dinner. "I don't know that she knows too much, though, but you're welcome to ask. She'll definitely tell you whatever she can."

When they had managed to eat everything Thayer had fixed, the men cleaned up the kitchen in silence before settling into the living room for the rest of the evening. Knox flopped into one of the armchairs, picking up his paper while Memphis and Thayer took the couch. Memphis began lazily scrolling through the Netflix options as Thayer snuggled into his side. Settling on some action movie on low, he tossed the remote on the coffee table, sliding his good arm over her shoulders.

"Do you think it's political?" Memphis finally asked.

"I keep thinking it has to be because of the blackmail attempt, but I don't know what it would be," Knox answered. "I've combed through every contribution to the campaign, talked to the representatives of every political action committee he deals with, and even hunted down the various aides of the other senators. Nothing stands out. It could always be something confidential, but if so, I don't have access to that information."

"Maybe tomorrow something will turn up," Memphis said. "Anyway, I think Thayer and I are going to call it an early night. She can barely keep her eyes open. We'll see you for breakfast."

Memphis eased Thayer up until she stood groggily. "You head to bed, and I'll be there as soon as I walk Murphy."

She mumbled her good night to Knox before heading toward the bedroom.

"I'll deal with the dog." Knox stood up, crossing to the door. "I doubt I'll get much sleep tonight anyway."

Thayer watched as he walked over to the door.

"Murphy." When the dog leaped off his bed to greet him, he bent down, giving him a good head scratch. "Let's take you for a walk before I turn in, how about that?" He took a moment to hook the leash to the dog's collar by the door before letting him lead them down the stairs.

Thayer turned back toward the bedroom. She didn't worry about falling asleep herself tonight. Just knowing Memphis and Knox had her back made her feel safer than she ever had.

Curtis stood in the shadows with his two remaining men watching the senator's lackey and the dog walk off.

He had been stunned to hear the details of their assault on the cabin. He already knew several of his team had been found with fatal gunshot wounds.

That wasn't what was the most shocking, though. It was the added lines about an incendiary device that had caused the fire. He knew his men hadn't had anything that could cause the explosion and complete destruction of the house. But, if it wasn't his men, then who had shown up with a military-grade flamethrower capable of such destruction?

He was beginning to suspect that the two men guarding Thayer had more skills than he had believed. Curtis wouldn't make the mistake of underestimating them again.

It had been made plain to him that if anything happened to cause Lehman Group to fail to secure that contract, Curtis would be held responsible. Mr. Robert's veiled threat had left him with the impression that there was more than just his job in jeopardy this time.

He and his men had already cased out the warehouse. As best as he could see, the building was almost impossible to gain access to. There were no visible windows on the first floor and just two heavy steel doors.

He knew the apartment they were in was on the second floor, but it was too high off the ground to access. He had yet to find anywhere that made the old building easy to breach. They would need to eliminate Thayer's bodyguards while grabbing her somewhere else.

He watched as the man and dog came back into view. Vaguely, he could hear Knox Monroe speaking to the dog. He had to admit it was a beautiful animal with that long, dusty-golden hair. Maybe the dog he would spare.

Curtis watched as Monroe typed a code into the keypad before pulling the heavy steel door open and disappearing inside. He had already debated, then threw out the idea of using a passcode device on the system. There was no guarantee it wouldn't send out a silent alarm to the local authorities.

"I see no way to get inside, sir," his top man said, looking through the field glasses.

"No, but I have an idea. Let's return to the hotel early tonight for some rest. I think we're going to need it these next couple of days," he answered.

Turning away from the warehouse, he walked briskly back toward the dark SUV they had parked several blocks away. Curtis was more than aware that his deadline was quickly dwindling. They had to act soon. The clock was quickly ticking down on the SASC vote.

KNOX COULD ALMOST FEEL the goose bumps rise on the back of his neck. He hadn't seen anything when he had walked around the building with Murphy, but he had learned long ago to trust his instincts. Right now, they were screaming that someone had been watching him.

He quickly punched in the seven-digit code, pulling the dog through the door behind him. They didn't need to stand there like sitting ducks while he looked around at the darkness. Unhooking Murphy's leash, he bounded up the stairs two at a time, the dog on his heels.

Punching in the next code to access the apartment, he tossed the leash at the hook before crossing to the windows. He had shut off all the lights in the apartment, except for the small light over the stove, so he didn't have to worry about being seen by whoever was down there.

Knox watched for a while, expecting to see movement or, at the very least, taillights. Instead, he saw nothing but darkness. Still, he knew someone was out there. The showdown he had both wanted and feared had been set in motion.

Knox listened to the silence encase him in the apartment. He could hear Memphis snore slightly from the other bedroom, only interrupted when someone rolled over in the bed. Murphy sat patiently at his feet, looking up at him. He took one last look outside before turning with a sigh toward the bedroom.

"Come on, dog. We can't be of any use if we're sleep deprived."

By the time he came out of the bathroom, Murphy was spread out on the bed with his head resting on the other pillow. He had slept in Knox's apartment the same way for weeks.

"And that's why my love life has been so lacking lately. Do you know how hard it is to convince a woman to spread her legs lying next to a dog?"

Murphy let out a small huff as if he had a ready rebuttal.

Shoving the dog farther onto his side of the bed, Knox lay on his back listening to the snoring from the next room until he finally felt his eyes close.

CHAPTER TWENTY

Memphis was sitting at the bar in the kitchen watching Knox cook the next morning when Thayer came dragging into the kitchen. Judging by the dark circles under her eyes, she was as tired as they were. If the men hunting for her didn't kill them soon, the stress of waiting might just do it for them. That easy comfort they had both felt back at his cabin was now gone.

"Are you okay?" he asked. Knox turned around, studying her face, his eyebrows knit in concern.

"I'm fine, just tired I guess."

Looping his foot under the bar chair she had slid into, Memphis pulled her closer to him. Wrapping his good arm around her, he felt her melt against him as he placed a kiss on her head.

Knox set a plate mounded with eggs, bacon, and potatoes in front of her. Picking up her fork, she took a halfhearted bite.

"We're going to find him, Thayer. We *will* end this," Knox said, sliding his own breakfast on his plate.

Standing with the empty pan in one hand, clutching the spatula in the other tight enough to turn his knuckles white, Memphis worried he would break it in two. "Actually, I think he's already here."

Memphis and Thayer put their forks down, staring up at him.

"How? Did you see or hear something?" Memphis asked.

"It was a feeling I got taking Murphy for his walk last night. I'm pretty sure there was someone watching us, but I never saw him," Knox said. "I think we might need reinforcements."

"I can contact my foster brothers. Maybe with their help, we can finally end this. They know this town better than anyone."

Knox nodded once in consent before digging into his breakfast. The two men had already discussed this possibility with Jay earlier. He hated to get them even more involved, but Memphis couldn't see any other way.

An hour later, they had all gathered around the dining table.

Memphis had introduced Knox to the newest face at the table, a large man named Randall. Shaun had explained that Randall was Miss Beulah's biological son, who left for college the year she decided to take in foster kids.

It was his apartment they were currently staying in. He had finished his undergraduate degree at Vanderbilt before receiving his MBA from Harvard. Returning to

Tennessee, he now ran a successful real estate development firm in Nashville, specializing in rehabilitating old warehouses into modern lofts.

Knox had learned that Randall was the enforcer in the foster home. If you caused too much trouble for Miss Beulah to handle you, Randall would mysteriously appear.

While everyone was getting drinks before finding their seats, Memphis quietly told him about the time Randall straightened him out. He had been driving the car of his current girlfriend's father when she decided to give him a hand job. Memphis crashed it into a tree in front of a cop. They had both been drinking, but since the cop was a friend of Miss Beulah's, he hadn't been hauled to the station.

The cops called the girl's dad, then took him back to the foster house. When Miss Beulah answered the door, they explained the next time Memphis did something like that, they would haul him to juvenile detention. They would overlook it this time, though, as a favor to her. Randall showed up two days later to "explain" to Memphis how his behavior needed to be altered.

Memphis told Knox he would never forget the beating Randall gave him, but he didn't do anything like that again. Looking at the man, who was only a little smaller than he was, Knox could see where he would intimidate the hell out of some kid, but none of the men sitting around the table seemed scared of him, only respectful.

"How do you know they're here?" Randall asked, narrowing his eyes on Knox.

"I just do. Call it a hunch. Regardless of whether you believe in hunches or not, I think we need to proceed like they're in town." Knox couldn't explain it without sounding like an idiot, so he decided his best recourse was to say as little as possible. It threw him completely when Randall just nodded before continuing.

"Okay, let's assume they are here. How do we protect Memphis's woman?" he asked. Knox had to stifle a laugh, watching Thayer puff up.

"Excuse me, I have a name," she said.

"I apologize," Randall said, turning slowly to Thayer. "How do we protect Memphis's woman, Thayer?"

Shaun tried to quiet Ben across the table when he started to giggle. Memphis had explained to Knox that Ben was on the autistic spectrum, but it manifested itself differently from most people's traits. He laughed at inappropriate times, asked too many personal questions, and shut down if he thought someone was angry with him.

Memphis also pointed out that he was loyal, unreasonably smart, and one of the best firefighters in the city. He understood how fire behaved better than anyone the Memphis fire department had ever seen.

"So, she *is* your girlfriend, right, Memphis?" Ben was grinning at Memphis as everyone went silent.

"Yes, Ben," Memphis said with a smile.

"I told you so, Jay. You owe me ten bucks," Ben answered, his grin even wider.

"Ben!" Jay chastised. "It's not appropriate to discuss the pool in front of Thayer." Ben's eyes grew wide as he looked at her.

"What the hell? How come I didn't get notified there was a pool going?" Memphis asked.

"Enough," Randall said, patting Ben's hand on the table. "Just remember, Ben, not everything needs to be shared in public. Now let's all try to shut up long enough to hear what the giant at the end of the table has to say."

"I'm sorry, Thayer," Ben whispered loudly to her before turning to listen to Knox. She waved at him with a smile.

"Anyway," Knox began when everyone had settled. "The only way to catch him, I believe, is for us to either see him following you or for him to make a move. The fact he hasn't been caught yet leads me to believe he's perfected his surveillance."

"Do you think he'll try to break in here?" Thayer asked.

"It's possible," Knox answered. "I think we need to always have someone here at night to watch the apartment. My men and I can't follow you all day, then stand guard all night as well. We're going to need more help."

"I'll set up a rotation schedule, so everyone takes a turn at night. Memphis and Thayer will also be exempt, of course, so they can function during the day," Jay said, accepting the legal pad that Randall slid across to him.

"Thayer, you and Memphis need to establish your routine. Eat lunch in the same area every day, shopping or appointments in the vicinity as well," Knox said. "We'll pick somewhere that requires you to park in the same lot every day, so you walk to everything. The men will shadow you while I scout for anyone who takes a little too much interest in your activities."

The other men joined Knox in deciding what activities would be best. With a city map spread out on the table, they soon decided where they needed to run their "operation."

THAYER SAT QUIETLY, listening as her every move was planned out. After a while, she got up to look out the window. Looking around, she didn't see anything that looked out of place. Was it possible he was watching her right now? She startled when she felt an arm snake around her waist.

"Are you okay?" Memphis whispered in her ear as she leaned back, absorbing his heat. She hadn't realized she was shivering until now. "I know how badly this must suck. I'm sorry."

"I'm just so pissed off. How dare they put everyone's life in danger?" She swiped at a tear angrily as it escaped. Memphis gently turned her into his embrace. Slipping his arm out of the sling, he folded her against him, safe in his arms. "I think the worst part is I don't even know why. Why are they so bent on getting to me?"

"I don't know," he said, kissing the top of her head. "But none of us will rest until we find out. You deserve a life where you don't have to look over your shoulder." He set her away from him, holding on to her arms. Bending so they were eye to eye, he added, "I promise you, I'll do whatever I have to until you feel safe again."

She looked into his stormy green eyes, laced with conviction. She knew he meant what he said. It's what scared her the most. She had almost got him killed already. When she nodded, he pulled her into a kiss. With one hand resting on her hip, he fisted his hand in her hair behind her head, angling it just right to deepen the kiss.

Memphis gave her no chance to think even one more dark thought when his tongue insisted that she open to him. She felt him press his body against hers. Every inch was hard planes and heat and urgency.

A gasp escaped her when she felt his hand travel up her side to rest on her breast, his thumb lightly brushing over her erect nipple. She wondered for a brief second if he was healed enough to wrap her legs around his waist when she heard someone mutter a "holy smokes" behind him.

Reluctantly, they parted, both trying desperately to suck enough air into their lungs.

"Okay, no making out in the public areas," Knox growled.

Thayer grew red when she dared a look around Memphis's broad shoulders to find the entire table staring at them.

"She was thinking too hard. It was starting to freak her out. I had to shut that shit down," Memphis answered when he spun to face everyone.

"I don't remember ever getting that response when I was worried about something," Jay quipped, breaking any tension in the air.

"Well, pucker up, buddy. I'll be right there." Memphis smirked at him.

"Do I also get felt up?"

"I don't know. Show me your tits." Everyone jumped when Randall slapped both hands down on the table in front of him.

"I swear to God!" he said, looking down the table at Knox. "They revert to the age of fifteen when they all get together. Are we done? I have a business meeting in half an hour. As long as I'm in town, I might as well try to get some things done."

He stood, motioning the others to leave as well. When the apartment was empty except for the three of them, Memphis let out a big breath. Knox sat down in the armchair with a smirk trained on Memphis.

"What?" he asked.

"He's right. You do act like a teenager around them."

"I know. I don't know what our problem is. It's stupid. I bet you're glad now you didn't have to put up with me growing up."

Knox only shrugged. "Would have livened things up. I don't think it would have been so bad. I could have used the help to restore my first motorcycle."

"I didn't know you were into motorcycles. It makes sense, though. What was your first one?" Memphis sat on the couch, pulling Thayer down next to him. "Did you know about this?" he asked her.

Murphy jumped on the couch, resting his head in her lap as she softly stroked through his fur.

"I did. You should see the beauty he rides now."

"Okay, so tell me about this fantasy life where I helped you restore your first one," Memphis said.

Thayer felt herself relax into Memphis's side as she listened to them discuss Knox's motorcycles. Murphy started snoring next to her as she felt her eyes grow heavy. She vaguely registered the fact that their deep voices became quieter as she slipped into a deep sleep.

When she woke up an hour later, Murphy and Knox were gone. She had slid down until her head was resting on Memphis's lap with a blanket pulled up to her shoulders.

"Sorry," she mumbled, stretching.

Memphis put down the book he had been reading.

"What are you reading?"

"Just something Knox tossed me before he took Murphy for his walk."

Thayer looked at the cover on the book, it was a romance.

"At first, I'll admit I scoffed but finally decided what the heck. I couldn't reach my phone without disturbing you, so what else did I have to do? Turns out, it has a pretty decent storyline, although I do question some of the more acrobatic-sounding sex. I considered myself reasonably athletic, but I'm almost positive I couldn't pull some of it off without breaking something."

Thayer laughed.

"Although I'm not opposed to rereading those parts just for purely scientific reasons, of course."

"Of course, for science," she said, rolling her eyes.

"My real question, though, is why was it on Randall's bookshelf?" Turning the book over, he studied the cover.

"That's your question?" she asked with a grin.

"Yeah," he said, tossing the book at the bookshelf. Miraculously, it landed on the top shelf.

"I don't know what is keeping Knox, I'll go check."

Standing quickly, Thayer's head thumped back down on the couch. When she sat back up, Memphis had already grabbed his jacket and was slipping out the door.

"What are you doing out here?" Knox asked, walking up to the door with Murphy at his heels.

"Sort of wishing I smoked," Memphis answered.

He had made it as far as the bottom of the stairs before sitting down. He had watched Knox tossing a ball to Murphy in the park across the street for half an hour. It was quite possible the dog actually preferred his brother over him now. Memphis shook his head at the thought of having a real blood brother.

"Did you finish the book? Is that why you're hiding out here? Where is Thayer?" Knox asked.

"She's fine, and I'm not hiding. I just needed some air."

"I'm sure you did after reading that book. I finished it last night after you went to bed. There's some hot shit in that thing. It's the same stuff Thayer reads on occasion. Thought you would want to know what you're competing against," Knox said with a wicked smirk.

Memphis shook his head. "I don't think I'm good enough to do some of that."

"Shit, I'm a pretty big man, and I don't think I could do some of it. Maybe if I found someone who weighed about ninety pounds. I'm afraid if I did, though, I'd rip her in half. I don't think any real man is that good." He slapped Memphis gently on the back, laughing as he keyed in the code to go upstairs.

"Might be worth the back surgery to try though." Memphis made sure the door was secure behind him before following Knox up the stairs.

"Got that right, little brother," the big man said with

a grin before keying the passcode into the lock on the upper door.

It was decided that Memphis and Thayer would wander around downtown for a while until lunch. The men spent a half hour deciding what parking lot would be the best before discussing the lunch possibilities. They spent the rest of the day wandering around until Thayer noticed Memphis starting to favor his side.

Meeting Knox back at the car, they drove silently back to the loft.

By the time they made it upstairs, Memphis had a pounding headache. Thankfully, Jay had shown up an hour before and had dinner waiting for them. He moaned at the first bite of creamy scalloped potatoes with ham. Jay had been the only one of the kids who had paid rapt attention to the cooking lessons that had been forced upon them. By the time he graduated from high school, he could cook as well as any gourmet chef.

"Everything go okay? Your people are in place downtown?" Jay asked between bites.

"They are, and no one saw anything out of the ordinary," Knox answered.

"This all feels very cloak and dagger," Jay added.

"It's the only way I can think to catch them. We can't just run to the cops about some group we think may or may not be in the area. Anyone need another drink?" Knox asked, pushing away from the table.

"Agent Tanaka still hasn't had much luck with the identity of who hired the men at your cabin. I'm afraid that's a dead end," Knox said, returning with another round of beer and a water for Memphis.

Memphis scowled at the realization that his brother was just as big of a babysitter as Thayer. Would one beer really hurt? He wasn't even on the heavy painkillers anymore.

"I'm not sure how you're going to explain to your insurance company that your house randomly burned down due to a fireball during an attack by hired gunmen." Knox smiled when Memphis laughed.

"Yeah, that's going to be interesting," Memphis said. "Thanks, buddy."

Knox scowled at his sarcasm for just a moment before a laugh bubbled up from the big man.

"Anytime."

OUTSIDE, Curtis stood against the wall of one of the other warehouses, looking at the windows on the second floor. Though the height of the second floor made it too hard to see anything more than what was pressed against the windows, he knew they were there. His men had followed them around the downtown area for a while before following them back here.

In the back of his mind, he knew they were setting up a trap. He also knew he was smarter than all of them put together.

There was no doubt in his mind that he and his men would have to, somehow, kidnap her off the street in downtown Memphis. They had counted at least four men watching her, including both Monroe and Prescott.

It would have to be a quick snatch and grab if they had a hope of getting away clean with her. It would be best to avoid any bloodshed in such a public area, though, he wouldn't be upset if Prescott was gutted at the same time. The man had become a very painful thorn in his side.

He had checked the company files for a safe house in the area but found none. It was no matter. It wouldn't be hard to find an abandoned house or building to hold her in. It wasn't like he had time to draw her death out much longer. He would need her caught, killed, discovered, and the press spinning their own sensational story in less than a week's time.

He had assured Mr. Roberts only that morning on his secured phone line that it would be no problem. Curtis hoped that was the case anyway. His reputation as a man who could get things done was starting to suffer.

Tomorrow he would look for the perfect place to take her. By this time next week, he would be lying low on some island where there was an endless supply of mojitos and bronzed women. Mr. Roberts wasn't the only one with the promise of a large payout when the contract was signed. Everyone at the company stood to make a small fortune, him included.

With a nod to his men, he turned for the SUV. Soon, he would be not only a wealthy man, but one who could name his price in the world of fixers.

Nothing could stop the smile that spread across his face as he climbed into the passenger seat. No doubt, his time had finally come.

CHAPTER TWENTY-ONE

"Better?" Memphis asked Thayer the next morning, standing in the middle of the optometrist's office.

"I don't know, I like your glasses. Like I said, they're very Clark Kent," she answered with a mischievous smile.

He smirked at her, putting his glasses in their case. "Yeah, well, Clark Kent just uses his as a prop so he can whip them off like a sexy reporter. He doesn't have to squint through them to see the damn lab reports."

"You don't know. He might be farsighted." She stifled a laugh as she watched him pay.

"So, the man can leap tall buildings in a single bound, but he can't see to read the newspaper? I don't buy it. Based on Superman logic, no one should know who I am in glasses anyway. I'm virtually incognito."

He twined his fingers through hers, pulling her out of the store. "Besides, does Lois Lane take one look at him wearing his underwear on the outside of his clothes and think 'yeah, I'd hit that?'"

Thayer burst out with a laugh as they walked down the street.

"I would like a cape though," he said with a grin, walking backward so he could watch her laugh.

With a mighty tug, she pulled him to her, wrapping her arms around the back of his neck.

"I think you would look amazing in a cape." Threading her fingers through his hair, she pulled him down for a kiss.

Memphis knew he should be more diligent about watching their backs out on the sidewalk, but he wouldn't give up even one kiss from Thayer willingly. Besides, isn't that what her father was paying the men in the shadows for?

He parted her lips, sliding his tongue inside, capturing her moan. Somewhere in the back of his mind, he also realized they would have to pry her fingers out of the death grip they now had on his hair. He would kill the first person who attempted that.

His hands slid down around her hips, squeezing a moment before pushing back.

"We need to stop before I take you against the front of his building." Memphis looked at her, her blue eyes glowing with lust.

Why had he decided to wait until after this was over before making love to her? He had to hold the world record for the bluest balls in history. Fuck, he was a complete idiot!

"Sounds like a solid plan," Thayer whispered into his ear, placing one more quick kiss on his lips before starting back down the sidewalk.

Memphis watched her for a second, shaking his

head before readjusting his now insistent erection to follow her.

They settled on a soul food restaurant for lunch, Memphis explaining that it would be similar to what she had eaten at Miss Beulah's. She argued with him that in no universe did chicken and greens always have to go together. He had the good sense to just smile when she moaned at the first bite of her lunch.

"How do you make every meal we eat sound like a soul-changing experience? I'm starting to get a complex since it sounds the same as when you come against my tongue," Memphis asked before slapping Thayer's back when she choked on her tea.

"Memphis!" She gave a wave of her hand to the other diners sitting near them.

"Sorry," he mumbled, looking around.

"Don't apologize, son," someone from one of the other tables said. "Take ownership of that."

Thayer turned bright red as they listened to the man laugh while his wife scowled at him. She covered her face with her napkin as her shoulders shook with laughter. When she slowly lowered her napkin, Memphis grinned at her.

"Oh, hell yeah, I'm owning it all right!"

They both burst into laughter again, only corralling themselves when the waitress asked if they would like dessert.

Choosing to share a piece of pecan pie, Memphis felt the knots in his shoulders loosen. Something about her always made him relax and forget everything but just being in the moment. He wondered if she was thinking the same thing as she let out a soft sigh.

"You're thinking about something awfully hard,"

Memphis said, startling her out of her own reverie. "Anything you can share?"

She looked up, spearing him with her soft blue eyes.

"I was just thinking..." she started.

"You were thinking...?" he asked when she grew silent. There was something important on her mind, and he wanted to hear it.

"I was wondering what it would be like to stay with you. I mean, for a while. After this is all over," she groaned. Glancing at him through her eyelashes, he was positive she could feel his heart fighting to escape his chest.

Had she just asked to move in with him?

"What about school?" he asked, barely believing there was hope for them to be together in the end.

"I think I can do a lot of it online. I won't know until I talk to my advisor." He reached over, cupping her cheek with a hand. Gently running his thumb under her chin, Memphis pulled her face up until their eyes met.

"I guess I'd better start working on getting internet."

He pulled her over into the most amazing kiss he had ever felt. It wasn't raw or rough. It was one of longing and promise. Sitting back, he continued to hold her face in his hand.

"It wouldn't have mattered if you didn't come home with me. I'd chase you across this whole fucking earth to be with you." Memphis smiled when Thayer turned red hearing the "awwws" coming from the tables near them.

"Son, you're making the rest of us look bad."

They started laughing again when they heard the

same man from before. Memphis stood, pulling Thayer up with him.

Winking at the couple who had been close to them, he added, "You think that's good, wait until I propose." He grinned at Thayer when her mouth fell to the ground.

Walking out through laughter, they headed toward more shops.

"Have we done enough for today? He's obviously not going to show himself," Thayer asked several hours later as they stood looking down the street.

"I think so. Let's go find Knox and see if he's heard anything." Taking her hand, Memphis led her back down the street toward the lot where they had parked. Suddenly, Memphis stopped, pulling her into an impromptu hug.

"Memphis, what are you—" Thayer began.

"Shh," he broke in while looking over her head. "I think we're being followed."

She started to spin around to see where he was looking when he tightened his arms around her.

"Don't do anything to give us away."

He felt Thayer try to relax as she stood in his arms. Soon, he released her, keeping one hand on her waist as he smiled. He kept his focus over her shoulder but tilted his head down slightly as if they were talking.

"Do you see him?" she asked softly.

"Not yet," he answered, growing silent again. He had only noticed someone shadowing them when he saw the same sweatshirt that had been in at least two of the stores from earlier duck behind a doorway a half block away.

"Wait, I think that's him." Memphis stiffened as he

pushed Thayer behind him. He already knew they had guns. He wasn't risking her getting hit if they decided to use them.

"What? What's wrong?" Knox asked, jogging up. He must have been shadowing them from a distance.

Thayer leaned out from behind Memphis to see where they were looking. Knox looked in the same direction Memphis was looking, as if they were communicating silently.

"That's him," Memphis said suddenly. "Jeans, black hoodie, cap pulled down. I swear he was following us."

"Take Thayer home, I'll go ask him a couple of questions." Knox started walking quickly toward a shadowy figure, who was working his way away from them.

They watched for a moment as Knox pulled a small radio out of his back pocket before Memphis took her hand, pulling her toward the parking lot.

They were quickly joined by another man as they jogged toward their SUV. When Thayer and Memphis were both secured inside with the engine running, the man ran back toward Beale Street.

Pulling into the parking area of the loft, they found Shaun waiting at the door with several tough-looking men watching the perimeter. Memphis shut off the engine and quickly climbed out of the vehicle. Thayer jumped out, meeting him at the front.

Taking her hand, he hustled her through the men, past Shaun, and up the stairs. It wasn't until he heard the door close firmly behind them that he took what felt like his first real breath since he had stopped her on the street.

Knox jogged down the street, trying to keep the man in the black hoodie in his sights. He had sent one of his men to make sure Thayer and Memphis made it to the SUV safely. The other one was trying to get ahead of the man so they could flank him, effectively cutting off his escape.

Knox knew Memphis wouldn't raise an alarm if he didn't feel there was a reason. If they could grab this guy, they would have someone to question. Best case was they would have finally caught the man in charge.

"Fuck, where did he go?" Knox mumbled, scanning the sidewalk. Fortunately, the area wasn't packed with tourists like it would be during the summer, but there were still enough milling around to make trailing someone difficult.

"Sir?" one of the men Knox had hired to help with shadowing Thayer said, stopping next to him.

Ignoring him for the moment, Knox continued to scan the shoppers around him until he caught sight of a black hood.

"There. Do you see the individual in the black hoodie slipping out of the doorway three stores down?" Knox asked, keeping a close watch on the man. He assumed it was a man anyway, he couldn't really be certain from this distance.

"You and Jones, when he gets back from securing Thayer, see if you can flank him. I'll push him toward you. We need to ask him some questions."

"Yes, sir," Fisher answered, crossing back over to the other side of the street, talking into his radio. Knox started down the sidewalk toward the black hoodie, lengthening his stride to close the distance between them. It was one of the advantages to his height. Not only could he see over most crowds, but he could also cover twice as much ground in half the time as most men.

He began to catch up when the black hoodie glanced into one of the reflective storefront windows. Obviously catching sight of Knox, he took off like a shot, rounding the corner of a side alley.

"Shit," Knox said, running after him.

Rounding the corner, he slid to a stop, finding no trace of the man. Jogging down the alley, he spied a door that led to one of the unrenovated buildings. Finding the door open, he stepped into the semi-darkness.

He stood still for a moment, getting his bearings before moving toward the interior. If the man had run in here, Knox couldn't tell which direction he had gone. The light wasn't good enough to check the floor for footprints in the dust, and he couldn't hear anyone running.

A sudden bang vibrated down from somewhere above his head. Knox tore through the rooms looking for a set of stairs leading up.

The building had obviously not been used as a store in a long time based on the graffiti on the walls. There were several layers of old spray paint under newer work in every room he passed. He had no doubt there might even be a squatter or several that made their home here at night, though he saw no sign of them now.

Rounding a corner, he finally spotted what he was looking for, a set of stairs winding toward the upper floors. Picking his way up the stairs, he tried to avoid the ricketier looking steps until he found a door. Pushing against it, he finally managed to burst through onto the roof.

Taking a quick glance around, he spied the man on the next rooftop over. The man ran like a gazelle, and Knox had no choice but to take after him at a full run. He just had to trust that his men were somewhere nearby.

Knox had never considered what it took to chase someone across a series of rooftops. It always looked cool in the movies, but reality was a whole other game. He had to skirt the huge air conditioners, exhaust vents, and debris that blocked him.

That was before he made it to the structural wall connecting the two buildings. It stood four feet tall and though not a huge obstacle, it did slow him down. Placing his hands on top of it, he hopped up just in time to see the other man sliding over the next wall.

"Hey," he yelled.

It wasn't like the guy hadn't figured out he was being pursued.

"I just want to talk."

It didn't do any good, the man disappeared over the next wall without even looking up.

Knox knew he would have to pick up the pace if he had any chance of catching the man. Where the hell his men were, he had no idea. His earpiece had fallen out somewhere while he'd been racing up the stairwell and was now dangling behind his back. He didn't have time to stop to fix it and pull the radio out of his back pocket, proving it was still there.

Dropping onto the next roof, Knox began working his way around the large air handler unit. He had played football in college. He knew how to weave. But then, that had been almost twenty years ago. Shit, had it really been twenty years?

He shook his head to clear that depressing thought from his mind and ran across the roof, avoiding the vents and a handful of angry pigeons. No amount of football training had taught him how to dodge pissed-off pigeons.

Hopping up on the next wall, he spotted the man still on the current roof near the other side.

"Fucking stop, and I promise not to break you in half when I catch you," he yelled.

Surprisingly, the other man simply picked up his pace. Fine, maybe that wasn't the thing to say, but this much running was starting to piss him off. At least he was slowly catching back up.

Knox saw him swing over the far wall before disappearing.

He noticed that this roof didn't have one of the monstrous air conditioners like the others. Instead, there was a large hole in the roof covered by a tarp to try and keep out the rain. Easing off the wall, he sent up a quick prayer that the roof would hold him. What he didn't need was to break both legs falling to the floor below.

Trying to stay on the far edge, he picked his way over to the next roof, or what he thought would be another roof. When he reached that wall, he found the building was separated from the next one by a small side alley. He guessed it was maybe seven feet across. It resembled a pedestrian walkway to more shops located at the back of the buildings.

Looking back up, he saw the man jogging across the next roof with the confidence of a younger person, knowing the old guy chasing him wouldn't even attempt the jump. Screw that.

Knox backed up, judging how much momentum he would need to make it across. Five feet wasn't really that far in the scheme of things.

With a roar, he sprinted at the wall, leaping up to use his right leg to push off with. Even with every ounce of strength he could muster, he still just barely managed to grab the wall on the far side. His legs and torso banged into the brick side while he clung onto the top.

Looking down, he chuckled. Where on the job description for watching after Thayer had it said that he must be willing to jump from one building to another?

He wasn't a superhero. He could produce a fireball with his hands, that was it, that was all he had to work with. He definitely didn't have the power to fly. The shit he did for his family even made him wonder sometimes about his sanity.

With a roar that matched the one he used when he jumped, he swung his legs, hooking the edge of the wall with his foot. Leveraging himself up, he rolled over the edge, landing with a thud on the roof. Yep, that radio was still back there, digging painfully into his ass.

Knox took a moment to catch his breath before standing up. The man was staring at him in surprise from the other side of the roof. At least he knew it was a man now. Really, he didn't look any older than Thayer. How did someone that young get mixed up in this? Surely this wasn't just some sort of unrequited love crap. No, he refused to believe that was it.

"I changed my mind. I am snapping you in half when I get my hands on you," he shouted. It had to be said. He was too angry now not to. He was also pretty sure that last stunt had left a couple of impressive bruises.

Like a deer, the kid shot off toward the other side with Knox after him. He climbed up on the far retaining wall and, with one more look at Knox, dropped over the side. Knox was only half a roof behind now and it only took him a moment to reach where the kid had disappeared.

Looking over the side, he found not another roof, but a twenty-foot drop onto some scaffolding. Knox stared at it for any sign of the kid exiting the labyrinth of pipe and wood at the bottom. Nothing. He didn't emerge at the bottom or appear running off down the alley.

Knox spotted his two men rounding the corner, sliding to a stop next to it. Fisher pushed under a piece of heavy sheeting surrounding the scaffolding but quickly emerged to jog down the alley. Knox moved across the roof, looking back out onto the main street, then around the back for any sign of him. The kid was simply gone.

"Anything?" he yelled down.

Fisher shook his head, gazing back up at him.

"Sonofabitch," he mumbled under his breath. "Okay, give me a minute to find my way down. We'll regroup and see if we can pick up his trail."

After a confirmation from his men, Knox turned around, looking for a door. He wasn't about to jump that far onto a questionable-looking set of scaffolding just to roll off the top onto the road below it. He might be crazy, but he wasn't stupid. Spotting the roof access door, he let out another line of expletives, finding it locked.

Looking back over the retaining wall, he yelled at the first one of his men he saw. "Jones, go get someone to open the damn roof access door." He watched Jones quickly enter the store below.

It was another ten minutes before the door was opened by a very angry-looking woman, Jones, standing off to one side.

"How did you get up here?" she demanded, blocking Knox's way. "No one is allowed on the roof."

"Ma'am, if you'll move aside, I'll get off your roof," he answered.

She glared at him, her arms crossed in front of her, for a few more minutes before letting out an exaggerated sigh. Stepping aside, she motioned with her arm for him to proceed her down the stairs.

"Thank you." Rolling his eyes at Jones, he quickly left to regroup outside in the alley. He found Fisher by the bottom of the scaffolding, trying to find any hint of where the kid could have gone.

"Anything?" Knox asked.

"The best I can figure, he slipped into one of the windows next to the scaffolding. My guess is he's from the area and knows these buildings and alleys much better than we do. We managed to keep him in our sights for a while, but we stopped when you didn't make it across that pedestrian walkway," Fisher answered.

Knox snorted. He had made it technically. It just took a little extra effort. "Jones, you head down the alley and check the next street over. Fisher, you continue down this street, and I'll head back the way we came. If we don't find any trace of him in half an hour, we'll head out," he said, pushing the earpiece back in.

Knox's men immediately headed out to follow his instructions.

Knox looked around the scaffolding a few more minutes before walking back to the front of the building. There was a very good chance the kid was holed up inside somewhere, but he wasn't about to ask the saleswoman if he could search it. He had barely come out of there with his ass intact as it was.

After half an hour, Knox had found nothing. He met the other two men in the parking lot by the dark SUV he had rented. They had been unable to find anything more than he had.

Climbing into the passenger seat, he laid his head back on the seat as Fisher pulled out of the lot. They would drop him back at the loft before heading back to their hotel for the night. He knew Memphis would be waiting for answers when he got back, but first he could use a shower. Trying to play an action star on a rooftop was sweaty work.

CHAPTER TWENTY-TWO

Thayer learned when they pulled up to the loft that not all the kids Memphis had been in foster care with grew up to be veterinarians or doctors or even firemen. Some, like Shaun, grew up to be the head of a very successful car theft ring.

Memphis told her quietly when they walked into the loft that the men outside guarding them were members of Shaun's car-jacking team. He refused to pull his guys from his various chop shops off their jobs to help.

"Does Miss Beulah know about it?" she asked as she followed Memphis to the kitchen.

He pulled out two cold bottles of water from the refrigerator, offering her one. Shaun had told them he would be upstairs as soon as he was done organizing his men.

"We all do, but he's not going to change. He's been enthralled with cars from the moment he learned to drive."

"But what happens if he's caught or hurts someone?" she asked, taking the water.

Memphis shrugged. "He only takes cars that are in parking lots or car sales lots, and he goes to jail if caught. Look," he said, pulling her down onto the couch next to him. "We don't condone his behavior, but he's still our brother. So, we turn a blind eye."

"But I thought you said Randall straightened all of you out when you got into trouble."

"He tried, but even Randall can't fix everything. We take comfort in the fact that he didn't get into trafficking drugs or people. He's not a bookie or an enforcer for someone. Sometimes you just have to pick your battles."

Thayer shook her head. The idea that everyone was fine with Shaun heading up an illegal organization baffled her.

Memphis had told her that after Randall and his older sister, who was married and living in Chicago raising kids, had both moved out, Miss Beulah had decided to become a foster parent. With her husband long since passed away, she quickly grew lonely in the big house.

When a caseworker she went to church with asked her to prayerfully consider opening her home to more kids, she agreed on one condition. She wanted the kids everyone else considered lost.

Jay was the first child she took in. He had been taken away from a crack-addicted mother who happily gave up her parental rights.

Memphis had been placed there next, followed quickly by Ben. Ben had been found scavenging through a neighbor's trash for food when his parents left him alone for the final time.

Shaun, Hettie, and Samantha came shortly after to fill out the bedrooms. Hettie and Sam were the only girls, so Miss Beulah had given them a room on the first floor near her with their own bathroom. Other kids had shown up as they had aged out, but the six of them had continued to remain close.

Randall had been concerned that his mother had bitten off more than she could chew, so he originally came home every weekend. But when he saw she was still able to command this group of "hopeless" kids, he started stretching his visits to once a month. Except when someone dared to disrespect his mother, then he swept in with a vengeance.

She wondered what Memphis's life would have been like if Knox had managed to find him after his mother died. He hadn't shared with her what had happened in the other foster home, but she knew it was bad just by the way his foster family avoided the topic.

"I'm going to start dinner." Thayer stood up from the couch, crossing into the kitchen. She had to have something to do to keep herself busy until Knox returned, or she would go crazy. She already felt like she had fallen down a rabbit hole. She had all the vegetables chopped for stir-fry when she finally heard the door unlocking.

"Any news?" Shaun asked, walking through the door.

"Nope," Memphis answered, sprawling on the couch.

With a shrug, Shaun pulled out his phone. Thayer wanted to scream at how calm they were.

Finally, she heard the door open again. Knox walked in with a scowl on his face. She was overjoyed at seeing even that emotion. It had been the longest hour of meal prep she could ever remember. Memphis had calmly remained on the couch reading another one of Randall's books while she fretted the time away.

"Did you catch him?" she blurted out, running to the door the moment Knox stepped inside.

He was sweaty and dirty, but she hardly noticed as she searched his face for an answer. "No, sweetheart, but it wasn't for lack of trying," he answered.

She felt her face fall, he had finally been the break they needed, and Knox had let him get away.

"Let me go clean up, and I'll tell you all about it over dinner."

She managed to muster a smile at him before he crossed the room, heading for the bathroom. She started the stir-fry with a feeling of defeat.

"I've got everything secured for tonight. A couple of the guys are going to hang around for a while, just to make sure there aren't any surprises," Shaun finally said, looking up from his phone.

"Good. Thanks, Shaun," Memphis answered.

"Yes, thank you, Shaun," Thayer added. She didn't have to like what he did, but she was still grateful for his help. She guessed the old adage, "necessity makes for strange bedfellows," was true. If Memphis trusted Shaun, then there must be more to him than just a car thief.

Knox emerged about the time dinner was ready in a pair of sweatpants and a T-shirt. His hair was damp, and he smelled much better than when he had walked by her earlier. Sitting down, she barely tasted her food as he regaled them with his rooftop chase. She questioned his description of leaping effortlessly across an alley from one roof to another, but she decided the real story wasn't important.

"All those damn buildings are nothing but a labyrinth in that area," Shaun said when Knox had finished. "If he's from down there, you'd never have found him. Those kids can slip in and out of those buildings without anyone ever knowing. I can ask around tomorrow about him, but I wouldn't hold my breath."

Taking her last bite, Thayer noticed Knox yawn. "We'll clean this up if you want to turn in. I think after this evening's excitement, we could all use a little extra rest," she said.

"That sounds like a good idea," Knox answered. He pushed his chair back from the table, standing up. "We'll talk about a new strategy tomorrow. Good night."

They all watched as the big man headed off to the bedroom.

"Murphy," Shaun said.

The dog picked his head up from the dog pillow he lay on.

"Looks like it's you and me tonight. Come on."

Murphy happily joined Shaun at the door where his leash hung. Snapping it onto his collar, Shaun opened the door to take him out.

"Looks like that leaves us to clean up," Memphis said.

"Looks like," Thayer agreed.

"I'll make a deal with you."

She cocked her head at him. His deals were always interesting and usually benefited her in some way.

"You head on into the bedroom, and I'll deal with this. When I'm done, I'll come help you 'relax' so you can fall asleep quickly."

She laughed at both his use of air quotes and a wink. She liked the sound of that deal, though. With a grin, she backed toward the bedroom, only turning around when she passed the couch. It wasn't too sexy looking to run into the wall behind you.

Thayer was sitting on the bed leaning back on her hands, her long blonde hair falling in loose waves down her back when he walked through the door. She had changed into his long shirt, opting for nothing more than a silk thong underneath it.

Memphis stood staring at her so long that Thayer began to feel self-conscious. It was obvious he liked what he saw, judging by the growing bulge in his pants. Finally, with a slight shake of his head, he stepped forward, pushing her legs apart until he was looking down at her. His hand reached out slowly, running through her hair, down her neck and over the top of her breast.

Thayer couldn't stop the gasp that escaped her lips when his hand returned to fist in her hair. Slowly, he pulled her up from the bed against him as he pressed their mouths together. With every gentle thrust of his hips against her, she could feel the heat pooling between her thighs. Why had she told him she wanted to wait? Her mind had said she wasn't ready yet, but every inch of her body begged her for more. Except there was one thing stopping her.

"There are absolutely no condoms in this entire

apartment," she moaned against his mouth. She could feel his smile.

"Been searching?" he asked. "I'm curious, Miss Kent, what did you have in mind during your desperate hunt?"

Thayer could feel the fire in her face. She would have a better chance of being indignant at his taunt if he wasn't kissing his way down her neck.

"I wouldn't say I was desperate," she said.

She knew her words might have more impact if they didn't end on a moan. Pulling his sling over his head, he moved his hand to replace the one already holding her hair. His other traced down her body, sliding between her thighs. She bucked against his hand as he made a slow circle over the damp silk.

"I beg to differ. Feels to me like you're very desperate." His touch was light, pushing her closer but not close enough to drive her over the brink.

Every time she would get close, he would stop. It was enough to drive any woman mad, but just as she was opening her mouth to share these thoughts, he stepped back. Unbuttoning the first three buttons of his shirt, he pulled it over his head with a pained grunt.

"You have to watch your arm," she said. "It's still trying to heal."

Rolling his eyes, he tossed the shirt into the corner of the room before trying to wrestle out of his pants. Based on the way he was now holding his injured arm, Thayer had no doubt it hurt.

Sliding onto her knees, she pushed his hands away. She quickly had his belt off and his pants open. It would be so easy in this position to slide his throbbing cock into her mouth.

Thayer stole a glance up at his face, finding him watching her with a look she couldn't interpret. Could he read her mind and was waiting to see what she would do? Slowly, she rose off the ground, her gaze never wavering from his. He didn't need to worry. She would never do anything to intentionally hurt him.

MEMPHIS HAD THOUGHT his lungs would simply cease to function when Thayer kneeled on the floor. He didn't know what he would do if she reached for him. Soon, he would have to tell her everything.

But when was the right time to tell the woman you love about the abuse? When did he explain that, while other boys his age were just starting to discover their sexuality, he was being sold to both men and women looking to satisfy their depraved needs? Would she push him away in disgust once she knew?

He had managed to live through an especially bad weekend when Mr. Howard, his social studies teacher, had found him in the school bathroom with a knife in one hand and blood dripping from the other.

He had always wondered later if he had begun cutting himself to work up the nerve to finally slit his wrist deep enough to end the pain. Mr. Howard had pressed his hand over the deepest cut, pulled him out of the stall and hauled him to the nurse's office.

The nurse, principal, resource officer, and two city police officers had all been staring at him in that small office by the time he was bandaged up. Speaking barely louder than a whisper, he told them it had all begun with a blow job.

The several months were followed by caseworkers, attorneys, and finally psychiatrists before he was moved to a mental health facility. He had given up any remaining hope he had of a normal life when he was brought to Ms. Beulah's doorstep.

Sex for him after that was just a physical release. He had fucked his way through high school, college, and, for a while, the Army. It always made him feel empty afterward, so he decided to stop. Then, during his time in vet school, he had a chance to breathe. Everyone was so busy, he could simply keep his head down and work.

By the time he bought his vet practice, he had been made painfully aware that he would never love someone any deeper than he loved his foster family. But then he had found Thayer in that dark dungeon.

"Where did you go?" Memphis heard Thayer whisper, breaking him from his thoughts.

Looking down into the large blue eyes, he smiled. Cradling her cheek in his hand, he felt his heart miss a beat when she turned to place a kiss on his palm.

"I'm right here," he said quietly before taking a deep breath. "So, no condoms, huh? I guess we'll just have to improvise." Shoving his thoughts down deep, he grinned before spinning her around, so his back was to the bed. Easing onto the bed against the headboard, he motioned for her to join him.

"Come here," he said.

When she reached the edge of the bed, he wrapped his arm around her, pulling her on top of him. She let out a small squeal when she landed straddling his lap.

"Take off these panties, sweetheart."

Standing on the bed over him, Thayer awkwardly

stepped out of them while Memphis tried to prevent her from falling off the side.

When she sank back down to her knees, he pulled her into a kiss. Every time he kissed her, she moaned, making him just want to do it again. This time, as his tongue explored every inch of her mouth, she began to grind against his cock.

"How?" she asked in shock as he slid the shirt down her shoulders.

With a shrug, he mashed their mouths together again. It was just a matter of distracting her while he unbuttoned it, but he couldn't reveal all of his secrets. Every relationship needed some mystery.

His hand slid from her hair to cup her breast, rolling her nipple between his thumb and finger until it peaked to a hard point. Thayer moaned, rubbing against him faster.

He lay back on the bed, thrusting his hips up as he pinched her hard nipples just the way she liked it. He smiled, watching her as she moaned above him, her hands on his chest, holding her up.

Her head was thrown back with her eyes closed as she worked up and down his length, heading toward her climax. When he felt her start to shake, he sat up, sucking her nipple into his mouth, biting gently as she cried out his name.

"That's it. We can never have actual intercourse," Thayer announced, collapsing against his chest, still trying to catch her breath.

"Why is that?" he asked, not sure he wanted to hear the answer.

"I think my head will explode. If a simple rub off can be this mind blowing, what would the rest be like?"

"Simple rub off?" Memphis chuckled. Sometimes it took all of his effort to keep up with her train of thought.

"Rub out?"

"I was having a problem with the word simple."

"Oh, sorry," she answered, resting her head on her hands, watching him. "A very complex and thought-provoking grindfest." He laughed, making her head bounce. "I'm sticky," she added.

"I don't doubt it. Want to help me into the shower? I have some new tricks to try out with my tongue."

"Hum, I don't know. I would hate for you to slip and fall?" She smiled when he looked down at her.

"You just get your sexy ass in the shower. Let me worry about the rest."

CHAPTER TWENTY-THREE

Knox lay in bed staring at the ceiling. At least he had managed to sleep until midnight before his dream about missing the other roof jerked him awake.

He rubbed his hands together, throwing a small fireball at the ceiling. It always burned away before it made it back to him. It was his equivalent of tossing a ball at the ceiling, only he'd never had to worry about breaking his nose this way. He had only caught his bed on fire once and that was in high school. His mother had not been amused in the least.

He listened to the loft, but all he could hear was snoring from the room next door. Getting back to sleep seemed to be out of the question. A walk might help him clear his mind or at least help him work through what happened just a few hours ago. If he could have just caught up on that rooftop, there was a chance this would all be over now.

Getting out of the bed, he pulled his jeans back on and hunted around for a shirt. Dressed, he nodded to the dog who had moved into his room at some point while he slept. Quietly, he opened the bedroom door the rest of the way. At least the mystery of how Murphy got into his room was solved.

Trying to be as quiet as a two-hundred-and-fifty-pound man could be, Knox carried his boots into the living room, where Shaun slept on the couch.

"Where're you going?" Shaun asked, watching Knox with one eye open.

Knox had learned from Memphis that Shaun never slept very deeply, having learned at an early age that bad things happen when you let your guard down.

"I need some air," Knox grunted, lacing up his boots.

"This isn't a good neighborhood to walk in at night." When Knox stood with a smirk, Shaun just shrugged before pulling the blanket farther up his body. Murphy met Knox at the door, so he fished the leash off the hook.

Checking that the outer door was secured behind him, they started down the road.

He walked out of the industrial park toward the few bars and shops in the area. Randall had told him there was the start of a renewal of the area, but as far as he could see, they had a long way to go. Quite a number of the old buildings he passed were empty and seemed to be more in need of a wrecking ball than a renovation. He guessed that was why he was a math teacher and not a developer.

He had only been walking for fifteen minutes when Knox felt someone following him. They were at least half a block away, but he could tell they were closing in slowly.

Reaching down, he unhooked Murphy's leash. If there was going to be trouble, he didn't want the dog to be unable to get away. Using the opportunity to take a quick glance back, he saw that there were at least four young men following him. He figured he could take two, three if he had to, but four might be a stretch.

Ducking around a corner, he walked a few feet before turning around to wait for them. The only weapon he had was a nasty-looking knife he kept razor sharp, but, with any luck, he wouldn't have to use it.

Within a few minutes, the men jogged around the corner after him, sliding to a stop when they found him facing them. He wasn't sure if the word "men" was accurate. They looked more like a couple of boys up to no good.

"Yo. Give us your green, old man, and we'll let you walk away." The biggest of the thugs held a baseball bat, tapping it on his hand as he spoke.

"You think I'd walk around here flush?" Knox asked, holding out his hands. With any luck, he could bluff his way out of this without any bloodshed.

"Give me your fucking money," the man repeated with a snarl.

Knox prepared for the onslaught.

Snapping his fingers at Murphy, he gave him a hand signal to go back to the loft. Memphis had shown him the hand commands the dog would respond to when they were sitting around one evening. Murphy would respond not only to hand and voice commands but also whistles. The damned border collie was smarter than most people he knew.

"Listen up, blow by, I don't have any money," he growled when Murphy was a safe distance away. "Turn around and walk away before you get hurt." Knox's lip curled up as he glared at the leader of the crew, daring him to engage.

Gripping the bat with both hands, the punk swung at Knox. Catching the bat with one hand, he pulled the kid to him, swinging his fist at his face.

He missed seeing the pipe that swung at his side, though, until it connected with his hip. With a grunt of pain, Knox spun, kicking at where the other man's head should be. The crunch of bone told him he had connected.

The first man had picked himself back off the ground and rushed Knox, tackling him to the ground. He managed to not crack his head on the ground as he let the momentum help him flip the man over his head. Spinning, Knox straddled the man, punching him in the face twice before he went limp.

With a roar, he stood up to face the other men, only to find one lying on the ground and the other two gone. Leaning against the wall holding his arm, while blood slowly ran down his face from a cut over his eye, stood Memphis.

"Don't you know a bad neighborhood when you see one? Pretty sure I heard Shaun warn you," Memphis said with a smirk. "Do you think they were waiting for one of us to be alone? It seems a little late for muggers, even around here."

"Nah, they were just a couple of kids looking for money," Knox answered.

Pushing off of the wall, Memphis flexed his arm several times, checking for damage. "What were you doing anyway?" Bending, Memphis hooked the leash he'd found back on Murphy's collar before turning back toward the warehouse.

"Walking," Knox grumbled, following with a slight limp. *Were* they waiting for one of them? He had told Memphis no, but now he began to question it. They seemed too young, but then the guy he chased on the roof was young looking as well. It seemed like whoever was orchestrating this was always one step ahead. If Memphis was right, they were getting more daring.

"I wouldn't mind if you didn't bring any more problems to our doorstep than what we already have right now. I don't yearn to get in a fight on a daily basis like you seem to. We have enough to worry about without you wandering into more shit."

"No one asked for your help," Knox growled, knocking Memphis against the wall as he passed him.

"I'm not just going to sit by while my dumbass brother gets himself shanked. I know we just met, but you're the only blood family I have. Which is completely fucked up."

Memphis was smiling at Knox when the big man abruptly came to a stop, spinning around with a scowl. Knox poked twice at Memphis's chest with his finger before opening his fist to pat on him with the palm of his hand. When Memphis grinned, Knox just turned, walking toward the warehouse with a shake of his head.

"We make it out of this shit show, I'm getting drunk," Knox growled, climbing the stairs to the loft.

"Oh, fuck yeah," Memphis agreed, trudging up behind him. "In spades."

"It doesn't make any sense. Whoever is doing this has to be well connected. How would they have found out so fast that Thayer was at my house then be able to hire people capable of snatching her? Are you sure her father doesn't have a powerful enemy?" Memphis asked the next morning over breakfast.

"I've looked at everyone we could think of. None of them has done anything that can be traced to this. It could be some radical, but they are usually not this organized," Knox answered.

"I just don't understand what my father or I could have done that was bad enough to merit all this," Thayer said in frustration. "Knox, was I that bad a person in high school? Was my father so horrible that he deserves me dying?" She wiped away a tear.

Knox reached across the table, taking her hand in his.

"Thayer, do you remember when you would get in trouble in high school, and I would make you spend the next day in the gym working on self-defense?" Knox asked. Thayer nodded once. Not only had it kept her in shape, but it had allowed him to let her go off to college, knowing she could fend off even the most skilled advance by a drunk college man.

"Please don't make me go through some routine just to prove I can still do the moves you taught me. The thought of seeing my breakfast again is less than appealing."

Knox laughed, shaking his head. "Did that ever seem like much of a punishment?"

"Not really," she answered, confused.

"That's because you never did anything truly worth punishing. If you had been a bad person, I would have been the first person to tell you, and I would have found a way much worse than working out for punishment.

"You are not to blame for what's going on, and as far as I can tell, neither is your father. He's well-liked by his constituency, respected on Capitol Hill, and a decorated Navy captain. You don't get there by being an asshole. At least not a corrupt one."

Thayer laughed. "Only you would just lay it out there. I can't remember anyone else ever explaining that at least if my father is an asshole, he's a decent one." Standing, she stacked their empty plates before crossing to the sink. Knox and Memphis stood to help, but she waved them back down.

"So, what is the plan after the weekend?" she asked, placing their dishes in the dishwasher. "We can't stay here forever."

"No," Knox agreed. "I think we go home. Memphis has a business to return to, and I can protect you better in Connecticut. It's not great, but it's all I've got for now."

Her eyes cut to Memphis. Knox noticed he had been strangely quiet through the entire conversation. Taking a deep breath, Memphis looked up, his bright-green eyes searching Thayer's face.

"I think Knox is right. He has better resources at home to protect you. I think it's time to change tactics."

Knox could almost hear her heart breaking. She thought she meant something more to Memphis. Shit, even Knox could see that, and he was no expert on matters of the heart. No, the look of pain in Memphis's eyes as he continued to watch her spoke volumes. But, for now, they had to be smart.

"Okay," she said quietly. "I understand. I don't like it, but I understand."

"THIS SIDE STREET appears to be our best choice." Curtis was pointing to a large map of the downtown area spread out on the bed. "Every day they walk back down here to the waiting car. There is a period of just a few minutes when they are on their own. The sheeting protecting pedestrians draped over this door should hide what's happening from the parking lot."

His men nodded, studying the location.

"O'Neill, did you make arrangements for this door to be left unlocked?"

"Yes, sir. I paid the construction foreman this morning and scouted out the location. There is plenty of room to park inside the building with a roll-up door that opens onto the back street," he answered.

"Perfect. You and Davidson will follow them like normal tomorrow. I'll get everything ready here," Curtis said, pointing at the building. "After you help me secure them at the secondary location, you'll be free to go. I will handle it from there. As always, you can expect payment within twenty-four hours after the job is done."

With a nod, the two men left the room to return to their own for the night.

Lying awake last night, Curtis had hit on the perfect place to kill Thayer. If he staged the scene just right, it would look like Prescott had killed her himself.

In researching both Prescott and Monroe, he had stumbled upon an old newspaper article about an abuse scandal involving the house Prescott had lived in. It would be perfect. Everyone would think he had gone mad and had taken Thayer with him, killing them both when they reached the house. It would create a scandal just in time to take the senator out of the discussion about the contract.

Curtis scrolled through all of the information he could find on the old foster home. Noticing that the house still stood vacant in one of the sketchier neighborhoods, he decided to research the ownership.

Pulling up the tax records, he discovered one Randall Jackson had bought it a few years ago. The only permits filed were for demolition, but it had expired a while back. As far as he could tell, the house still stood vacant on the property.

Old newspaper articles showed pictures of the house. Armed with those and the address from the records, Curtis left his room to find it. He had to make sure it wasn't being used by squatters or as a crack house, though that would only add to the media circus. This had to work. He was running out of options.

Pulling up to the front of the dilapidated house, he fished the flashlight out of the side pocket of the SUV. He debated the gun in the glove compartment, but he had his knife with him for protection, so he left the gun there. He always preferred a knife anyway. It made the fight more personal.

Curtis walked around the house, trying doors, until he finally found a broken window around the back. Pushing it up, he slid into what appeared to be an old bedroom. The walls were covered with random graffiti, so he assumed it had become a favorite hangout of the neighborhood kids.

It didn't take him long to make a quick sweep through the first floor before climbing the stairs to the remaining bedrooms. He wished he had found out which room Memphis had been terrorized in, it would have been more poetic, but he supposed any of them would do.

He chose the back bedroom on the top floor. The window was shrouded by a large tree which would keep any prying eyes from seeing them, and it was the farthest from the road.

Testing the sheetrock around the room, he knocked a hole in two places, allowing him to wrap a rope around the corner post. This would work for his purposes. All he needed were a few more items and he would finally be ready.

He climbed back out the window with a smile. By the end of the weekend, this would all be over, the senator would be destroyed, and Curtis's new lifestyle as good as guaranteed.

CHAPTER TWENTY-FOUR

"Last day, I promise. After today, you can go home while Knox tries to flush them out." Memphis had been up since dawn thinking about what happened after they called this off today.

He knew Thayer would return home while he headed back north to his practice. It didn't mean he liked the plan, he just knew he needed to do whatever was necessary for Thayer. Knox was still baffled why he couldn't find even a trace of who was hunting her, but then, neither could the feds.

"We could just stay in bed today," Thayer moaned, pulling the covers tighter around her. "You could take off all of those bothersome clothes and slide back in here with me."

She had flopped over, reaching for Memphis when she saw Knox standing in the doorway, his big arms crossed over his chest with a scowl on his face. "Ugh," she said, rolling back over. "You're always such a cockblock."

"She said it, not me," she heard Memphis say from the bathroom door with a laugh.

"Uh-huh," Knox growled, turning around to head back to the kitchen.

Memphis picked up his boots from the end of the bed, sitting down on the edge to put them on.

"Can we at least eat lunch somewhere new today?" Thayer asked as she crawled across the bed to him. Swinging a leg around, she straddled his lap as he worked to tie his left boot, snuggling into his chest.

"We can. Someone is very crabby this morning." Memphis observed, kissing the top of her head.

Sitting back, Thayer gave him her best sneer before pushing him back on the bed, pinning his hands above his head.

He lay looking up at her with a smile as she bent forward to kiss him. Jay had swung by yesterday to check his arm and side. As long as he didn't get too rowdy, he was back to somewhat normal.

"Whatever," she said before swinging off of him. Sitting back up, he watched her walk into the bathroom, wondering if he would survive letting her go home.

For all of their talk about her staying with him, he still knew in the back of his mind this would be over soon. The thought made his chest hurt in a way he had never experienced. For the first time in his life, he had fallen completely in love.

With a sigh, he hoisted himself off the bed to walk into the kitchen. Knox already had sausage set out while he continued to cook up a stack of waffles. Walking over, Memphis picked one up, leaning back against the counter where Knox was cooking.

"So, if nothing happens today, you think she'll be safe at home?" he asked as the big man opened the waffle iron to check on his latest creation.

"I do. She can be surrounded by security there." Knox set the fresh waffle on the plate before adding more batter to the iron. "I'm sorry, this is how it has to be."

Memphis looked over at him expecting a smirk, but Knox was serious.

"I really am."

But they both knew her safety was more important than the feelings Memphis had for her. They had stayed up late last night after Thayer had fallen asleep on the couch discussing all their options.

"No, I get it. I don't like it, but I get it." Knox nodded as Memphis took a deep breath, plastering on a smile for Thayer as she walked out of the bedroom. He knew until Knox found someone, he really wouldn't totally understand the problem Memphis was having with this.

"Papa Bear made waffles!" Thayer shouted out, planting a quick kiss on Knox's cheek before scooping up one of the plates laden with waffles. Memphis heard the grumbling from Knox, but he also caught the smile when he thought no one could see him.

"Did I hear something about waffles?" Ben asked, sitting up on the couch.

Murphy stuck his head up from where he had been stretched out over Ben's feet. With a woof, he hopped over the back of the couch, trotting over to Knox. Shoving a waffle in his pocket, Knox shut off the iron before grabbing Murphy's leash from the hook by the door.

"I'm walking the mutt before we leave." Hooking the leash to Murphy, Knox gave the dog a piece of the waffle before pulling open the door.

"That dog's going to be so spoiled by the time I get him home, I won't be able to do anything with him," Memphis said, popping another piece of waffle in his mouth.

WALKING DOWN THE STAIRS, Knox hunted around for any sign of the men from the other night. Reaching a school playground he had discovered on one of their walks, he unhooked Murphy, letting him stretch his legs for a bit. The dog only made one lap around the playground before he returned to wait for Knox to produce the ball he knew he always had in his pocket.

Knox threw the ball until his shoulder started to ache. He was actually going to miss this stupid mutt when he went home tonight. Memphis had already decided to stay another day before driving his receptionist's Bronco back north. Knox had planned to have the senator's plane waiting for them the second they finished their last stroll around the downtown area.

With a whistle, Knox called Murphy over, securing the leash to his collar. According to Memphis, you could control this dog with an entire series of whistles, but he hadn't had time to learn all of them yet. Yeah, if he ever found another dog this smart, he might have to buy it. Murphy sat at his feet, using his nose to push at Knox's hand.

"What is it," he said, kneeling. "Not gotten enough attention today?"

The dog's feathered tail thumped on the ground as Knox rubbed down his golden coat.

Pushing back up from the ground, he gave the hand signal to heel. Murphy quickly fell in step next to him as they slowly walked back toward the loft. He hated to admit, even to himself, that he was going to miss living here surrounded by Memphis's foster family. As much as he enjoyed living by himself, it often got lonely.

Returning to the loft, he had a moment of panic when no one seemed to be upstairs. He knew that Ben had to report to work this morning, but where were Memphis and Thayer?

Remembering Randall had mentioned a home gym on the first floor, he soon found them playing a round of horse on the makeshift basketball court.

He stood in the shadows, watching them laugh as they came up with crazier shots after every letter. It seemed Memphis's arm was healing nicely based on his layup technique. He watched as the ball missed the hoop. It was a good thing his brother had settled on baseball.

Knox shook his head, smiling at their ridiculous antics, not sure when he had seen two people more suited to each other. Even with his brother a solid dozen years older than her, his laid-back attitude seemed to complement her more driven personality.

How, after everything Memphis had gone through over the years, he could still be so unjaded was beyond him. He guessed it had to do with DNA, but if it came from their dad, he hadn't gotten any of it. In the back of his mind, he wondered if things were different, would Thayer ultimately leave with Memphis?

"If you kids are done with your game, maybe we could go hunt a kidnapper?" he growled at them.

They were starting to get a little too into each other in the filtered lighting, and Knox had experienced enough of that to last him a lifetime.

Thayer just smiled over at him while Memphis rolled his eyes. Somehow during their time together, he had lost his power of intimidation over both of them, if he had ever had it in the first place. He'd have to think about that. What was the point of being a giant if people weren't terrified of you?

Setting the ball down, they followed him out the door.

"Remember to give us a fifteen-minute head start to get into position before you leave the parking lot," Knox said, walking to the front of the building.

As he suspected, one of his men was already waiting in one of the black SUVs for him. They had followed the same routine every day, with Memphis and Thayer waiting until they had their shadows in place before leaving, but it never hurt to go over the rules again.

"Yeah, we know," Memphis mumbled, standing next to the Bronco.

Knox grunted before climbing into the SUV. As he headed out of the industrial park, he turned around to catch one last glance of Thayer wrapped in Memphis's arms.

"Maybe today's the day we catch them," Fisher said.

Turning back around, Knox stared out the windshield.

"Maybe."

"So, what do we look at first today?" Memphis asked, pulling Thayer out of the Bronco in the parking lot downtown.

They had parked in the same place they had been parking for the entire week now. It stood to reason that following a routine would make whoever was hunting Thayer comfortable enough to make a move. That was the hope, anyway. So far, it had proven to be wrong.

"Does it matter? What could there possibly be left to see?" she answered, taking his hand as they walked toward the shops. "At least I get to walk around outside for a couple of hours. I have a feeling that will come to an end when I get home."

"Let's do this then. I'll buy a blanket, then we'll pick up some food and have a picnic in the park by the river. We can watch the barges being pushed up the river."

"That sounds like a perfect idea," Thayer agreed enthusiastically. Anything to break up the monotony of walking the same streets again.

Picking up sandwiches from the Peabody Deli, complete with an assortment of desserts to sample, they walked to the nearest riverfront park. Finding the perfect spot with views of the Pyramid and the bridge from Arkansas, they spread their blanket out on the ground. Since it was the weekend, the park was full of families enjoying the pleasant afternoon.

"This isn't bad, right?" Memphis asked, opening up the picnic. "Let's see what our money bought us for lunch." The deli had packed the basket for them with a variety of items. Memphis pulled out two large sandwiches, chips, and fruit. "Root beer? Nasty. This must be yours."

"You don't drink root beer?"

"No, that stuff is gross."

"Oh, but your Powerade is better?"

"Toilet water is better." He grinned at her as she wrinkled her nose in disgust. "You know I'm going to miss giving you a hard time, right?" Memphis handed her a bag of chips, reclining back against the tree they sat under.

"You can always come visit."

"Yeah," he said halfheartedly, looking back down at his sandwich.

They finished their lunch in silence before Memphis scooted down, placing his arm over his eyes to catch a nap. Thayer watched him for a while, but she finally turned to watch the barges make their slow way up the river pushed by tugboats.

She sat quietly for a long time, sitting on their blanket until the park slowly started to empty, the families heading home for dinner. Looking over her shoulder finally as the sun neared the horizon, she found Memphis watching her.

"I guess we should go," she said without moving.

His green eyes moved over her as he sat up. "I guess we should," he said, standing.

Reaching down, he pulled her to her feet. Wrapping his hand through her hair, he pulled her into a kiss. She knew this would be it. When they reached the parking lot, they would each go their separate ways. As much as she wanted to stay by his side forever, she had to think of what was best for them all.

His tongue delved into her mouth, twining around hers as they held each other desperately by the river. When he stepped back, they were both breathless.

Picking up the blanket, he folded it into the basket. Taking her hand in his, they walked slowly back, savoring their last moments together.

CHAPTER TWENTY-FIVE

Knox had left his men to follow Thayer all day while he saw to the arrangements for their return home and checked on the people following up on the few leads they had found. Security at the senator's house had been increased, with more men patrolling the perimeter as well as more cameras in previously blind areas to protect her better.

He was now standing in the parking lot by the rental SUV, waiting for her and Memphis to show up. They were already a few minutes late from the agreed upon time, but he wasn't concerned yet. When a light rain began, he returned to the inside of the vehicle to wait.

Checking his watch again, he growled, realizing they were now fifteen minutes behind schedule. He assumed they were sucking face somewhere out of the rain. They had five more minutes before he went to jerk them away from wherever they were holed up. He shouldn't be expected to babysit them anymore at their ages.

Knox was flipping through a magazine he had picked up at a local bookstore when his phone buzzed in his pocket. Fishing it out, Knox saw it was Fisher.

"Fisher, where the fuck are they? The plane is waiting," he barked into the phone. He was greeted by a moment of silence before Fisher cleared his throat.

"Are they not with you? They should have been there fifteen minutes ago," the man answered.

"You're supposed to be watching them. Why don't you know where they are?" Knox closed his magazine slowly as panic began to squeeze his chest.

"They ducked into that construction overhang on the way back. I assumed you would see them emerge on the other side. It's less than a block," Fisher said.

Knox could hear Fisher starting to run through the phone as he jumped out of the SUV. Without responding to Fisher, Knox ran toward the construction area at the edge of the parking lot. Racing behind the plastic, he slid to a stop. Neither Memphis nor Thayer were anywhere to be seen, but there was a trail of blood on the sidewalk.

Noticing the trail disappear behind a door, Knox tried the knob, finding it unlocked. Swinging it wide, he waited for Fisher to enter with his gun out before following. It only took a second for his men to sweep the empty building to determine no one was inside.

There was, however, a blood trail surrounded by several shoe prints left behind in the dust. They ended by a roll-up door at the far end of the old empty building.

Jerking the roll-up door open, Knox followed a set of tire treads out into the street where the rain had washed them away in the direction they took.

Looking first one way, then the other, he realized with growing dread that they could be anywhere by now. The only hope he felt was the knowledge that he hadn't found either one of their bodies lying dead inside, though the amount of blood indicated someone had received more than just a scratch.

Running his hand through his hair, Knox knew he had no more idea where they could have gone than who had taken them. How could he have been so stupid as not to have checked the building earlier? He had found it locked every other day. Why was the one day he let his guard down the day it was left unlocked? Anyone could have hidden in here knowing they would walk past it on the way to the parking lot, just waiting for an opportunity.

Now he hadn't just lost Thayer. He had lost Memphis too. He stood in the rain with rivulets of water running down his neck, trying to decide what to do next.

"Sir, it looks like there were more than just three based on the footprints." Knox spun around, returning inside the building. Fisher had been looking for anything that would help track them.

"I would speculate that this is Mr. Prescott's blood. It seems to reason that they would have to have incapacitated him first to control them. It doesn't look like there was much of a struggle either." Knox walked over to where Fisher was kneeling in the dust. "Mr. Prescott, if uninjured, would have put up more of a fight."

"Do you think he can survive long based on the blood loss here? How much do you think there is?" Knox wanted to scream. Whomever this was had simply been playing with them all along. How had they still managed to remain one step ahead?

"If it is Mr. Prescott, and he can get it stopped, he should survive. If I'm wrong though, and it belongs to Miss Kent, I just don't know." They stood staring at the blood trail for a few minutes as Knox worked at putting some kind of plan together in his head.

"The car tread doesn't look like anything special, so that's no help." Knox looked around the building before adding, "They had to have been watching for a while to know Memphis and Thayer would use this route back to the car. You didn't see anything?" Fisher shook his head.

"Then I guess we should call everyone to the loft. Maybe they will have some idea of where we go from here. I'll see what my guy with the FBI can find out."

Memphis woke up tied to the corner of an old room in an abandoned house in a bad state of disrepair. It only took him a second to realize why the room looked vaguely familiar.

It hadn't been his. That one was down the hall on the right, but it had belonged to another child sent to live in this house.

For the life of him, he couldn't figure out why he would be tied up here until he saw Thayer sitting in a chair across the room from him. She had been tied up and gagged. Memphis couldn't just see the fear in her eyes when she looked at him, he could feel it pouring off of her in waves.

He knew his first instinct at being trapped here

again should be panic. He should be frozen from the trauma, but instead of fear, it just made him angry. He had fought his way out of this hell once. He could do it again if he could just not bleed out first.

He was dizzy and nauseous, but that could be attributed to the crack on the head he had received after trying to prevent himself and Thayer from being dragged into a car inside the building.

Assessing his injuries, he was positive that except for the cuts and a goose egg forming on his head, he was okay for now.

They had just popped under the construction awning to get out of the rain as they headed to the parking lot when some man had jumped out from behind a door, slicing Memphis across the chest with a knife. It had been so fast he had barely had time to react.

Thayer had fought when they grabbed her, so he laced another cut down Memphis's upper arm, making her freeze. After that, he simply had to hold the knife at her neck to make both of them comply.

"You're not dead yet, I see," a man said to Memphis as he walked back into the room. "That's good. I'm not sure dying from a crack on the skull could be explained as easily."

He walked over to Thayer, grabbing a fistful of her hair when she tried to squirm away from him. Pulling her head back, he looked down at her.

"Don't worry, it'll be over soon. I have an island waiting for me."

"Who the fuck are you?" Memphis asked in a shaky voice. He really was going to have to do something sooner rather than later while he still had some strength left. Maybe he had lost more blood than he thought. "What do you want with her?"

The man turned her hair loose to stare at Memphis for a minute before laughing. Twirling a wicked-looking knife, the man slowly walked over to Memphis, squatting down in front of him.

"Who am I? I'm the man hired to make sure her father doesn't block the signing of a very lucrative contract. I had it all planned out. The kidnapping of his only child, only to be found right before the contract appeared before the committee, making him miss the vote as he rushed to her side.

"If I just killed him, it would have brought too much attention down on us. But a quiet kidnapping would have destroyed him without too much of a fuss. If that didn't work, I would have had enough to create a sensation in the press to prevent him from continuing to block it moving forward."

"All of this was over a fucking government contract? You have hillbillies right out of *Deliverance* kidnap her, send thugs to my house at night to kill us in our sleep, and now this? How much did they promise you if it passes?" Memphis looked at the man in disbelief.

"Enough to set me up for a while," the man said with a smile that sent shivers down Memphis's back. "But it's even more than the money. It's the prestige of doing a job no one else could pull off." Chancing a glance at Thayer, Memphis saw a look of recognition dawn on her face. She must have heard of whatever contract he was referring to.

Turning his gaze back to the man, Memphis watched as he took a deep breath, trying to calm down. "I thought this location seemed almost poetic for what I have planned." Slicing another bloody groove down Memphis's thigh, he stood with a laugh.

"Poor orphan kid with an undisclosed drug addiction snaps at the thought of his captive girlfriend leaving him. He kills her, then himself, in the house where it all began. I think I read somewhere that you liked to cut yourself too. Sound familiar?"

"You're insane," Memphis growled out. "Those demons left a long time ago. I've seen way worse shit than what happened in this house since then." At least he still sounded tough, even if he was having a hard time staying conscious.

He had been working on the rope that bound him to the corner, but it stubbornly held fast. If help didn't find them soon, they would wind up dead.

"I have something to get from the car. I'll return shortly, then we'll get to experience the live last performance of the two star-crossed lovers. Complete with one of them having a tragic descent into madness." Memphis watched him walk out of the room.

"Are you okay?" he asked, looking over at Thayer.

When she nodded her head, he started to phase away to find Knox.

He stopped when he heard Thayer whimper. "Hey, I'm still here. I need to go find Knox while he's gone. Can you hold on?"

She nodded her head again.

Memphis wished he could assure her everything would be okay, but if he couldn't get Knox here in time, they wouldn't be. No matter what happened, he wouldn't lie to her. This was bad. Settling back, he slowly slipped away as her wide blue eyes watched.

KNOX HAD CALLED Jay on the way back to the loft to explain what had happened. By the time he pulled up to the converted warehouse, everyone was there waiting for details.

No one had any clue where to start looking or even how to put out a report on the car, since they didn't know what he was driving. Hell, they didn't even know if it was a man or a woman or a mixture of both who had finally managed to abduct them out from underneath their noses. At least they had a starting point from where they were abducted.

He had called Dex, the FBI agent, who had insisted on being kept in the loop. With no license plate or description of the vehicle, there was very little he could do to trace it.

After arguing back and forth for what felt like an interminable amount of time to Knox, Dex had finally agreed not to call in the local FBI office. The last thing Knox wanted was to pressure someone into hurting Thayer and Memphis before he could locate them. With the promise of searching through the traffic camera footage, Dex wished him luck before hanging up.

Spreading maps across the table of both Memphis and the surrounding area in Tennessee and Arkansas, Knox and the rest of the men poured over them, running through one theory after another. After fifteen minutes of discarding every option laid on the table, Knox felt himself nearing the end of his sanity.

Needing to clear his head so he could think, he

hooked the leash to Murphy's collar and told the others he was walking the dog.

He stormed the few short blocks to the nearest elementary, with Murphy close to his side. It was as if the dog could sense something was wrong with his master.

Arriving at the school playground, he unhooked the leash, letting the dog run. He watched as the dog made a halfhearted lap around the outer fence. There had to be some way to find them in this town. If Dex couldn't find the vehicle, he wasn't sure what to do next.

"Knox!" a weak voice cried out, startling him out of his thoughts.

Looking around, he spotted Memphis sitting behind him, only it wasn't really his brother, just the specter of him.

Knox stood looking at the gash running across Memphis's chest, oozing blood. Another one ran down his bicep and still another down his thigh. The wonder at Memphis being able to find him in this school ground was only a passing thought.

"Memphis?" he asked, taking a step toward him.

"No time. He's coming back. Tell Randall the old house. He'll know." With that, he faded back into space.

Whistling to Murphy, Knox broke into a run, heading back toward the loft. He felt the dog running next to him as they approached the SUV still parked in front of the loft since they had walked to the park. Opening the door, he waited for the dog to jump in before following him. Flying out of the parking lot, he dialed Randall's phone, impatiently waiting for the man to pick up in the loft.

"They're being held in some old home. Memphis

said you would know where," he barked out when Randall answered.

Knox fought to rein in his fury as he waited for Randall to recognize what Memphis was talking about. All he wanted to do was punch the closest thing next to him. Murphy barked in the back seat as if he mirrored Knox's frustration. Finally, Randall came back on the line.

"I think I know where they are. I'm sending you the coordinates now. We'll meet you there."

CHAPTER TWENTY-SIX

Thayer watched as Memphis returned to the room. She knew it would take a lot out of him, but she was terrified when he seemed much weaker than he did only a moment ago.

The man had left a slice down his thigh when he stood up earlier, just missing a major artery. Memphis didn't need to lose any more blood than he already had. She watched in silence behind her gag as he fought to maintain consciousness when he returned.

The man returned shortly, carrying a tripod that he set up in front of Thayer. She watched as he adjusted the equipment, then opened a bag he had left on the floor.

It had finally occurred to her what contract he was referring to. She remembered her father worrying over a new military contract that was being reviewed by the SASC he was part of in the Senate. He hadn't told her anything about the particulars, but he had mentioned that the company leading the bids had a less-than-stellar reputation. She knew he had been in discussions with his committee on awarding the bid elsewhere. Whoever won stood to make a fortune.

"What are you doing?" she heard Memphis ask weakly. He was so pale, she wasn't sure how much longer he could hold out.

Pulling out two syringes using gloves, he filled both with something murky from a small jar. Thayer could not understand what he was doing. If he wanted them both dead, why not just kill them back at that construction area? Why go to all of the trouble to bring them back here?

"The senator has to be destroyed enough he misses that meeting. He's a stubborn sonofabitch with a stellar reputation, so it has to look good enough to fool even the crime scene experts. No detective with nothing better to do than to start asking questions is going to derail me. It has to be a death sensational enough to fool everyone. You understand."

He turned his terrifying smile toward Thayer. "I debated a snuff film, but that's really not my style."

She could feel the shiver run down her spine at his words.

"Good to know there are at least some limits to your depravity," Memphis said.

Thayer didn't understand why he would continue to provoke the man.

Walking over to Memphis, he laid the point of the knife on his shoulder before slicing it down his chest. Thayer tried to scream to leave him alone through her gag, but Memphis barely flinched this time. Kneeling down, the man studied Memphis for a moment.

"Maybe I should do a snuff film. You could watch me rape your girlfriend, then kill her. I could still pin that on you."

Memphis spit in his face, kicking out at him with his good leg. With a laugh, the man rose to his full height, wiping the spit off of his face. Thayer was screaming as loud as she could through the gag at the man to get him away from Memphis. Walking back over, the man set his nasty-looking knife on a small table next to the syringes.

"How do you plan to do it? It's not like we'll be around to tell anyone," Memphis said.

"Oh, it's really quite simple. I'll shoot her up with a lethal dose of ketamine mixed with a healthy dose of speed. It would be easy for you, being a veterinarian, to get your hands on both. No one will be surprised to hear you've been siphoning it out of your cabinet a little bit at a time.

"I'll send the same through your veins, leaving the needle in your arm. I'll stage the scene afterward for the greatest dramatic effect, of course, after you're both dead. A tragic lesson in being led astray by an unstable man."

Thayer began to beg for their lives, even though her words only came out as a garbled mess. She knew neither her father nor Knox would ever believe that they had died of an overdose, but by the time they proved differently, it would be too late. Her father would be destroyed.

Shaking her head, tears streaming down her face, she tried her best to reason with him. If she could just make herself understood, maybe she could buy them a little more time. Knox had to be burning the city down by now, looking for them.

"I love you," Memphis said weakly, pulling on the restraints holding him against the corner post of the bedroom. Her eyes snapped to his face. "Remember that..." he added with a smile. "Whatever happens, I love you."

No, she didn't want to hear that. She wanted him to whisper those words while holding her on a beach somewhere or even standing ankle deep in the middle of a pen of pigs. But not here, where she couldn't speak around the musty rag pushed into her mouth.

She felt a hot tear roll down her face again as she prayed he could see into her heart. That he could understand that she had fallen in love with him too.

Hearing a short bark downstairs, Thayer saw Memphis nod. What was he trying to tell her? Was it Murphy with the cavalry?

Stepping to the door, the man pulled out a gun from his waistband as he looked down the stairs. Putting his finger up to his lips, he warned Thayer to be quiet. Hearing nothing more, he must have decided there was no threat and returned to the table.

She watched as he returned the gun to his waistband. The knife he had been using to cut Memphis was still resting on the table as he picked up the first syringe, turning to face her.

Stepping up, he pushed her sleeve up above her elbow, wrapping a piece of tubing around her bicep. He untied her one arm from the chair, giving her a chance to fight him if he hadn't grabbed it tightly with the other hand.

"This vein should work," he said, thumping on her arm.

Thayer fought with everything she had, even though the effort was laughable, with her legs and the other arm still tied. At least she would know she hadn't gone down without a fight. Somewhere in the back of her mind, she knew Knox would be proud of her. He had taught her to never back down.

"You should make the news from coast to coast. Nothing will stop me..."

Thayer stared up at him when he stopped talking, making a gurgling noise instead. For a moment, she couldn't figure out what was wrong with him. She jerked her arm out of his grasp as he turned the syringe loose that had been hovering over her arm just moments before.

Suddenly, she saw a stream of blood trickle out of his mouth. When he fell to his knees, Thayer tried to scream as she watched Memphis's shadow slowly disappear from behind him.

KNOX HEARD the thump upstairs as he searched through the rooms on the first floor. He had been apprehensive at not finding anyone guarding the exterior of the house, but he wasn't taking a chance of stumbling on any surprises.

Motioning Murphy to his side, he quickly moved to the stairs, keeping his gun ready. He was impressed at how fast the dog could clear a room using his superior sense of smell to hunt for threats. As they neared the top of the stairs, he thought he could hear muffled screaming coming from one of the rooms.

"Murphy, scout." He watched as the border collie shot off down the hallway, hunting for the source of the noise. Hearing him bark, he moved quickly down the hall, entering the last bedroom.

Thayer was tied to a chair crying as she fiercely fought to reach the knife sticking out of the back of a man. He was lying on the floor at her feet, surrounded by a growing puddle of blood.

Knox kneeled, feeling for a pulse, finding none. The man had a knife buried to the hilt in his back at an angle that would have hit his lungs and his heart.

Studying it even more closely, he realized it was a method of immobilizing, often taught in hand-to-hand combat. He also knew it took a great deal of strength to stab someone through the back at that angle. Whatever had happened in this room had resulted in at least one death. He just prayed he had arrived before there were any more.

Looking up at Thayer, he found her almost frantic. She was trying to tell him something while struggling to pull the tape off of her mouth.

"Memphis!" she yelled with a sob.

Turning, Knox saw his brother slumped in the corner, tied to one of the corner posts of the room, with Murphy licking his face in a desperate attempt to wake him.

Quickly cutting through Thayer's remaining restraints, he followed as she rushed to the corner where Memphis sat. Knox reached behind him to cut on the rope that held him in place. Thayer tore off a piece of her shirt to try and stop some of the blood oozing out as he slumped forward onto the floor.

"Thayer!" Knox barked, bringing her eyes up to his. "Are you hurt?"

When she shook her head, he pulled her to her feet. Taking Memphis's arm, Knox pulled him onto his shoulder in a fireman's hold and turned toward the door. Blood seemed to seep out of everywhere.

"Go," is all he said to Thayer, motioning to the door with his head. With Murphy in the lead, he followed her down the stairs, arriving at the front door at the same time Randall did.

"Let me have him," Randall said, taking Memphis off of Knox's shoulder. He handed him off to Jay and Ben.

"Take him a couple of blocks over so this looks like he was jumped, but not too close to here. I'm going to have enough questions to answer as it is. We need to make this look like an unrelated incident.

"And Ben, make sure he doesn't bleed out before the EMTs can get there." Turning to Shaun, he ordered him to get Thayer back to the loft and keep her there until he returned.

"What are you doing?" Knox roared as he watched Memphis being carried toward a waiting SUV with Murphy close at their heels.

Thayer was screaming at him as Shaun held her to him in a bear hug, walking her to his waiting car.

"I assume the person or persons who orchestrated this is dead somewhere in the house?"

Knox nodded once.

"Do you want any of this mess to blow back on the

senator? This type of scandal could still sink the election. The press will hound Thayer relentlessly until she can't breathe when this is leaked out. And how do you think Memphis will fair under FBI questioning?" Randall asked Knox, shoving him in the chest back toward the house.

"How is it not going to blow all over them? The guy that's been after Thayer is dead upstairs. He had a knife run through his chest from behind, and I know Thayer didn't do that. Memphis's blood is everywhere. How do you think he's going to escape being questioned?"

Suddenly, he realized what dragging Memphis into the news would do to the man.

"Fuck, the military could make Memphis disappear just to make sure no one else finds out what he's capable of," he said quietly as Randall nodded slowly.

"Or he could spend the rest of his life under the FBI's thumb. We need to make all of this disappear for everyone's sake. The senator does good work in Washington. He doesn't need this scandal. Neither does Thayer. I promise Memphis will get help, and we'll keep Thayer safe.

"But this needs to be covered up. We'll still find everyone involved in this and destroy them."

Knox stood still, looking at Randall for a moment, trying to digest his words. Maybe he was right, but he could hear sirens in the distance already and soon it wouldn't matter. They would all be embroiled in a mess. "What do you suggest we do?" he simply asked Randall.

"You burn this fucker to the ground. Now, Knox. I'll pull whatever strings I need to make it look like a drug deal gone wrong or a bum who lit a fire in the house. You deal with this. I've got the rest."

With a nod, Knox trotted to the back of the house, rubbing his hands together. With a roar, he threw his first fireball through the bedroom window at the back of the house.

Crashing through the glass, he heard a whoosh as the old house caught fire. He threw four more fireballs, completely engulfing the house before Randall pulled him back to the front of the house.

They quickly moved across the street, watching as fire trucks pulled up in front of the house. Somehow, Ben appeared near one of the trucks, announcing that the house would just have to be a complete loss. He managed to convince the chief it was too risky to search the old, abandoned house for anyone inside.

Knox had worried about putting any of the firemen's lives at risk when he was told to burn it. He was grateful that Ben was watching the situation carefully.

"Jay had the ambulance on its way before we even had Memphis out of the car," Ben said quietly as he joined them across the street.

"We didn't have to go that far to find somewhere the cops would believe he got mugged. Jay got some of the bleeding stopped on the way there. His pulse was faint, but he still had one when I left. Jay stayed to watch from the shadows, just to make sure. They'll take him to Memphis Memorial."

"Have you heard if Shaun and Thayer are on the way back to the loft?" Randall asked Ben, checking his phone.

"Yeah, Shaun just texted that they were headed to the hospital to wait for Memphis." Ben just grinned when Knox scowled at him. "He said one punch to the balls trying to wrestle her into his car was enough to convince him she'd be fine there."

Randall shook his head as he patted Knox on the shoulder. "Let's go. Ben will see to this." Turning to Ben, Randall added, "They'll find at least one body in the rubble from the second floor."

Ben nodded once before turning back to the fire. He rejoined the men fighting the blaze as Randall and Knox drove away from the curb down the street.

On the ride to the hospital, Knox called the senator, explaining just enough to fill him in on what had happened and assure him that Thayer was safe. Knox agreed with him that he would do everything within his power to return her to Connecticut as soon as possible, but that it had been a long night, so he felt she needed to rest for a couple of days.

After calling the pilot to inform him that he could shut down the plane for the night, Knox sat back with a sigh.

"What's the plan this time? You hauling her back to her daddy? Seems to me you might have a hell of a fight on your hands," Randall asked.

"You know, I think I'll let her decide what she wants to do. I'm too tired to fight anymore."

Randall grinned, looking out the windshield. "You might not be so bad after all," he said, receiving a snort from Knox in response.

Walking through the curtain in the emergency room at Memphis Memorial, Knox stopped short when he saw Memphis lying in the bed covered in a network of black stitches. There was an intern bent over him hard at work, like he was sewing a patchwork quilt.

"He looks like Frankenstein's monster," he said to no one in particular.

"They think he'll have somewhere around three hundred stitches when they're finally done. He's lost almost a third of his blood. Much more, and he would have gone into shock."

Knox turned to look at Thayer as she spoke from the corner of the room. She was curled up in a chair, looking exhausted.

"How is he still alive?" he asked her, receiving only a shrug of her shoulders. He took a step closer to the bed where Memphis lay covered in nothing but a sheet pulled up between his legs to his waist. His hair had fallen onto his forehead, and Knox reached out automatically to brush it back.

"He'll be okay, Knox. You know how tough he is," Thayer said with a smile at the gentle gesture.

"Fuck yeah, he is. My little brother is no pussy," Knox proclaimed quietly as he turned to look at her over his shoulder with a smile.

Thayer snorted a small laugh, letting Knox know that she would be okay too.

"Let me take you back to the loft to get some sleep. I'm sure he'll be out for a while." He waited patiently while Thayer considered her options.

"No," she said after a moment. "I think I'm right where I need to be."

Knox smiled at her, nodding once before he walked out of the room. Knox wasn't surprised by her answer. She was right where she belonged. Wherever Memphis was. Knox knew she would choose to stay with Memphis, knowing she would love him into the next life with everything she had.

Knox walked back into the room carrying a chair.

"Mind if I sit with you while they finish?" he asked quietly.

"I would love that," Thayer responded, watching Knox set the chair against hers in the tiny space.

The big man sat down, pulling out his phone. Slumping down in the chair, he crossed one ankle over the other while checking his messages. "Knox?"

"Yeah, sweetheart?"

"How did you find us?"

"Memphis found me in the park with Murphy."

"Have you wondered how he did that when he didn't have anything personal of yours?"

Knox looked at her with confusion before turning his gaze back on his sleeping brother. How indeed?

"I think it has to do with the fact you share the same DNA. Maybe, it's just a brother thing," she added.

Thayer laced her arm around his large one, squeezing his hand as she lay her head on his shoulder. Without a thought, he leaned over, placing a kiss to the top of her head. A brother thing, shit, he liked the sound of that.

Memphis was resting quietly when they finally moved him to a room. It wasn't much bigger than the curtained area in the ER, but at least it was private.

Thayer had been drifting in and out of sleep when the door slowly opened, bringing Knox to his feet in an instant. Easing into the room, Senator Kent looked over at his daughter in relief. Without a second thought, she jumped up, throwing herself into his arms. Folding Thayer against him, he held her close, looking over at Memphis.

"Christ," he said quietly, taking in the stitches

covering Memphis's body. "I spoke to the doctor on the way here, but I had no idea it was this bad." Holding Thayer away from him, he looked her over with concern etched on his face. "Are you all right?"

She nodded at him. Fortunately, she had changed into a pair of scrubs one of the nurses had been nice enough to bring her. Her other clothes had been covered in blood. "I'm okay, Dad. If it wasn't for Memphis, I don't know what would have happened."

The senator hugged her closer.

"I owe him everything," she whispered.

"No, *I* owe him everything," he answered her. "Knox updated me on what happened. It seems you've found a good man, sweetheart. You stay with Knox. I'm going to go talk to someone about finding a better room with a cot for you. I would send you to get some rest, but I doubt your stubborn streak would allow that." He smiled at her as Knox gently led her back to her chair.

Walking over to Memphis, the senator laid his hand gently on Memphis's shoulder, giving it a light squeeze. Without another word, he left the room in search of someone in charge.

Knox knew that James Kent would leave no stone unturned to provide for Memphis's recovery now. The senator had found someone he respected lying in that bed. A man who had summoned the last of his strength to save his daughter and he would be loyal to Memphis forever.

Knox returned to his seat next to Thayer. Wrapping his arm around her shoulders, he pulled her against him. He finally felt, even with Memphis drugged out of his mind in a hospital bed and Thayer looking more exhausted than he had ever seen her, he could truly breathe again.

He watched as Memphis's chest slowly rose and fell in his sleep. Against all odds, his brother had turned out to be one of the best men Knox had ever known.

Thayer had finally told him everything that had happened. If Memphis hadn't plunged that knife into the man's back, she wouldn't be sitting here snuggled up against him. With a sigh, Knox settled deeper into the chair, listening as Thayer's breathing slowed into an easy rhythm with sleep.

CHAPTER TWENTY-SEVEN

Knox knew he should have been surprised to find the tall FBI agent from Washington, DC, sitting in Memphis's room when he walked in two days later.

His brother still looked like something out of an old horror flick and was doped up on painkillers, but at least he was awake now. Knox had finally convinced Thayer that Memphis would be fine if she returned to the loft at night to get some rest.

Agent Tanaka stood up from the chair next to the hospital bed when Knox and Thayer walked in.

"Miss Kent," he said, offering her the chair. "I'm glad to see you safe and healthy. I spoke to your father yesterday, so I know he was very excited to see you unscathed." Thayer smiled at him before sitting down.

"What brings you here, Agent Tanaka?" Knox asked.

"Please, call me Dex. I was wrapping up a few loose ends. Thought I would check on Dr. Prescott as well as fill you in on recent developments. After all the excitement surrounding Memphis's recent mugging," Dex said, raising an eyebrow toward Knox. "I realized there might be some questions you had that fell through the cracks about what was happening with your kidnapping case."

He split a look between them. Knox knew that Dex didn't believe Memphis had been mugged for even a moment. The man was too smart for that, but he seemed to be fine with the subterfuge.

"I would very much appreciate that, Dex. Please have a seat." Thayer nodded to the small couch along the window. Senator Kent had insisted that they be moved into a large room saved for VIP guests.

When everyone had settled and Memphis had drifted back off to sleep, Dex brought them up to date on everything he knew. Pulling a folder from his briefcase, he handed it to Knox. Inside was every scrap of information the FBI had on the case.

"Officially, this is what we know. DNA extracted from the body in the fire told us that came from a man named Curtis Floyd. He had a rap sheet of mostly minor crimes in California.

"He was currently employed by the Lehman Group, an international conglomerate with its hand in a multitude of manufacturing companies. They were in line to receive a contract from the US government, totaling somewhere in the vicinity of a little over twenty-five billion dollars.

"That was, anyway, until this morning when your father managed to block the vote. It has been awarded to another company that favors a more...ethical business model, let's just say."

"I can't believe I never saw it," Knox said in barely contained disgust. "It was just about money this entire time."

"Sometimes, the most heinous crimes are committed for the most mundane reasons. I wouldn't beat yourself up, I missed it too." Dex said quietly, studying the large man sitting next to him.

"We served a warrant at the Lehman Group's headquarters yesterday, which appears to be leading to the arrest of several at the very top of the company. Mr. Floyd's remains, however, were identified yesterday in a fire at an abandoned house registered to a Jackson Development Corporation here in Memphis.

"Odd that the CEO of that company just happens to be the son of a woman who runs a foster home where your man lived," Dex added, motioning to the bed where Memphis slept.

"Anyway, the official story is he was hiding out there while waiting for his next chance to grab Miss Kent when he was discovered by a couple of gang-bangers looking for easy money or a place to shoot up. He was pretty crispy, but the medical examiner believes he was stabbed before the house was set on fire to cover up the crime.

"So far there has been no trace of accelerants, but I'm sure something will turn up. I doubt they'll put much effort into finding out since the house had no fire insurance, so we can rule out arson for profit, nor were there any witnesses. Whatever they decide, as far as I'm concerned, the case is closed.

"Unless either of you has anything else to add."

Dex waited patiently to see if either Knox or Thayer would correct his version of the story. Knox knew there were so many holes in the details that a truck could drive through them, but he also knew no one would be served by uncovering them. When neither of them spoke, Dex stood up, straightening his suit.

"Miss Kent," he said, nodding to her. "It's been a pleasure seeing you again. I hope next time our paths cross, it's under better circumstances."

"Thank you. If my family can ever do anything for you, please do not hesitate to call." After escorting the man out of the room, Knox turned to study Thayer. "What?" she asked, looking up at him coolly.

"Nothing," Knox said with a smile. Somewhere along the way, he had missed when the sweet, shy girl had grown into the strong, confident woman he was looking at.

He would leave for home tomorrow. She no longer needed a babysitter. Knox knew her place was here with Memphis. He was a good man who would take care of Thayer, just like Knox had over the years. But where Knox thought of her as his kid sister, Memphis loved her on a much deeper level as the amazing, capable woman she had become.

He felt Thayer reach out to take his hand.

"It's going to be okay now, Knox," she said, smiling at him.

"Yeah, I think for the first time in what feels like a long time, it really is," he answered, squeezing her hand before sitting back on the couch to read his paper.

Memphis stood outside the door with his finger hovering over the doorbell. He was still debating in his mind about whether he wanted to know more or not. It wasn't like he hadn't survived through life this far without having answers.

"Have you changed your mind? You don't have to do this, you know." Thayer stood next to him at the door, watching as he wavered over the doorbell.

"No, I'm good," he said, pushing the button.

Within minutes, the door was thrown open by a vibrant woman dressed like she was more likely on her way to attend a concert at Woodstock than receive guests.

"You must be Memphis. Come in!" she said with exuberance.

Shaking her hand, Memphis stepped back, letting Thayer walk through the door. The woman gave Thayer a hug before showing them into a brightly painted living room.

"Can I get you something to drink?"

Memphis and Thayer declined, settling onto the couch across from the chair she sat down in. She stared at Memphis for a minute before shaking her head. "I can't get over how much you resemble Knox. He showed me a picture of you, but I didn't really see it until now."

"Ms. Monroe, thank you for letting us drop in like this. I'm not sure what I hope to learn about my father, but Knox said you might be able to tell me a little about him. My mom would never talk about him."

Memphis looked at the woman studying him. It was a mystery how anyone this apparently free-spirited and friendly ever produced someone as grouchy as Knox. Though Knox had tried to warn him that his mother was a bit different than most, he hadn't been as prepared as he thought.

"Please call me Sunny. Have you eaten, or can I get you something to eat? I can't tell you how good it is to see you again, Thayer. Even after everything that's happened, you still have the most beautiful aura around you. It's simply glowing. Love looks very good on you, my lovely."

Memphis couldn't hide his grin. Thayer had read him the riot act, when he was finally coherent enough to understand what she was saying, for waiting until they were about to die to say he loved her. He had explained that there was never a bad time to tell her he loved her, imminent death or no.

"Thank you, Sunny. I've missed hearing about your adventures. I think you've given Knox more than one heart attack since we've talked last," Thayer said. She had regaled Memphis with stories about the infamous adventures of Sunny Monroe on their way to Kentucky. He had been skeptical of some of the more outrageous ones until now.

"Well, I'm sure you didn't drive all this way just to listen to an old woman ramble." Memphis snorted a laugh. She couldn't be a day over sixty and looked even younger. He was almost positive she would never know even one day of being an old woman. She had too young a spirit for that.

"I didn't know your father for very long, just a weekend, really. What a weekend that was," she said with a reminiscent smile. "That was back in my wilder days. I can tell you he was tall and so good-looking."

With a wink at Thayer, she added, "Must be where you boys got your good looks."

"Did you ever see him exhibit any special gifts like throwing fire or phasing to another place?" Memphis asked.

"No, he just seemed like your typical charmer. He was only around for a little while, though, so I knew little more than a name. I was working at the PX on base when he got in my line to check out. He flirted, I flirted, and before I knew it, I had agreed to meet him that night at a concert in Louisville," she said. "We spent the whole weekend holed up in a hotel, and nine months later I had Knox."

Memphis sat for a few minutes in silence, feeling that the more he learned, the more mysterious his father became.

"There was one weird thing. I got a postcard that asked me to name the baby Knox. There was no return address, just his name. I didn't have any other names picked out, so I thought, what the hell."

"What was the postcard of?" Memphis asked.

"Somewhere up north. I don't remember, it was a long time ago." He was starting to understand Knox's frustration trying to follow a trail with little more than a vague description to work with.

"How did you find out about me?" he finally asked.

"A letter showed up out of the blue one day from your mother. He must have told her about Knox. It asked if I knew where his dad was, that it was important she find him. It just had her first name with a phone number. I called her, but I didn't have any idea where he was. I was sorry to hear she had passed."

She reached out, squeezing his knee. "I'm sorry I

didn't think to insist we meet. She sounded like a lovely person."

"She was, thank you," he said quietly.

Thayer took his hand, holding it tightly.

"We never exchanged more than first names, and she never told me that she was dying of cancer. I told Knox that night about what had happened. He wanted to leave immediately to go find y'all, but I had nothing more to go on. He began hunting for you that night. He must have been around thirteen then."

She paused, staring off, lost in the memory. "He was so excited to learn he had a brother. He called that phone number every night for a week before it was disconnected."

"It must have been about the time she was hospitalized. She passed away about a week later."

They all sat in silence, thinking about what could have been if his mother had just shared their last name. He could have simply passed from one loving parent to another without the pain between.

It didn't matter now. He had survived and come out the other side stronger than before. In the end, he still had time to build a strong relationship with Knox, and that's all that counted.

"How about I make us some coffee?" Thayer asked, standing up.

"Oh sweetie, all I have is herbal tea. I'll come help you. I also have some whiskey to make the tea go down easier," she whispered loudly to Memphis. He couldn't help laughing at the wink of conspiracy she added on the way past.

When the tea was served, they turned to lighter

conversation, laughing over stories of Sunny's latest exploits. She shared several stories about Knox growing up, including his inability to get a homecoming date since he stood a solid foot taller than all of the girls by sophomore year of high school.

"So, could Knox always create fire with his hands?" Thayer asked, sipping the last of her tea.

"No, he must have been around twelve when we discovered it quite by accident. He had been reading about Merlin at school and decided to try his hand at casting spells.

"I guess he was rubbing his hands together when a fireball appeared, he panicked, throwing it at the back shed. Burned the thing to the ground before the fire department showed up to put it out.

"I had to make up some elaborate story about how it caught on fire. They didn't buy it, but they couldn't prove any different either." She shrugged with a laugh.

"That's about the age I was when I phased the first time. It must have something to do with puberty. Completely freaked me out at the time. One second I'm sitting in my bedroom, the next I'm in front of this girl's locker at school. I had swiped her scarf when she wasn't paying attention and had it in my hand. Fortunately, it was at night, so the school was closed."

"Oh, I just remembered something. I do have a picture of your father if you would like to see it. I had this little camera at the time I took everywhere. Another couple at the concert offered to take our picture with it. I didn't even remember I had it until months later when I got the film developed," she said.

Memphis sat forward on the couch with a nod.

Standing, she flitted into the other room, returning with several scrapbooks.

Flipping through pages, she came to a grainy picture of her standing next to a tall man in what must have been Louisville. Memphis studied it, trying to see the similarities between them. Sunny was right, they did get their looks from their father. Pulling out his phone, he took a picture of it before looking at the page across from it.

"Is that Knox as a baby?" he asked, pointing out the naked baby that lay on his stomach on a fluffy rug to Thayer.

"Oh, I have to have a copy of this." She laughed as he took a picture of it too.

"This scrapbook might also interest you," Sunny said quietly, handing him another one she had been holding.

Opening it, Memphis turned to the first page. He was shocked to find a school picture of himself. Looking up at her quickly in confusion, he flipped to the next page, finding a newspaper article about the first foster home he had lived in.

Slowly looking through the book, he found a copy of his graduation announcement from high school, pictures of him playing baseball at college, a copy of his discharge papers from the military and a snapshot of him receiving his vet degree.

"What is this?" he asked, looking through it again.

"It's everything I took off the wall of Knox's room when I moved. He kept everything he could find about you tacked up on a board. Even after he left home, he would bring stuff home with him to put up. I put it all in that scrapbook when I moved in here."

"That's crazy. If he knew this much about me, why didn't he just tell me who he was?" Memphis looked over at her, but she only shrugged at him.

"He thought you were better off the way you were. You seemed to have finally made a good life for yourself. I guess he didn't want to do anything to mess it up."

"Well, that just makes him an asshole," he exclaimed, slamming the book down on the table. "I'm sorry," he said to her. "I guess I don't understand."

"Oh, don't apologize to me. I had the same argument. It makes me happy that you finally know. I'm just waiting to see what you do with the information. Whether he'll admit it or not, he's waited a long time for you to become a part of his life. Do me just one favor, meet him at least halfway."

They turned their conversation to other topics. Memphis needed a break from a past he was just now getting to know. It would take him time to figure out how to handle everything going forward. He could tell her one thing, though, he had no doubts that he would go as far as he had to for Knox. He wasn't taking a chance on losing even one more family member from his life.

Memphis talked Sunny into joining them for dinner, then returning to her house where they visited until late that night. After promising to return again soon, they left her to return to the hotel.

Memphis lay awake long after Thayer had drifted off, looking at the picture of his father on his phone. He didn't have to think about what it meant to have found out that he had a brother. Knox might be overbearing and seriously obnoxious, but he already loved having him around.

He was still trying to wrap his head around everything that had happened between them. He still didn't have all of the answers about how their relationship would work. He just knew they could count on each other to have each other's back. Just like brothers should.

CHAPTER TWENTY-EIGHT

"Just how long were we gone?" Memphis asked in jest as they stood in front of his truck.

It had been almost three months since they had fled this small farming community in Minnesota. There had been complications from an infection. Then the stitches had had to stay in longer than originally thought.

Jay had insisted they stay in Tennessee until he was positive the skin Curtis Floyd had flayed open on Memphis had completely healed. He still had twinges, but everything seemed to be holding together.

The detour to Kentucky had also added several days to their drive back. They had decided to return the next day to spend more time with Sunny. Memphis couldn't really explain why he wanted to get to know her better.

Maybe it was the fact that she shared a small similarity of experience with his own mother. It also helped that Sunny was just a fun person to be around. He assumed all the fun had been used up on her, leaving none to infuse into Knox's DNA.

The FBI had closed the case on Curtis Floyd, thanks to Dex's help. Floyd had had a long history as a hired gun to the top bidder. His immediate boss, Brent Roberts, had stumbled upon Curtis when he tied up a problem for the man while on business in Los Angeles.

It still made Memphis shiver every time he thought about how close they had come to dying for nothing more than a paycheck. He knew it would take a long time to get over the need to look over his shoulder all the time to make sure no one was sneaking up on them.

Knox had flown home to Connecticut shortly after the fire had been ruled an accident where he began hunting for his next teaching job. Unfortunately, he had to resign from the job he'd held at Thayer's old school because of all the time off while he was involved protecting her.

He brushed off her apologies to him, saying it wasn't like she had asked to be kidnapped, then shot at, then kidnapped again. He had mentioned several times about moving closer to them anyway. Thayer had kept him informed on Memphis's recovery with an update the big man insisted on at least twice a week.

Even Senator Kent had returned to business as usual, splitting his time between Washington, Connecticut, and the campaign trail. He had managed to avoid a large media circus, thanks in part to Randall Jackson's quick thinking.

Thayer had told Memphis one night after talking to her father that he was being approached for a possible run at the White House during the next presidential election. She wasn't sure he was interested, loving the job he had now, but he wasn't ruling the possibility out.

"Are you sure this is the right place? We didn't fall down a rabbit hole on the way?" Thayer asked as she stood next to him with the same confused expression on her face that he had.

They had arrived in town late the night before, having driven the Bronco back from Tennessee. Stopping by the vet clinic, Memphis had picked up his truck before they checked into the only hotel in town. Knowing he no longer had a house for them to stay at, it was the only option.

Now, they were standing in front of what should have been the burned-out rubble of Memphis's cabin. Instead, there was a beautiful new cabin standing in its place.

Turning in a slow circle, Memphis shook his head. It was the right place. Taking Thayer's hand, Memphis led her up the steps onto the porch. Murphy had taken off to chase rabbits in the small wood behind the house as soon as they arrived.

"You don't think the county seized my property, do you? Let some developer turn it into a vacation house?" Memphis asked, looking over at her.

"If so, your dog is now trespassing," Thayer answered with a shrug.

Memphis turned back to the front door, noticing for the first time that he could hear Murphy barking from somewhere inside.

Fishing his keys out of his pocket, he studied them for a moment before realizing there was a new one on the key ring. He had no idea when it could have appeared, although he did remember asking his receptionist to put together a new set of keys for him since the last one had been inside the cabin when it burned to the ground.

"Well, here's hoping no one meets us with a shotgun."

Sliding the key into the lock on the new front door, he raised his eyebrows at her when it opened. Once inside, he took a minute to look around. Murphy came bounding out of a back room toward them, barking happily.

The front door opened into a large living room. There was still a fireplace on the left wall, but this one was at least twice the size of the previous one. Slowly following Thayer to the right, he discovered a large gourmet kitchen with an adjoining dining room large enough to feed at least a dozen people comfortably.

"Look, Memphis. There's a note taped to the fridge," Thayer said, waving toward a large stainless steel double refrigerator. Taking the note down, Memphis followed Thayer as she headed down the hallway toward the back of the house. There were two bedrooms with a large bathroom between them, an office, and finally a master suite at the end.

The entire house had been furnished, so Memphis sank down on the end of a large king-size bed, opening the note.

Brother,

It seems only right that since I was possibly the reason your house burned down in the first place, that I be the one to fix it. Notice there is no confession of guilt, however.

I called in a few favors the day you left here in the Bronco, hoping that you would get to return shortly. Even then, I had a feeling you would need more room than your original floor plan provided.

It's amazing what the locals were willing to do when they heard their beloved new veterinarian's house had been destroyed by a random fire. They should be expecting you back at your clinic next week.

You might have to get off your ass for a change and do some work.

Knox

"Three months seems a little aggressive, even for Knox," Thayer said, looking over Memphis's shoulder at the note.

Murphy ran through the room, disappearing out the dog door onto a deck attached to the back of the house. Memphis stood, shaking his head.

"I agree, he had to have had several crews working around the clock. But you won't hear me complaining." He tossed the note onto the new dresser. "Am I supposed to carry you over the threshold?" he asked Thayer. "It is a new house after all."

"I think that's only if you're married. I've never heard anything about that if you're just living together." She laughed. "Besides, I know you still need a little more time to heal before lugging anything heavy around."

"I wouldn't be opposed to that, you know."

"To what? Lugging around a bunch of weight?"

Memphis rolled his eyes at Thayer's words. He could only stand fighting with her over how perfect she was in his eyes so often.

"To us getting married." He looked back over the note. "Though, if you're just sticking around out of some sort of obligation for helping you, then I don't know."

Thayer cocked her head at him. Standing up, she crossed her arms over her chest. Cocking one hip out, she watched him pointedly ignoring her, though, to be perfectly honest, he really wanted an answer.

It was silly, but somewhere in the back of his mind, he wondered if she stayed with him out of some misplaced loyalty. She had stayed by his side the entire time he was in the hospital, only leaving when Knox and Randall physically carried her out so she could get some sleep.

She had stayed with him when he had moved back into the bedroom at the loft, waiting on him until he was able to take care of himself. But even after everything, he couldn't help but worry.

"Do you think I'm here just because you found me in some pit?" Thayer asked softly. When he didn't answer, Thayer walked slowly toward him until she was standing as close to him as she could get without touching. "I do love that you rescued me...three times."

He met her eyes with his deep green ones.

"But, Memphis, that's not the only reason why I love you. I also love you because you're kind, funny, sweet, loyal, smart, fierce, protective, and a thousand other reasons. So, yes, I do love you for saving me. But if that's all you think you mean to me, then I'll go right now."

Memphis sat silently searching her face like he would find what he was looking for in her eyes. If he couldn't trust her when she had just poured out her heart to him, then maybe there was no hope for them.

Thayer made it as far as the doorway to the bedroom before he sprang from the bed. Wrapping a strong arm around her waist, he picked her up off the floor. With a squeal, she found herself bouncing on the bed before Memphis was on top of her looking down.

"You said you love me, and that's all I need to hear. I love you, Thayer. I have from almost the first moment I saw you. I know I still have a lot of shit from my past to deal with, but you're my future, and I really like where my future is headed."

He dipped his head down, sealing his lips to hers. When he licked over her bottom lip, she opened for him, allowing him to devour her.

"I do think we should get married, though, just to guarantee you stick around for a while," he said when they finally came up for air.

She had just started to laugh when he leaned down to kiss her again. This time though, his hand found the buttons on her flannel shirt, working them open one at a time. It was technically still his shirt, but he had given up trying to wrestle it away from her.

Spreading her shirt open under him, his hand found her breast, plumping it under her bra. Without warning, Memphis sat back on his knees, pulling her into a sitting position with him.

He frantically wrestled with removing her shirt and bra like she was on fire. When he had tossed them onto the floor, he pushed her back down with his strong hand, following her until he could pull her taut nipple into his mouth.

He flicked her hard nipple with his tongue, sucking on it until she moaned with need. Just when she began to beg, he moved to the other side, repeating his ministrations as he desperately pulled on the button of her jeans. With a pop, he released her breast, sitting back up on his knees, feverishly pulling her jeans past her knees.

"Please, please, please," he began to plead as he stood up from the bed, pulling his shirt off in one quick tug. Moving to the nightstand, he opened the top drawer with a smile.

"Fucking best brother in the world!" he exclaimed, pulling out a row of condoms in triumph. Thayer couldn't hold in her giggle, watching him. Tossing the condoms at her, he yanked his jeans open, hopping back toward the end of the bed while trying to take them off.

Thayer tore one of the packages open before handing it to him at the end of the bed. She sat up on her elbows watching him roll the condom onto his throbbing cock before he grabbed the cuffs of her jeans, giving them a hard pull to remove them. She was pulled off of her elbows with a laugh as he worked her panties down her legs.

"What do you keep mumbling?" she asked him as he tossed her farther onto the bed.

With a grin, he followed until he was lying above her.

"I have no idea. I didn't know I was talking. Probably begging my dick to hold on." His mouth crashed back down onto hers as they desperately ground against one another.

He had explored every inch of her body over the last couple of months, but he never got tired of feeling her soft body pressed against his. This time, when her hands roamed over his chest, they were both reminded by the scars left behind what they had almost lost forever to a madman.

"Memphis, I need you in me," she whispered into his ear as he kissed her neck.

Balancing on one arm, he slid his fingers through her folds to check if she was ready for him. When he slid his fingers into her entrance, using his thumb to rub her clit, she arched up to him in a moan. Pulling his fingers out, he fisted his cock, running it through her folds as she writhed under him, trying to pull him closer.

"Easy, Thayer. I don't want to hurt you." Plunging his tongue back into her mouth, he entered her in a gentle thrust. Thayer wrapped her legs around him when he stopped moving, trying to force him deeper. He moved his mouth back to her breast, sucking on her nipple as he thrust in farther.

"Memphis!" she gasped when he took her virginity.

He shifted his weight when he stopped moving to look at her. Reaching between them, he started playing with her clit again, slowly pushing deeper as she relaxed.

He could feel the orgasm trying to build inside her as she began to quiver around him. Reaching down his back, she raked her nails up him, making him thrust hard.

Not needing to be told twice, he started rolling his

hips, pulling almost out before driving back in. Memphis removed his hand from between them to steady himself over her as he pumped harder and harder, burying himself to the root with each thrust.

"Fuck, you're amazing," he growled as he pulled back before slamming back into her. Sitting back on his knees, he pulled her up on his thighs slightly before leaning back over on his hands. With each thrust in this position, Memphis could feel his cock rub against a place deep inside her that made her arch up toward him.

When her orgasm hit, it dragged him under in a wave of ecstasy unlike anything he had experienced in the past. She had been right when she told him they might explode. There was no doubt in his mind that he would never be the same again.

Memphis slumped over her, desperately trying to hold himself up on his forearms as he panted next to her ear.

"Are you okay?" she whispered.

"More importantly, are you okay?" he asked, rolling off of her onto his side. "Wait here." Memphis climbed off the bed, walking into their new bathroom to dispose of the condom.

Digging through a linen closet, he found two towels. They would have to make a trip to the city to finish their new house, but at least someone had thought of a few basic necessities to get them by for now. Turning on the walk-in shower, he waited for it to reach the right temperature before returning to get Thayer.

Leading her back into the bathroom, he eased her into the shower in front of him, grabbing the travel-sized soap that had been left there. Pulling her against his chest, he held her as the warm water cascaded down their bodies. Turning in his arms, Thayer laced her hands around the back of his neck, running her fingers through his hair.

"You know you can't leave now, right?" Memphis asked, looking down at her. "Remember, I told you, once I buried myself in you, I would never let you go. I'm in too deep now, I'd never survive." He eased his mouth down against hers in a soft, gentle kiss. "I love you so fucking much," he whispered, standing back up.

Thayer smiled up at him as he held her.

"I love you, too," she said quietly as they stood in their new house, letting the stress from the last six months slowly run down the drain until all that was left was just Memphis and Thayer. With a happy sigh, she looked at him. "What do you have planned for the rest of our day?"

He palmed the soap in his hand, working it into a lather on Thayer's back as he considered.

"Well, I probably need to stop at the clinic to get a feel for what I'm walking back into on Monday. We had also better go grocery shopping so we can eat for the rest of the week.

"Then, just in case you're interested, I had a reliable source text me that the Browns have a new litter of puppies ready to be weaned if you'd like to go see them. That's where I got Murphy from." He had bent down, washing her lower body as he spoke.

"Can we? I would love to see Murphy in puppy form!" she said with a little happy dance.

"Absolutely, rinse off so we can go." Memphis laughed when Thayer bounced out of the shower, quickly pulling him behind her. He barely got a chance to shut the water off before she was throwing a towel at him.

With their clothes back on, Thayer made a quick check of the kitchen to get an idea of what they needed from the store later.

After locking up the new house, Memphis opened the driver's side door of the vet truck. Murphy jumped in first, settling happily next to the passenger window to bark at the scenery as it passed him by.

Thayer followed him, stopping in the middle of the bench seat, hooking the seat belt. She had folded up the console in the middle earlier so she could sit next to Memphis as he drove.

He cringed a little, wondering what kind of mess he would have to clean up later in the back seat. At any one time, you could find anything from syringes to bubble gum to a pair of gloves shoved into the console. It would be worth it, though, to have Thayer so close as he drove.

Memphis climbed into the driver's seat, starting the truck so it could start warming up. He had checked that Thayer's mud boots and coveralls were still in the back of the truck. Someone had obviously cleaned them for him before returning them to the same spot. He would have to remember to thank his receptionist for more than just the use of her Bronco for so long.

Sliding the truck into reverse, he laid his arm on the back of the seat so he could use the side mirror next to Murphy a little easier. The large vet box in the bed of the truck rendered the rearview mirror next to useless.

Thayer snuggled against his side, sliding her hands between his thighs in an effort to get warmer. He sat for a second, taking in the scene inside his truck. Sliding his arm around Thayer, he placed a kiss on her head.

He wondered if this was what all of the obstacles in his life were leading up to. He tried not to allow the hardships in his past to bring him down. What doesn't kill you makes you stronger has been his mantra for a long time.

It made sense now. He had had to be even stronger than he thought he could be in order to save Thayer. He had walked through hell for her and had come out on the other side, a little banged up, but not any worse for wear. Now, he had it all, and he was happy. Really fucking happy.

"Is everything okay?" Thayer asked, looking up at him.

With a gentle kiss on her lips, he squeezed her closer before turning around to take her to see the new litter of puppies.

"Everything is perfect."

EPILOGUE

FOUR MONTHS LATER

Knox sat at the table enjoying his afternoon coffee as he watched the boats making their way down the Thames River. Between the naval base and the Coast Guard Academy, there was always plenty to see in this part of Connecticut.

He was trying to decide if it was time for a change of scenery, though. Teaching math to high school students had always been the most rewarding part of his life, and he was itching to get back in the classroom. It was nearing the end of spring, so he needed to make a decision soon.

He looked down at his feet when he heard a grunt, followed by a whimper. Stretched out underneath him, Harry Styles kicked his paws as he dreamed.

Knox had not given the tiny ball of hair the name Harry Styles. After all, who named a dog after a member of a fucking boy band? It had been on the tag attached to the tiny collar he had shown up wearing.

He had been relaxing in his apartment one evening when a knock at the door had brought the tiny puppy into his life. A kid carrying a dog crate had handed Knox a bag of items, along with the crate, when he opened the door before disappearing.

There was no note with the puppy, but he had a pretty good suspicion of who had sent him the present since he looked similar to Murphy. Setting the crate on the ground, he had opened the door to see what emerged before making a decision on what to do with it.

He had let out a string of curse words when a tiny ball of fluff trotted out, yipped once at him, then peed all over his front entry. Thus began the love/hate relationship between Knox and Harry.

That had been almost four months ago. Leaning down, he rubbed Harry's side as the dog kicked his leg. Knox had just gotten him back from Senator Kent's house, where he had left him in the care of the senator's staff while they attended Thayer and Memphis's wedding.

They had managed to make it a whole four months living together before they found the nearest preacher to marry them. Their friends and family had been given a week's notice. Thayer had tried to talk him into staying with them for a while to visit, but the last thing he wanted was to be trapped in the middle of nowhere with two horny newlyweds.

"Do you mind if I join you?"

Knox looked up to meet the eyes of a man he had come to know fairly well during the case involving Thayer.

"Depends," he answered, pointing to the chair next to him. Knox watched the tall man as he placed his order for coffee. He was the agent with the FBI working out of the Washington, DC, office, which made Knox suspicious of why he was down here.

When Thayer was abducted, there was some confusion about which office would handle such a high-profile case. Finally, it landed on Agent Dex Tanaka's desk with the office in Massachusetts lending support since that was the state she had been in when she was kidnapped.

"What does it depend on?" Dex asked, sipping his coffee.

He had been a good guy to work with. The agent didn't seem to exhibit any of the superiority complex that Knox had run into in the past, he even bent over backward to access any information Knox had asked for to further the case along. He had immediately pulled up the satellite footage of Memphis and the surrounding area when they had gone missing without question.

"On what you're doing here," Knox answered.

Dex took another sip of his coffee, watching Knox over the rim of the cup. It was obvious the man wanted something, but instead, he simply cleared his throat.

"How has Miss Kent, or should I say Mrs. Prescott, been? I understand congratulations are in order," the agent said. He absently stroked Harry's head where it had come to rest on his lap the moment the man sat down. "She married the man you were working with to find her? Memphis wasn't it?"

Knox narrowed his eyes at him, he knew this man forgot nothing and knew damn well what Memphis's name was as well as the role he played in the entire affair. Although he had held up his end of the bargain and kept Memphis's name out of the official records.

"They were married a week ago." Knox motioned to the waitress for a refill. Settling in a little more to his seat, he prepared for what was beginning to look like a slow process. "So, what brings you to Connecticut, Agent Tanaka? Or am I just on the receiving end of a social call?" he asked.

"Dex, please." Dex took another sip of his coffee, looking out over the river. To Knox, it looked like the man was trying to organize what he wanted to say in his mind. "I've tracked you down to ask for a favor. I need someone with certain...shall we say...abilities that aren't obstructed by bureaucratic scrutiny."

"That sounds like a favor a sane man should run from," Knox responded, watching a Coast Guard training boat pass by on its way to the sound. "Of course, I've never been accused of being sane."

With a slight twitch to the corner of Dex's mouth, he turned toward Knox."That's what I'm counting on," he answered, taking another swallow of his coffee.

"About a month ago, I was made aware of a young woman who had been abducted off the street. When I looked into it, even though the local police told me she was just a troubled girl who ran away from home on a regular basis, something didn't quite add up. She would always eventually turn up at home after a short while or stay with a relative until things had simmered down.

"Her father agreed that she was troubled, but that in the past, she had always contacted him to let him know she was okay. I guess a runaway with a conscience, I don't know."

"You want me to go hunt for a runaway in DC,

Agent Tanaka?" Knox asked with a scowl. He couldn't imagine why his abilities would be needed for that.

"Dex. That's just it. I believe she wasn't a runaway this time. I started pulling files of known missing runaways in the area. Many of them, of course, wound up in the morgue or hospital or simply showed back up at home. But there are a significant number who simply vanished—enough to raise questions in my mind."

Dex reached down into the attaché case sitting at his feet, pulling out a small stack of files.

"The local police aren't very motivated to follow the few vague leads I've managed to put together, nor are my superiors. Mr. Monroe, I believe these girls are being kidnapped to be sold. I've managed to find a very thin trail that leads to the Houston area. It's nothing I can point to as proof, just a trail of guesses."

Knox took one of the folders off of the stack Dex had placed on the table. Flipping it open, he looked into the obstinate eyes of a girl in her teens. She looked like a typical rebellious teenager with her green-tipped hair and dark eyeliner.

He remembered the days of being stuck at fifteen years old. The kids teased anyone who was different from them until you learned to wrap yourself in a bad attitude just to get through the day. He had been much taller than the other kids and rail-thin with a single hippie mother and a dad who had been a one-night stand.

Looking back at the picture attached to the first folder, he thought about how he had been given the chance to grow up. He had made something good of himself with the help of that same hippie mom.

This girl deserved the opportunity to grow up too,

with the help of a concerned parent, to be something good. He studied the file for a few minutes more before slowly closing it.

"So, what do you need me to do?" he asked. Dex reached back into his bag, pulling out a set of wristbands in an evidence bag.

"Her father said she never went anywhere without these until she disappeared." He handed the bag to Knox. "It's part of why he knew something was very wrong. Her mother gave her the set for Christmas right before she passed away."

Knox sat silently holding the bag as he stared at the leather bracelets. Fuck, this story just kept getting worse.

"I thought maybe you'd talk to your brother, see if he can find any trace of her."

Knox's gaze snapped to Dex in surprise.

"Yeah, I know he's your half brother. I also know he has a rare gift for finding people. It pays to pay attention in my business. You never know when a piece of information may prove useful."

"Do you think she's still in the country?" Knox asked, looking back down at the picture he still held. If it meant guaranteeing the agent kept his brother's gift a secret, he would agree to anything.

"I don't know, but if there is a trafficking ring snatching girls off the streets of DC, I need to stop it before anyone else is taken."

Looking at Dex's determined face, Knox nodded once before closing the folder.

"I'll leave for Memphis's home in Minnesota tonight, but there is one condition," Knox stated, glaring at Dex. With a nod, Dex motioned him to continue. "No one finds out Memphis is involved."

"I remember, and I understand why. You have my word that I will keep his name far away from this. I would not want to jeopardize his life if the wrong people found out about him any more than you would."

"I will hold you to that," Knox growled, leaving no doubt that retribution would be swift if he ever found out otherwise. Between the two of them, Memphis had much more to lose if he fell into the wrong hands.

"It should take me a solid day to get there, I'll let you know as soon as I have anything to report." Standing up, he gathered up the folders, tucking them under his arm. Shaking Dex's hand, he grabbed Harry's leash before heading back down the river.

"Knox," Dex called out to him before he got too far. "I'll keep following the few leads I have here. Thank you...sincerely." Knox nodded again at him then set a brisk pace for home.

When Knox arrived back at his apartment, he quickly stuffed a couple days' worth of clothes and toiletries into one of the saddlebags that fit on his Harley. The files he got from Dex, he slid into a different bag securing them to the side of his bike.

Grabbing food, collapsible bowls, and the leash, he had to work at packing it all in the front of the sidecar he had reattached earlier. Harry happily jumped into the sidecar, waiting for Knox to attach his harness and slide a pair of goggles over his eyes.

After speaking briefly to his elderly landlord, Knox roared out of the driveway toward Minnesota. With any luck, he would make it to his brother's house in time for dinner tomorrow night.

He hadn't even made it out of the state before Harry started shifting around in his seat. Finding a quiet spot to pull over, Knox attached his leash, letting him out to stretch his legs. This is why he would never have kids. He had a horrifying vision of trading in his Harley for a minivan full of fighting kids pulling over every few minutes for someone to pee. With a shiver, he loaded Harry back into the sidecar.

He lucked into finding a local diner in Pennsylvania that allowed Harry inside as long as he sat under Knox's feet at the bar. The dog happily ate his food as Knox finished his eggs with hash.

Only stopping for gas, they quickly made their way through Ohio before Knox finally had to stop for a few hours of sleep. Parking outside the door of a cheap dive of a motel off the highway, they crashed on the double beds for a few hours before pressing on.

They weaved their way through Chicago the next day. Knox knew he could have gone around the city to avoid the traffic, but he had loved Chicago the few times he had been there. Harry must have felt the same way, barking the entire time they were downtown until he finally fell asleep curled up on the seat again. Maybe they would move to Chicago. It was as good a place as any, and he would be closer to both his mother and brother.

It was late afternoon when they finally dropped into Minnesota from Wisconsin. Knox's butt had grown numb hours ago, and Harry looked like he had simply melted inside the sidecar with his head propped on the side. They were both hungry as well as a little dehydrated.

As much as he loved a cross-country road trip, Knox

decided there should be a limit on how far you had to ride in a day. He couldn't remember being so excited to turn down a dirt road before, but with Memphis's house within view, he sighed in relief.

Roaring up to the front of the new cabin, he took a minute to admire it again. He still couldn't believe they had completed it so quickly. His old Navy buddy had really come through for him. The man now owned a construction company in Hartford that always had a waiting list. He had promised Knox he could get it done, and he had been true to his word.

Shutting off the Harley, he leaned over, unhooking Harry so he could jump out of the sidecar.

Knox dusted off his coat, tossing his gloves into the sidecar before climbing the steps. He could tell Memphis was home since his vet truck sat in the driveway next to the house.

Reaching the front door, he held up his fist to pound on it when the door slowly opened, revealing Memphis standing there in nothing but a pair of old jeans. He crossed his arms over his chest, narrowing his eyes at Knox.

"Knox."

"Memphis."

Though he had a smile on his face, his brother made no move to invite Knox inside. He heard Thayer say something from inside, but Memphis just ignored her, staring warily at Knox instead.

"Is this just a friendly visit?" Memphis asked, looking at the Harley sitting behind him. Murphy had already joined Harry in the front yard, roughhousing in the grass.

"Well, it's like this," Knox said, glaring down at his

little brother. "I need to ask a favor. As I see it, there are two ways this can go, the easy way," Knox said with a smile, pulling something out of his back pocket.

Holding up the taser, he waved it slightly in Memphis's face with a wicked grin. "Or the silent way."

Memphis smirked back at him as he watched the sparks dance between the tines. With a roll of his eyes, Memphis threw the door open, gesturing to Knox.

"Then, by all means, come in."

Keep an eye out for book two
Invincible
coming in May 2026!

A LOOK AT BOOK TWO:
INVINCIBLE

Can her strength save them all?

Tyler Buchanan has always been strong. Physically, she can outmuscle most men. As a welder at the Houston ship channel, she became known as a woman who gets the job done.

Then an FBI agent shows up at her door with a case that muscle alone can't solve. Girls are vanishing from Washington D.C. without a trace, and Dex Tanaka has followed a cold trail to the last person he'd ever expect to need. He's methodical. Skeptical. And completely out of options.

She said she'd help find the girls. She didn't say she'd fall for the man asking. But someone powerful wants those girls to stay missing, and Tyler's strength can move anything in the world. *It just can't protect everyone in it.*

AVAILABLE MAY 2026

ACKNOWLEDGMENTS

No writer can stand on their own two feet without being propped up by others happy to stay in the background. I'm no different.

I figured out quickly that *Intangible* was no easy book to write. Thanks to Meredith at Anessa Books for hunting down the plot holes and inconsistencies. I knew when she pointed out what a jerk Knox was and then later admitted he was growing on her, I had the big guy nailed.

Never would I consider presenting you, my dear reader, with a story that wasn't polished to near perfection without trusting Ellie at My Brother's Editor to remove all those apostrophes and random commas. She also has to make sense out of my written Texas drawl. Bless her!

As always, I couldn't do this without my valuable, amazing, and underpaid cover designer, Rachel. It's been a blast to grow together in this crazy business. I couldn't possibly have a better cohort in crime.

A very special thanks to the rest of my family. Thomas, who always spews out phrases like "good job, babe, you got this, and you deserve tacos." Wilson for answering all of my many vehicle and weapon questions. Madison for also wondering why none of the cowboys that apply at our ranches look like ones featured on Man Candy Monday.

Last, but never least, thank you to all of the ARC readers, bloggers, and readers that make this worth the blood, sweat, and tears. You make it worth every long day hanging out in the world of make-believe!

A SAMSON

suspenseful romantic

Avery Samson grew up on a ranch outside of a small west Texas town. Since she could remember, she's had her face stuck in a book. High School graduation found her leaving ranch life for the big city.

After living all over the state of Texas, she now finds herself back on one of the family ranches near Dallas with her husband, surrounded by cattle. A lot of them. They're everywhere! When not crafting swoon-worthy romantic book boyfriends, you can find her streaming the latest British mystery or heading on her next adventure.

averysamson.com

www.ingramcontent.com/pod-product-compliance
Lightning Source LLC
La Vergne TN
LVHW030916080826
845145LV00013B/2928

* 9 7 8 1 9 6 9 8 7 6 3 2 5 *